A TREASURY OF FOLKLORE

WATERLANDS, WOODED WORLDS AND STARRY SKIES

A TREASURY OF FOLKLORE

Waterlands, Wooded Worlds and Starry Skies

Dee Dee Chainey &
Willow Winsham

BATSFORD

CONTENTS

AUTHORS' NOTE

In this collection of customs and stories, we have tried to build bridges between people from all places. We wanted to show how people tell similar tales wherever they are from. In order to do this, we have unearthed stories from across the globe and gathered them together here. Many of the stories in this book were chosen to highlight this issue of cultural appropriation, and we have tried to explain how such stories have been appropriated, and the damage that this does.

With this in mind, we have tried to use sources from the culture in which each tale or tradition originates, preserving the essence of the tale in language that would be familiar to those who share its heritage. And while it is sometimes more difficult for the reader, we have used the names people call themselves, and the words that these people would choose to tell this tale, since these are important things. It is a mark of respect and acknowledgement that these stories belong somewhere, and belong to the people of that place. For traditions and stories from living traditions, we have made sure to use the present tense, and not erroneously mark these as a thing that is past. Folklore refers just as much to the living, breathing folk groups and customs we see all around us today.

We have purposefully chosen folklore that uncovers the similarities between our different cultures. Yet we have preserved the details of each tale, hoping to display the intricacies that make each folk group so mesmerizingly different, to evoke the places where this folklore originates, and to celebrate their individuality.

We would like to thank everyone who has shared their tales and traditions with us, and we hope we have done justice to the wonderful folklore that unites us all.

INTRODUCTION

When we first envisaged the Treasury of Folklore book series, we imagined it as one book covering all types of physical landscapes where humans live across the world. The material we uncovered, however, greatly surpassed what could be contained within a single book. Yet now, we finally have the opportunity to compile much of this folklore in one special volume: a compilation of our favourite folklore contained within the three original books in the series.

We started the series in search of understanding. We aimed to explore how humans across the globe create customs, beliefs and tales around the places they live in. Although the details of these beliefs and customs vary from place to place, the truth that we unearthed is that, in so many ways, we are all inherently the same. We discovered that we, as humans, all share primal fears and dreams, no matter where we live, how we dress, or what we choose to name the monsters of our myths and legends. Gazing across the ocean into the vast horizon, we all long for the treasures and pleasures that the wide world around us can offer. We all dread the unknown as we gather around our campfires in the darkness of the nighttime forest. We all stand in awe of the eternity of time under the glimmer of ancient stars, wondering about the unwritten future of our own short lives.

Here you will not find a collection of stories, but a pathway leading into the world of folklore in all its forms: a breadcrumb trail of tales, traditions and beliefs from around the world. We have gathered these together around the timeless human themes they speak to. You will find folk magic with hope and fear at its core; customs that ease the pain of loss, and traditions performed from grief and an eternal longing for the impossible. You will hear tales of temptation and jealousy; myths and legends of our innate fear of divine retribution and death. We explore the hidden meanings that simmer below the surface of our folklore – the wisdom of communities across the world passed down through the ages, and the lessons they convey for each new generation that follows.

While including folklore of all kinds, from all places, across all times is an impossible feat, we hope this small collection will help you to delve more deeply into the subject. We invite you to use this understanding to pick up the trail of the tales and traditions of the places familiar to you. By forging the path of your own folklore journey, you will uncover the hidden depths and meaning beneath the stories and customs of your own communities, and gain a deep understanding of how folklore shapes your life, relationships and the world around you.

Join us as we dive deep into the heart of these stories, beliefs and traditions, and uncover the shared humanity that binds us all.

WATERLANDS

SEAS AND RIVERS
Wonderous Waterlands

From the earliest times, the sea has been a major part of life for many people around the globe. Humans walked across continents, and traversed the seas, to settle the shores of distant lands that belonged only to the beasts of the earth. Since the ice receded, and tundra spread over our planet, island and coastal communities sprang up and their lives and livelihoods relied on the sea, as they still do today. From folklore, myths and legends we can see that people have always viewed the sea as majestic, with a power to consume all. It is a regenerative, creative force that churns outside the bounds of time, roaring its way through land, animals and humans alike. In the face of this, people look at the sea with an all-consuming awe, and see the gods and goddesses of creation shimmering in its depths.

For thousands of years, great heroes and heroines from across the globe have traversed the seven seas, battling pirates and monsters for the prize of treasure, fame and the promise of a life of adventure and the lure of unknown shores. On their voyages, archetypal heroes are often favoured by gods of the sea and are witness to miraculous beasts, underwater worlds and palaces, and to fabled islands. Whether these heroes on great voyages seek fame, fortune or pirate treasure, it's certain that the lure of the ocean and its secrets are as old as time itself.

A resounding theme in ocean folklore is the unknown, and the innate human fear of what one cannot see lurking under the waves in far-flung seas. Many stories tell of ghostly bells, still ringing from the depths of sunken towns that were swallowed by the sea – as if the inhabitants still go about their daily tasks, submerged under the dark waters among the waving seaweed fronds. For many on the biting shores of the Northern Hemisphere, the sea is a place of raging storms, ghostly mists and strange noises that pierce the frosty beaches on dark nights and conceal hidden threats to life and land. For those in the southern seas, there are endless tales of sea monsters and temptresses in the clear waters and sweet lagoons, who lure men to their doom.

When we look at sea folklore from around the world, we find it is often used to explain the unexplainable: unquenchable feelings of lust, illegitimacy, disappearance, bad luck, death, starvation or a fruitless yield. Folklore indeed teaches us that the sea is dark, illicit and full of temptations. The ocean can offer the things of our wildest dreams – treasure, love, a different life – but to get these we must face our darkest nightmares: the terrifying things that lurk beneath the surface in our subconscious minds. When we face these, and defeat them, we win the treasures of the deep and see sights most can only dream of; yet one thing that folklore teaches – make no mistake – is that the treasures of the sea always come with a price.

Similarly, rivers hold a great deal of symbolic meaning across the globe. Rivers are boundaries and barriers, yet we can transgress these with the help of the gods and their rituals. In myth and legend they help us travel between worlds or spiritual realms. The rivers of the Underworld accompany the dead on their journey through Hades in Greek myth, and in Scandinavian lore one must wade through rivers on a journey to the land of the dead. In traditional Sámi tales of Finland and Sweden, double-bottomed *sáiva* lakes act as doorways to their Underworld, with shamans able to speak to the spirits of the lakes, who could help protect people and ensure a plentiful fishing haul if offerings were left for them.

Rivers and lakes are the things of the sea, but tamed; they have similar dangers, but their dangers are tempered and we humans are offered a choice, a forked path, through which to choose our fate. If we fail, we will metaphorically be lost in our own human frailty, and the gifts and wisdom of the otherworld and its gods are taken from us. Such gifts offer opportunities to transcend our lower selves, and raise us up to be godly, with super-human powers and skills. They show us the amazing things that are on offer to us, and there for the taking – if only we do things in the correct way and choose to act with wisdom and kindness.

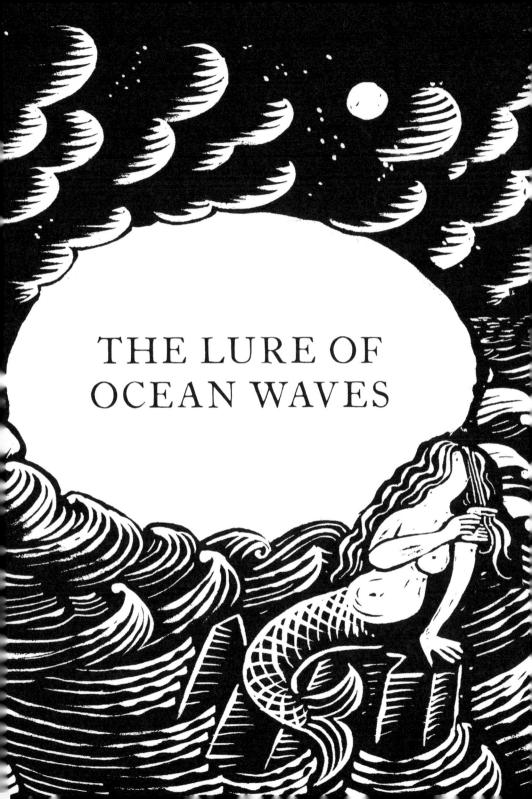

THE LURE OF OCEAN WAVES

FAMOUS FLOODS

Some of the most famous flood stories are those of Noah, who makes an appearance in the Christian Bible, Jewish Torah and Islamic Quran. Yet did you know that a devastating flood that almost extinguished humankind is a motif that resounds through myths from all corners of the ancient world? Many nations share a story of a great deluge, and while there are multiple versions of the myth, we see common threads running through them all. Many flood myths appear to be tales of the gods' punishment for the errant ways of humans, or for over-population, while others tell of the repopulation of the earth or human origins. One item that appears almost consistently is a boat or vessel that saves a few chosen people as a reward for their piety or wisdom, often filled with all the plants and animals needed to rejuvenate life across the earth. The stories commonly tell of a brother and sister pair, yet some have bewitching details all of their very own, unique to the land where they originate.

We find the roots of Noah's deluge in earlier stories, like that of the ancient Near Eastern *Epic of Gilgamesh*, which was passed down from the Sumerians to the Assyrians and Babylonians. It describes Utnapishtim as a great ancestor who survived a terrible flood and was granted immortality. Utnapishtim was instructed by the god Enki to build a giant boat; everything that was not within the ship would be destroyed by a great flood. Afterwards, Utnapishtim sent out three birds: a dove, a sparrow and a raven. Only the raven did not return – a sign that the flood was over. As a reward for his faith, the gods gave him and his wife the gift of immortality.

Many of the Noah stories follow this pattern, yet some have quirky details unique to their country of origin. Noah appears in traditional Indigenous tales of the Dreamtime flood, *woramba*, from the Fitzroy River area of Western Australia, where it's said that the *Ark Gumana* carried Noah, along with Indigenous Australians, finally settling on the flood plain of Djilinbadu. It's believed that the idea of the ark ultimately landing in the Middle East was a lie, to keep Indigenous Australians in subservience. However, another Australian story gives a different explanation for the flood. The medicine man Grumuduk, who could call the rains and cause plants to grow and animals to be fruitful, was kidnapped by a plains tribe. On his escape he vowed that whenever he walked on an enemy's territory, salt water would follow in his path.

Strangely, mice often find themselves in starring roles in the flood myth genre. A Russian folk tale recounts how the Devil told Noah's wife to prepare a strong drink in order to discover Noah's reason for building the ark, which indeed she did, finding out the secret that God had entrusted to him. She was also responsible for the Devil, who had transformed himself into a mouse, secreting himself away on the ark and gnawing holes into the bottom.

An Indigenous flood story from northern Siberia also mentions mice. Here, seven people survived the flood on a boat, yet a horrendous drought followed it. They dug a hole, which filled with water, yet all but one man and one woman died from starvation; these two had eaten mice to save themselves. The whole of humankind are descendants of this pair.

The boat is a recurring symbol in many stories. In Hindu tradition, a demon stole the sacred books from Bramha; humanity, in its entirety, became corrupt, apart from the seven Nishis and Satyavrata, the prince of the maritime region. One day, when Satyavrata was bathing, the god Vishnu came to him in the form of a fish, warning him of the great deluge that would come to destroy all that was corrupt on the earth. He told Satyavrata that he would be secured in a capacious vessel, and instructed him to take with him the seven holy men, and fill it with all the plants and animals of the land. With this, Vishnu disappeared, and over the next seven days Satyavrata did as he was commanded and prepared for the waters. Indeed, within a week the rains began. The rivers broke their banks and the oceans flooded the land, bringing a large ship floating towards them. Satyavrata bundled the holy men on board, along with their families, and all the herbs and grains he had been instructed to bring, along with two of each animal. The great Vishnu came again to protect the vessel, by transforming into a giant fish and tying the boat tightly to himself to survive the flood. When the waters subsided, Vishnu killed the demon that had stolen the holy books, and taught their lessons to Satyavrata.

In the flood myth from Cameroon, the prophetic animal is a goat, rather than a fish. The tale tells that a woman was grinding flour one day and allowed a goat to lick it up. In gratitude, the goat warned her to take up her possessions and flee before the flood ensued.

Some flood stories take an even more fantastical turn. For the Soyots of the Republic of Buryatia in Russia the world is carried on the back of a giant frog or turtle. While this idea might be familiar to many, it might surprise you to know that it's told that the creature moved just once and from this tiny act the cosmic ocean flooded the earth; in fact, the creation stories of Eastern Siberia say that if the world frog moves even a little, the world will shake violently, and earthquakes can rain down on humanity.

We also find that many myths link a worldwide flood with giants. Berossus, a Chaldean writer, astronomer and priest of Bel in Babylon in the 3rd century, adds to the Noah story by describing the antediluvians that were left after the flood as a depraved race of giants; all except 'Noa' that is. Instead, Noa revered the gods, and resided in Syria with his three sons: Sem, Jepet and Chem. He foresaw the oncoming destruction in the stars and had set about building a ship to save his family. Remnants of the boat are still said to exist where it settled, on the peak of Gendyae or Mountain, and bitumen was still taken from it to ward off evil well into the 19th century. Similar tales of an antediluvian race of giants exist in Scandinavian flood traditions, where Odin, Vili and Ve defeated the primordial giant Ymir. All but two of the giants, Bergelmir and his wife, were killed in a great flood that arose from the blood of Ymir's gushing wounds. All giants are descended from these two.

Stranger still, elves appear in a Chingpaw flood story from the northern region of Myanmar. In this tale, brother and sister Pawpaw Nan-chaung and Chang-hko fled to safety on a boat, taking nine cocks and nine needles with them. Once the rain had ceased, they threw one of each from the boat, until they came to the last pair. On throwing these overboard, they finally heard the cock crow and the sound of the needle hitting the bottom. With this they were able to return to dry land, and soon came upon a cave in which two elves had made their home. The siblings stayed with the elves in their cave, and all was well with them; that is until Chang-hko gave birth, and left the infant in the care of the elfin woman while she went out to work. This is where the story takes a gruesome turn: the woman was a witch! Faced with the incessant wailing of the child, the witch took it to a crossroads where nine roads met, chopped it to pieces and scattered the body about, yet keeping a little with her, with nefarious intent. On her return to the cave, the elf-witch made a curry from the remaining parts of the babe, feeding it to the unsuspecting mother. When she discovered the truth, in her utter dismay, Chang-hko fled to the crossroads to plead with the Great Spirit to avenge her child and bring it back to life. The Great Spirit deemed this impossible, but instead promised to transform the remaining pieces of her child into the next generations of humankind – one branch for each of the nine paths – making her the mother of all nations to ease her pain.

MERMAIDS, SELKIES
and Spirits of the Deep

The folklore of the sea is filled with tales of half-human hybrids; these creatures, often exceedingly beautiful in either looks or voice, exact a strong allure over those they come into contact with. Whether beguiling with their beauty or with the exquisite nature of their singing, these creatures can be both benign and terrifying, helping humans if it serves their purpose, or luring them to a wet and watery end if the mood takes them.

Seductress or Saviour?
The Timeless Lure of the Mermaid

Tales of mermaids have frequented folklore, children's literature and popular culture in recent times. The origins of these long long-haired, fish-tailed, half-human beauties, however, stretch back surprisingly far into history.

An Assyrian myth from 1000 BCE tells of Atargatis, a beautiful fertility goddess. One of the many tellings of her story describes how she fell in love with a handsome young man, but tragedy was not far behind. Some say he was unable to keep up with her love-making, while other versions of the tale say that it was the birth of her human child that caused her great shame. Whatever the cause, the outcome was the same: Atargatis killed her lover and, unable to stand the guilt, she threw herself into the sea. Her desire was to become a fish in penance for her terrible actions, but it was not to be. Her beauty meant that the transformation could only be half-complete, and the grieving goddess found herself with her old human head and body but, below the waist, with the tail of a fish.

From then onwards, mermaids have become a staple of popular culture and belief, spreading throughout the world in numerous forms and incarnations. Some mermaids were said to have shown kindness towards humans. The mermaid encountered by an old man in Cury, Cornwall, rewarded his lack of greed by granting him many mysterious powers and bequeathing a magic comb that was passed down through the generations of his family. More often than not, however, mermaids receive bad press and their relationships with humans are reported as decidedly negative; for instance, the Brazilian Iara or Yara is known for tempting sailors down to her palace under the waves to a watery end.

Christopher Columbus famously recorded a sighting during a voyage in 1493, declaring the 'mermaids' he had witnessed as: 'Not half as beautiful as they are painted.' This scathing assessment might be explained scientifically; it has since been thought that what he had actually seen were manatees, sea cows or dugongs.

Perhaps the best-known and most well-loved mermaid is Hans Christian Andersen's *The Little Mermaid*, a story inspired by earlier mermaid folk tales, in which the famous storyteller used fairy-tale tropes to conjure a magical narrative beloved by many today. Written in 1836 and published the following year, Andersen's mermaid has been represented in dozens of incarnations and variations over the almost two centuries since she first appeared on the printed page. Often reimagined and retold for modern audiences, the tale is one of many now at the centre of debates about gender, sexuality and feminism in folk tales and literary fairy tales. The mermaid is commemorated today by a statue that rests at Langelinie, Copenhagen, Denmark; fashioned out of bronze, she is a copy of the original designed by Edvard Eriksen and erected in 1913.

The Little Mermaid:
A Tale from Denmark

Once there was a mermaid, the youngest of six princesses, who lived in a beautiful kingdom beneath the sea. Her mother was dead, but her father, the Merman King, ruled with the support of their grandmother from a breathtaking palace made of coral and amber and a mussel-shell roof. Although the youngest of the sisters, she was the most contemplative, calm and content.

Each of the princesses had a small garden, and while the others filled theirs with all manner of beautiful things, the youngest mermaid had nothing in hers but flowers that were like the sun and a marble statue of a beautiful boy. She was greatly taken with the human world above, begging for tales from anyone who might know anything of what went on there. Such stories only increased her fascination, and the little mermaid longed to see it for herself. This was not a forlorn hope; when each princess reached the age of 15 they were permitted to rise up above the waves and sit on the rocks by night, to watch the ships and experience a little of the world of humankind.

One by one her sisters had their turn, and the youngest mermaid watched and waited and listened to their experiences, each passing year only increasing her desire and longing to see for herself. Finally, when she felt she could wait no longer, her turn came. Sunset had just passed when the little mermaid rose up through the ocean for the first time, to find a calm sea and golden streaks fading in the sky. Drinking in the fascinating sights, the sound of a party in full swing on a nearby ship caught her attention; captivated, she swam closer for a better look.

She spied a young prince celebrating his birthday, and, to the mermaid, he was the most attractive sight she had ever seen. She watched and watched, enjoying the brightly coloured rockets that were set off in his honour, the lights and flashes and gaiety little short of magic in her eyes. The mermaid could not tear herself away even after the last strains of music had long faded, the ship now in darkness as the night went on. So she was there to witness the sudden breaking of the calm: an unexpected storm rolling in, shattering the peace of the night. Waves crashed higher and higher, rolling over the deck, the ship at the mercy of the tempest.

As the little mermaid looked on, the main mast was snapped like a piece of kindling, the helpless vessel tossed onto its side as those onboard flailed desperately in the water. Despite great danger from floating debris, the little mermaid found the prince, holding his head out of the water and keeping him safe as the storm finally died down. As dawn broke she took her precious prize to the nearest land, setting him on the beach carefully before retreating to watch. Before long, the prince was discovered by a young woman, who ran for help, and the mermaid watched sadly from behind a rock as he was carried off to warmth and safety.

The mermaid returned to her home but could not forget the prince; quiet and withdrawn, she pined for the young man and the world she had left him to. When she admitted the cause of her sadness to a sister, word soon spread, and it was revealed that the location of the prince's kingdom was known to another mermaid. The princesses took their sister there, and the little mermaid now spent her evenings near the palace, watching what went on there and waiting for glimpses of her prince. Instead of soothing her troubled heart, more and more she wished for an immortal soul like humans possessed; alas, being a mermaid, this was not to be. Instead, like any mermaid, she was destined to spend 300 years beneath the waves, before her form would be dissolved into foam.

Was there nothing she could do to gain a soul, she asked her grandmother one day in despair. There was only one thing, the old woman told her: if a mortal man loved her more than anything in the world and married her, her body would then become infused with his soul and she would achieve her wish. It could not be, however, for she had only a tail – and how could a mortal man love someone who is half fish?

That night the mermaid decided to seek help elsewhere. There was a terrible sea witch known for her great powers, and the mermaid set off to ask for her advice. The journey was terrifying and hard, through bare grey sands and bubbling mud, with trees and bushes that were alive, grabbing and pulling at those unwary enough to get too close. Horrified, the mermaid saw in the mud the bones of animals and humans who had drowned. It was so tempting to turn back and return to her lovely home, but the determined little mermaid continued on her way.

Finally she reached the house of the sea witch, who already knew the reason for her visit. It was foolishness, declared the witch, but if she was determined to go through with it, there was a way that it could be done. To swap her tail for human legs and have the chance to gain an immortal soul and be with her prince, the witch would make her a potion; before sunrise came she must swim ashore, sit on the beach and drink it. Her tail would then divide and shrivel, becoming instead the two legs she so coveted. It would come at a price, however, the witch warned. The process would be painful and feel like she was being run through with a sword. Not only that, every step the mermaid took on her new feet would feel like treading upon knives as she went. She would, however, without doubt, be the most beautiful girl the kingdom had ever seen.

A more faint-hearted girl might have balked at this, but the mermaid stood firm and agreed, her love for the prince so great she was willing to suffer anything to have the chance to win his heart. She would not be able to reverse the process, the witch warned: she would never be a mermaid again and would therefore never see her family under the waves. Also, if she didn't manage to convince the prince to love her, she would not gain a soul, and on the first morning after his marriage to someone else her heart would break before she instantly turned into foam in the sea. Even to these terrible conditions the mermaid agreed, but there was yet more. As payment, the sea witch demanded the girl's beautiful voice in the form of her tongue. Again the little mermaid did not hesitate, and her tongue was duly cut out, the witch making the promised potion for her.

Grief-stricken at the thought of not seeing her family again, but hopeful for what was to come, the mermaid made her way to the beach. Drinking the potion down she felt the first stab of agony course through her as the witch had promised. It did not matter, however, as the prince himself appeared at that moment and, as she looked at herself, the mermaid gleefully saw that her tail was gone, human legs now in its place.

Intrigued, the prince asked her name, but of course she could not tell him that or anything else about herself. Instead, she was taken to the palace, where she was given clothes and looked after as a valued guest. The prince became very fond of the little mermaid, and the pair were

inseparable. She slept on a velvet cushion outside his room, and he took
her riding with him, climbed mountains as they explored the kingdom,
and she smiled and looked on him with love even as her feet bled. The
prince did love her in return, but, alas, as a child, not as a future wife, and
the proposal of marriage she so longed for and needed never came. For the
prince confided in his silent confidante that he was in love with the girl
who had discovered him on the beach after the fateful storm, and he could
now love no other. This news nearly broke the mermaid's heart, especially
as without her tongue she could not tell him that it was she who had saved
his life that night, and was powerless to reveal her identity.

As time went on, rumours started to circulate that a bride had been chosen for the prince. Yet the mermaid did not worry, as he had told her that because there was only one girl for him he would never wed. To keep up the pretence, however, he made the voyage to where his prospective wife lived in a neighbouring kingdom; the mermaid – his constant attendant – accompanied him on the journey. In a terrible stroke of fate for the mermaid, it turned out that the princess was the very same girl who had helped save the prince; overjoyed, the prince at once consented to marry her and preparations for a grand wedding were soon underway. The mermaid played her part with smiles and all signs of happiness, even as her feet bled and the pain in her heart grew ever greater as she knew that this marriage would bring with it her death.

One night, the mermaid received a visit from her sisters. They were barely recognizable as their hair was shorn off; out of love for the little mermaid they had made a bargain with the sea witch, swapping their hair for a knife that would save their sister's life. She had only to stab the prince with it when he slept and the spell would be reversed; the little mermaid could then return to her 300 years as a mermaid and an end dissolving in the foam.

The mermaid took the knife and crept into the room where the prince slept, a smile on his lips as he dreamed of his new bride. Gazing down at him, she felt her heart almost burst with love, and in that moment she knew she could not carry out her task. With a final look at him she turned and left, throwing the knife far out into the sea. A moment later the mermaid followed, throwing herself into the deep water, where she dissolved into foam.

Despite the witch's dire prediction, however, all was not over for the little mermaid. She was greeted by the daughters of the air, spirits who had been offered the chance to strive for 300 years doing good deeds in order to earn an immortal soul. If they were successful, they would reach heaven, and the little mermaid, through her suffering and selflessness, would now have the chance to do the same. Gladly, she accepted the offer, bidding farewell to the earth and sea below as she rose up into the clouds above.

THE KING OF HUMBUG: P.T BARNUM AND THE FEEJEE MERMAID

Being elusive creatures, it isn't often that the opportunity arises to see a mermaid in the flesh. In 1842, however, visitors to New York were presented with just such a chance, when the now infamous Feejee Mermaid went on show at Barnum's American Museum, through the connivance of arch-hoaxer P.T. Barnum. Believed to be of Japanese origin, the 'mermaid' – measuring an estimated 45–90cm (1½–3ft) long – was actually the desiccated body of a monkey sewn to the back half of a fish. Despite disappointment expressed by some visitors, the exhibit was a hit, with Barnum's profits doubling in the first month the 'mermaid' was on show.

Not long afterwards, the mermaid mysteriously vanished; some stories say it perished in a fire, while others are convinced that, against all odds, it escaped this ignoble fate. Is a similar mermaid in the possession of the Peabody Museum at Harvard University in fact the original Feejee Mermaid?

The Mermaid to Serpent Queen: The Many Guises of Mami Wata

Mystical, ever-changing, many things to many people; the African water deity known as Mami Wata is a complex and multifaceted spirit. Most popularly depicted as half-woman, half-fish, with long, wavy black hair, her likeness to the popular and seductive mermaid of legend and folklore is immediately inescapable, highlighting the hybrid and shifting nature of folklore between different times and continents. Her nature is like that of the sea itself: powerful, changeable, alluring, both willing to give, and to take away. She is worshipped throughout West, Central and Southern Africa, as well as within the African diasporas: throughout the Caribbean, Latin America and the USA.

Her origins are often debated, but it is generally accepted that Mami Wata is not indigenous to the African countries that have become her home over the centuries. With a long tradition of part water creature, part human deities in such areas, however, it is unsurprising that she has thrived and taken root there.

The primordial water spirit, noted for her overwhelming beauty, Tingoi (or Njaloi) has been identified as a precursor to Mami Wata, and forms the link between sea, water deity and serpent. Sometimes depicted as a mix of serpent and fish, Tingoi has the head of a human woman, long, black locks of hair and a stunning appearance, not to mention the powerful lure she holds over those who follow her, heavily suggestive of later mermaids of European lore and Mami Wata herself. Receptiveness to such beings was already present when, in the 15th century, through contact made from trade and conquest, the mermaid was taken by African peoples and reimagined, emerging as the fully African Mami Wata.

Another link between Mami Wata and mermaid lore is through the connection both have to mirrors. The image of a mermaid combing her luxurious locks while admiring her reflection is a common one, and Mami Wata is likewise often depicted with her own treasured glass. Mirrors are also used by her followers to make contact with Mami Wata;

they form an important piece of Mami Wata worship and identification and are present at her shrines. Mirrors represent the reflective surface of the water, but also allude to her ability to transgress boundaries. They are said to attract her to them because of her vanity, drawing her presence to wherever she is needed. Her devotees mirror her in their worship: recreating her underwater realms within their sacred spaces, impersonating her in rituals, and even entering possession trance states to gain her favour. However similar some of her traits may seem to mermaid traditions, though, the worship of Mami Wata is very much a living belief, one that has been called a 'uniquely African faith' that developed in times of trade with the wider world.

In possession of many powers, Mami Wata is generous and bountiful, bestowing them upon those who follow her, well-known for bringing wealth and fortune to those she favours. Fertility is also said to be in her boon, despite her own infertile and childless state. Another power possessed by this deity is that of healing, in both body and mind. It is said that the most favoured of her followers have sometimes been taken down to her watery realm beneath the sea, returning to their life on dry land changed beyond recognition forever.

Despite her great power for good, there is a darker side to Mami Wata. While giving gifts in one moment, in the next she can and will take them away, striking with sudden wrath those who displease her. Illness, suffering beyond measure, even death itself is said to come at her hand. There is also said to be a limit to her bounty; to those she grants wealth, beauty is beyond their grasp, and those upon whom she bestows fertility, wealth will never be theirs. Mami Wata is a powerful female, nurturing and sexual potency fully co-existing within this most complex of deities. Yet she is also prone to jealousy, demanding faithful celibacy from men in Zaire in return for wealth, and it's said in Ghana that she can even kill a man's wife. For the Igbo of Nigeria, Mami Wata can also punish with illness, especially if feeling slighted at not receiving enough attention from her followers.

Although unpredictable, one of the many lures of Mami Wata is the very fluidity of her nature. The Krio of Sierra Leone look to the Moa River as the source of all life; the river is wild and unpredictable, mirroring the nature of Mami Wata who lives within it. Capable of morphing and being formed into whatever is needed by each individual person who calls on her, Mami Wata's appeal is that she can be many things to many different people at any given time. Her shifting and hybrid nature is illustrated in a physical sense in an Efik sculpture of Mami Wata, where she is represented as a mixture of woman, goat and fish, while in her hands she holds a snake and a bird. In some locations, Mami Wata is found in a plural form, as Mami Watas, and even in male form as Papi Watas.

Mami Wata has enjoyed a resurgence in attention in recent years, and there has been a general increase in interest in African deities. Such interest in Mami Wata in particular has also been spurred on by popular singer Beyoncé's fascination with the deity and allusions to Mami Wata in her album *Lemonade* and her own personal depiction of the goddess. An exhibition examining Mami Wata was held at UCLA in 2008, while the MAMI exhibition of 2016, held at the Knockdown Centre, New York, examined the different ways six women-identifying artists related to and identified with Mami Wata.

Some suggest that there is a less positive facet of Mami Wata: that far from empowering women of colour, the idolization of the spirit is actually harmful, reinforcing the derogatory image of Black women as 'manipulative eye candy'. Largely, however, her reception is seen as a positive thing, capturing the imagination of and empowering many as the powerful water goddess is reinvented afresh for a modern audience.

The Selkie-folk, the Shapeshifting Seals of the Northern Seas

For those that live on the shores of the icy waters of Orkney and Shetland, the raging waves and skerries provide an atmospheric backdrop to tales of the selkie-folk. While originally dark, malevolent creatures, selkies later became renowned as beautiful and gentle, often found dancing on the sand under moonlit skies. Selkies emerge from the waves as seals, only shedding their magical skin when they reach the shore, transforming into human form as they cast it away. Many tales tell that if the skin is taken and hidden the selkie cannot return to the sea to live with their selkie-kin, and must stay in human form until it is returned.

One such folk tale is remembered in a famous Orcadian ballad, 'The Great Silkie of Sule Skerry'. In this tragic tale, an Orkney maiden falls in love with a selkie man, who abandons her shortly after she gives birth to their child. Seven years later, a seal appears to her and tells her that he is her lover, only to dive once more into the sea. Another seven years pass, and the seal appears once more. This time he gives the gift of a golden chain to their son, who goes with him to live in the sea. The woman remarries, and many years later her husband is out hunting one day and shoots two seals. On returning to the house, he gives his wife the gold chain that he found around the neck of the younger seal. She realizes that her husband has tragically killed both her son and selkie lover.

Male selkies were often blamed for the disappearance of young women who wandered too close to the seashore alone at night. Many disappearances were put down to the girls being whisked away and taken as lovers by selkie men, who easily conquered the mortal women with their seductive powers. Indeed, women used to paint crosses on their daughter's breasts to ward off the selkie-folk when they set out on a journey across the sea; yet a selkie lover was often coveted.

Selkie nymphs were said to have snow-white skin and large, dark eyes, and be just as irresistible as the males. Old stories say that they often sat on rocks in groups, basking in the sun, and if disturbed they would hurriedly slip back into their skins and swim away. 'The Goodman of

Wastness' tells of a man who refused to marry a woman of his own kind, but set about stealing the skin of one unfortunate sea-maiden after stumbling upon a group of them one day. The selkies leapt into the sea and swam away, yet all but one had donned their skins and returned to their seal form. As he bundled her skin away and turned to leave, he heard the maiden weeping, begging him to give back what he had stolen. At her pleading he instantly fell in love with her, and implored her to stay with him as his wife. She agreed, but only because she couldn't return to the sea without her skin, which he refused to return. As the years passed the couple had seven children and were content. Yet each time the man left the house his wife would search high and low for the skin that was stolen from her on that fateful day long ago. One day, when she was searching as usual, her daughter asked her what she was looking for, to which she replied, 'A skin to make shoes from,' to help her daughter's injured foot. The daughter said she had seen her father take out the skin a time ago, when he thought her to be asleep. The selkie wife rushed to the place, pulled out the skin and ran to the beach. And, slipping it on, she leapt into the sea to return to her selkie husband.

Many children on the Orkney Isles have been said to have 'selkiepaws' – webbing between their fingers and toes. For instance, there are accounts of a 19th-century midwife who attributed this to their selkie parentage, and repeatedly cut it away to prevent fins forming from their tiny hands.

To Summon a Selkie Lover

M any folk have yearned to meet a selkie lover over the years, and when the secret method of calling one to you was uncovered, it was passed down from generation to generation as prized knowledge, as it is now passed on to you here. First, you should wait until the perfect time to meet your lover, this of course being high tide. When this time has come, you must go quickly to the ocean waves. Once you have reached the shore, you should shed seven tears into the sea – no more, and no fewer. At this, a potential selkie lover will appear in front of you in the waves. But be warned: sadness follows many who take a selkie as their life-partner, as most will always yearn for the waves until their days are done.

MONSTERS FROM THE DEEP

Tales of monstrous sea creatures span the centuries, appearing as early as the dawn of writing itself. Many sea serpents embody creation and primordial chaos, and can be found in end-times myths from across the globe – stories that tell of the end of the world. Tiamat is one of the first, described in ancient Mesopotamian tablets known as the *Enûma Eliš*. Seen as a great dragon, she is sometimes a creator goddess, while a symbol of primordial chaos for others – a thing that has filled humankind with dread since the earliest times. The myth tells of the joining of Tiamat, the personification of the saltwater ocean, with Apsu, the god of the fresh water. These two ruled together at the dawn of time, and were primeval waters in the cosmic abyss. Younger gods were born from this union, living within the body of the great Tiamat and making a great noise, which angered Apsu, hence he planned their demise. When the younger gods found out about his intentions, Marduk and Enki killed Apsu in revenge, and a great battle between the gods ensued, ending with Tiamat's death – a symbol of the new gods overcoming the watery chaos that existed at the beginning of time. Marduk created the heavens and the earth from the two halves of Tiamat's body on her death, and created people as slaves to the gods from the blood of her lover-son, Kingu.

According to Jewish tradition, the fearless Leviathan of the *Talmud Bava Batra* is said to be a multiple-headed sea serpent or crocodile, which emits a noxious gas from his mouth that makes the waters boil like an apothecary's mixture. Breathing fire, his scales are his pride and his teeth are terrible. What many people haven't heard of is his female counterpart; it was said that if the two mated the world would be destroyed, so the female was salted and preserved to be fed to the righteous at a glorious banquet on the Day of Judgement. Tasty!

Tales of primordial snakes and serpents come from many mythologies. Jörmungandr, the Midgard Serpent of Norse mythology, is one of the children of Loki along with Hel and Fenris-Wolf. He was thrown into the sea that encircles Midgard by the gods because of a prophecy that great misfortune would befall them due to Loki's offspring. At this, he grew so large that his body now encircles the entire visible world and he can grasp the end of his own tail with his maw. As sworn enemies, Thor is destined to slay Jörmungandr when Ragnarök – the battle at the end of the world – arrives.

Surprisingly, giant squid are not in fact mythical sea monsters at all, despite growing to the length of a school bus; the largest ever found measured close to a colossal 18m (nearly 60ft). One legendary creature often depicted as a terrifying giant squid is the Kraken, a sea monster hailing from Scandinavia. Erik Pontoppidan, an 18th century historian, describes the Kraken as 'round, flat, and full of arms, or branches', with a back 2.5km (1.5 miles) in circumference. It's said to resemble a series of small islands at first, with something floating around that looks like seaweed, and then, finally, huge tentacles as tall as a mast appear from the depths. The only way to escape his fearsome clutches is to row away before he surfaces, and then lie on your oars for safety. Apparently, fishermen have always been glad to find him, as his presence leads to an abundance of fish – yet the fishermen never stay in his vicinity for long, as even his retreat back into the sea causes whirlpools that will drag anything close down into the depths forever.

Sea monsters still capture our imagination today. A 1920s hoax told that a sea monster was to blame for the sinking of a German submarine in 1918, when Captain Günther Krech's vessel, *UB-85*, was damaged by a strange beast with 'horns, deep-set eyes and glinting teeth'. A contender for the wreck was found in 2016, yet historians from Bournemouth University said tales of sea monsters and the sinking of U-boats grew from the secrecy that surrounded precisely what took place during the first U-boat battles. Stories often arose as a result of journalists and ex-Navy men 'talking late at night, after having a nice time'. Sea monsters appear in contemporary culture, for instance the terrifying sea serpents of Robin Hobb's *Liveship Traders* trilogy (1998–2000), or the fearsome Kraken in *Pirates of the Caribbean: Dead Man's Chest* (2006), yet some reject all claims of their existence. Many dismiss them as mere oarfish turned legend, often citing the example that washed up on the shore of

a Bermuda beach in 1860 – initially called a sea serpent – as evidence. Yet sea monsters linger on in our imagination, maybe as they are often perceived as spiritual symbols of the subconscious mind and our hidden fears, quietly lurking deep in our nightmares to this day.

Scylla and Charybdis

We've all heard people say they're stuck 'between Scylla and Charybdis', but do you know there's more to the phrase than just being 'between a rock and a hard place'? In Greek mythology, Scylla was a terrifying monster that lurked in a cave on the Calabrian side of the Strait of Messina in southern Italy, while Charybdis lived on the Sicilian side.

Tales tell that Charybdis was a feared whirlpool that vomited ships and drowned seafarers by sucking water down to the depths of the abyss, then hurling them back up, 'lashing the stars with waves'.

Scylla was said to be a creature with a human face, with the tails of dolphins, while her nether regions were surrounded by the heads of ravenous dogs – yet this wasn't always so. Hers is a woeful tale of a beautiful virgin and a lover scorned. On being pursued by Glaucus, an unrelenting suitor, she was horrified to see his tail, making her question whether he was a god or a monster. Glaucus explained that he was certainly an equal of the watery gods. When sorting his catch in a field after fishing one day, he saw the fish eating the grass and then miraculously returning to the sea. On seeing this wonder he too ate a little and was then compelled to plunge into the waves forever. The gentle powers of the ocean took him as their brother, and prayed to Tethys to purge his mortal, earthly parts away by repeatedly reading a secret charm. Glaucus bathed in 100 streams, and became of the sea for evermore: falling into dark oblivion, he woke with a sea-green beard, azure skin and a fishy tail. At this story, Scylla scorned his love and fled. Glaucus went to the monstrous realms of the sorceress Circe to plead for one of her baneful love potions that would ensure that Scylla should feel the same agonies of love as he did. Hearing this, Circe revealed her own desires for him, and when rejected, vowed her revenge. Circe went to the cave where Scylla had sought shelter and poisoned the water there. Scylla was transformed into a monster forever, as her destiny decreed.

From that day hence, Scylla has plucked sailors from any passing ship that drew near to her to avoid the dreaded Charybdis, devouring them alive as the screams of her 'dark blue ocean hounds' echo from

the cave walls. Indeed, Odysseus himself had to navigate between the
two monsters, and was advised by Circe to sail closer to Scylla, or risk
losing his entire ship to Charybdis. He took her advice and only six of
his crew died – one apiece eaten raw by each of Scylla's heads. Many have
rationalized Scylla as the treacherous rocks of the Italian coast, which do
indeed devour wayward ships.

ISLANDS OF FABLE
AND MYTH

With the sea featuring prominently in the lives and cultures of
so much of the world, it is hardly surprising to discover an
underlying fascination with tales of mysterious islands among the legends
that pass down to us. Some of these are purely fictional in their creation,
while others are linked to either a former or existing geographical
location, ready to be discovered by an intrepid folklore explorer. Beware
of such a quest, however: these islands prove notoriously elusive to those
who wish to find them. Variously invisible, difficult to locate due to
shifting position and generally hard to pin down, they remain
a tantalizing focus for adventurer and myth-lover alike.

In Slavic folklore, the island of Buyan is home to several fascinating
characters and tales. The north, east and west winds are said to live there:
indeed, weather of every type is said to originate from Buyan. The island
is also known as the place where the sun both rises and sets each day, with
two goddesses, the morning star and evening star, helping the sun on its
way and welcoming it back each night.

Koschei, known as 'the deathless', is closely linked with Buyan, as the
island was the secret location where he hid his soul. Certain that the only
way to cheat death was to keep his soul and body separate, Koschei took
no chances. His soul was said to have been concealed with ever-increasing
intricacy: in some tellings it was to be found within a needle, within an
egg, within a duck. Despite his best efforts, Koschei could not avoid his
fate forever, and there are several versions of how he finally met his end.
In one he was killed by a blow from a small stone hidden in the yolk of
an egg – which in turn was hidden inside a hare, itself inside a duck.
Another slight variation on the egg theme is less complicated: Koschei
dies when he is hit on the forehead by the egg in question. A further
version tells how Prince Ivan breaks the egg containing Koschei's soul,
thereby causing his death.

Buyan is also said to be the location of alatuir, a mythical stone attributed with many magical properties. The most powerful of all stones, various sources describe alatuir as protecting a river of healing that flows beneath, and some say that a beautiful wound-sewing maiden also sits upon the stone, which marks the very centre of the universe. Like the island itself, alatuir is a positive healing force, said to be able to give happiness to those who come into its presence. It is hardly surprising therefore, given the stone's importance, to find it has a guardian. Gagana is a large bird with an iron beak and copper claws; along with Garafena, a magical snake said to be the oldest of all snakes in existence, the two guard alatuir and keep it from harm.

There are several theories regarding the origin and location of the mythical and paradise-like Buyan. Some hold that it is a location only in myth, while other sources state that tales of Buyan actually refer to the Baltic island of Rügen. There is also a theory that the term 'buyan' was originally used as an adjective or epithet for the concept of a fabled island, only later coming to be the name of a particular island itself.

Wherever its location, Buyan has an enduring and influential place in folklore. As well as featuring in several Russian tales, in the early 20th century Russian opera *The Tale of Tsar Saltan,* the Tsar's wife and son are mercifully saved from a watery death: cast adrift in a barrel by her jealous sisters, the pair are set ashore on Buyan by the sea, who has witnessed their plight.

Maui, Demi-God
and Creator of Islands

In the rich heritage of the folklore of the Pacific, there is perhaps no better-known figure than Maui. The trickster demi-god features in many stories across the islands. Generally accepted to have been the cleverest and most mischievous of several brothers, Maui, and the lands in which his tales originated, have close links with the sea. The tales of Maui and his exploits span thousands of miles of ocean, connecting the people and cultures of New Zealand, Hawaii and the Tahitian Islands, in an invisible yet tangible web of storytelling heritage.

It was said that Maui's brothers refused to take him fishing when they set out in their canoes. Perhaps it was because he was prone to playing tricks on his slower-witted siblings. Perhaps it was because they still had not forgiven him for returning to the family as the prodigal son and gaining a place as their mother's favourite. It might simply have been the fact that Maui was just not as good as they were at catching fish and would hinder their collective efforts. Whatever the reason, one day the brothers relented and allowed him to accompany them on a fishing trip out into the rich blue waters. Maui brought with him his beloved fish-hook, baiting it with a bird that was sacred to his mother. The brothers would have no cause for complaint about this particular catch: the fish Maui managed to hook was of such a great size that he asked his brothers to help him to haul it in. Unbeknown to them, clever Maui was also pulling the very land up from the bottom of the ocean. To prevent detection, he told his brothers not to look back; unable to resist, however, one did so, this act having far-reaching consequences. Not only did the line break in that moment, but so did the land – no longer a single perfect mass, behind the canoe lay a chain of rough, uneven islands, those we know today as Hawaii.

Interestingly, thousands of miles across the ocean, this tale of Maui has a Māori counterpart. In this version, after hiding away in the brothers' canoe, the disliked younger brother revealed himself only when it was too late to be set ashore. Although the brothers assumed he would

not be able to fish without a hook, Maui produced his own and, striking his own nose and using the blood as bait, Maui was soon rewarded with the biggest bite of his life. As previously related, the land was pulled up, along with the largest fish they had ever seen. In this tale, Maui left his brothers for a time, with strict instructions not to cut into the fish, but they did not listen. The consequences were disastrous. The fish thrashed about so violently in an attempt to escape that the canoe was destroyed, the brothers killed and the land left jagged and torn, making travel across New Zealand's North Island tricky to this day.

CLAIMED BY THE WAVES: Underwater Worlds

The Lost City of Ys

Another universal idea throughout global folklore is that of the sunken or drowned city or land, lost forever beneath the waves. Common features of such tales and legends include the belief that glimpses of these tantalizing worlds can still be seen or heard today, with talk of phantom bells or ghostly music drifting over the water, calling to us down through the ages.

Certainly, winning the prize for the best-known land to be taken by the sea is the mythical Atlantis: first mentioned by Plato in 360BCE, the idea of the lost civilisation has continued to captivate and inspire through the ages, bringing forth further stories across time and location.

It is hardly surprising that these tales occur with such frequency, with the ravages of coastal erosion and natural disasters such as tidal waves altering and reshaping the coastlines of the world over the centuries. For some, catching sight of a now-lost land is a good thing, while others are considered a curse. Those who are unlucky enough to see Cill Stuifín in Ireland on its reappearance every seven years are said to be fated to die within the following 12 months.

The Breton legend of the lost land of Ys, or Kêr-Is, is believed to have originated in the 12th century, developing over the following centuries to detail the fall of the ill-fated city built by King Gradlon to please his daughter, Dahut. Dahut was said to be greatly enamoured of the sea, but this proved to be something of a hindrance: Ys was built on low-lying land, and a dyke was erected to protect the city from flooding. At low tide the gate was kept open, but as the waters rose with each tide, the gate had to be closed and locked to keep the city safe. As a further precaution only one key to the gate existed, held by the king himself.

Despite her father's attempts to please her, Dahut was not said to be of good character; the young woman lived a wicked and decadent lifestyle, encouraging others to follow in her debauched ways. Dahut, according to rumour, drank, danced and fornicated, often murdering her lovers before they left her bed, and tales were rife regarding her terrible ways.

Although cautioned by Saint Winwaloe on the errors of the life she was living, Dahut remained resolutely unrepentant. As in most such tales, however, the king's daughter met her comeuppance. One day, a knight dressed all in red who was visiting Ys came to Dahut's attention. She summoned him to her chamber that night, and it might be presumed that Dahut once more had her wicked way with her handsome paramour. During the course of the night, a violent storm broke out, and Dahut told her lover about the dyke, the gate and the key. In some versions of the tale the red-clad knight (or the Devil, for so it was he) convinced Dahut to steal the key for him – in others the terrible deed is carried out by Dahut alone. The result was the same, the gate was opened wide and the high tide and storming waves rushed in, threatening to engulf Ys and all who lived there.

Alerted to the disaster, the king made good his escape upon his magical horse, taking with him his treacherous daughter. However, the very saint who had tried and failed to bring about reform in the unrepentant Dahut instructed the king to push his daughter – the demon who had brought such trouble on them all – into the water. Despite wavering, the king finally did so, before riding on to safety as the only survivor.

King Gradlon – a sadder, greyer man – found shelter in Quimper, France. A statue of him was erected there in 1858 and can still be seen today, visible between the spires of the cathedral.

The location of the ill-fated Ys is generally said to be beneath Douarnenez Bay in Brittany. Given the fluid nature of folklore however, by the 15th century the tale had relocated across the ocean, where tales began that Ys actually lay off the coast of Land's End, Cornwall. Further developments to the story in the 16th century identified this same land as

Lyonnesse, the home of Tristan, of star-crossed Tristan and Isolde fame. Later tellings have further conflated the tale with King Arthur's final battle with Mordred, the land being swallowed by a tidal wave.

Fascination with sunken cities is still going strong in the 21st century with Franck Goddio's discovery of the lost Egyptian city Thonis-Heracleion. Of great strategic importance, the harbours of Thonis-Heracleion were the focus of all major trade in and out of Egypt, and the city was also of religious significance. In the 8th century it was lost in its entirety: the city's statues, temples and artefacts were submerged beneath the waves, preserved and remaining largely forgotten until Goddio's history-making breakthrough.

Urashima Tarō and the Palace of the Dragon King

Many versions of the tale of Urashima Tarō exist, yet the seeds of the story appeared in Japan as early as the 8th century. The legend goes as follows: Urashima, a young fisherman, is walking home in the twilight after a day at sea, when he sees a group of boys torturing a small turtle. Now, while Urashima is known as a most skilled fisherman, he is also famous for his kind heart, so he rescues the turtle and releases it back into the sea. He thinks nothing more of it until the next day, when he sees the turtle again. She comes into his boat to thank him for his good deed, and makes an astonishing offer: to take him to the Palace of Ryūjin, the Dragon King of the Sea, where it is said that it is always a different season on each side. Urashima, of course, accepts. His day takes an even stranger turn when the turtle grows and grows until she is large enough to have him sit on her back. She carries him to the Palace of the Dragon King, deep in the depths of the ocean – yet on the way he doesn't become tired, nor do his clothes become wet.

On arrival, he is escorted through the gates of the great underwater palace by the guards, and inside sees the small turtle once more, now

transformed into a lovely princess named Otohime Sama, the Daughter of the Dragon. Urashima happily decides to stay with the princess as her husband. After a time, he begins to think of his elderly mother and father and misses his childhood home. He tells his wife of his sorrow, saying that he intends to visit his parents, and then return to her in the palace of the sea. The princess tells him that she will certainly miss him, but gives her blessing, and the gift of a box as a token of their love, which contains a very precious thing that will protect him from all harm – but only on the condition that he never opens it. Urashima accepts the box, and is whisked away on the back of a turtle to be delivered safely to the shore once more.

On his arrival he sees that his home is gone, and his mother and father are nowhere to be found. Dismayed, he asks if anybody remembers the fisherman Urashima Tarō. The people there reply that they do, yet only as a character in old tales of a man who was swallowed by the sea 300 years before, and that his parents died of grief. Urashima realizes that he has not been in the Sea King's palace for just a few days, but for hundreds of years, and all he knew and loved is now gone. Overcome with grief, Urashima returns to the seashore to wait for the turtle to collect him, yet it never comes. In despair, he thinks of his bride, and turns to the box – now his only hope of uncovering the secret of where to find her. Fatefully, he opens it. In a puff of smoke the elixir of everlasting youth blows away, and the years he has lost catch up with him at once; his hair turns white, his face wrinkles and his back bends with age. There, on the same shore where he met the turtle 300 years before, he falls down dead at the edge of the sea, never again to see his love – who still waits for him in the depths of the sea, in the glorious Palace of the Dragon King.

SCHEHERAZADE'S TALES: One Thousand and One Nights

Across the world, the sea holds the promise of gifts and opportunity, yet also of threats unknown. Treasures of the sea are depicted in just this way in *One Thousand and One Nights* – or *Alf layla wa-layla* – a collection of Middle Eastern tales dating back to the Islamic Golden Age. The book uses a frame story as a backdrop to many smaller tales – famously known as the *Arabian Nights* to Western readers.

This tale tells that Shahryār, the Sasanian king, is dismayed to find his wife has been unfaithful to him, and has her killed in revenge. He then decides to castigate all women, claiming they are all likely to be just as unfaithful. The king sets out to marry one virgin each day, consummate the marriage, and have her killed immediately on the following day, so that no wife can ever be unfaithful to him. One brave woman, Scheherazade, offers herself to the king willingly when no more virgins can be found. She comes up with a solution to prolong her life: to tell one tale to the king each night, but not give the ending until the next evening, keeping the man in suspense, and herself alive at each sunset. She can never be killed without leaving the conclusion to a tale untold, and in this way she survives for 1,001 nights. After this, versions of the tale differ, yet in all of them the woman survives at the decree of the king.

One tale from the collection, *The Fisherman and the Jinni*, reveals just how mercurial the waves can be with their gifts and dangers.

The Fisherman and the Jinni

Once there was a poor fisherman with a large family: a wife and three children. He worked hard each day, casting his nets four times, yet they often came back empty. One day was different. As he began to pull up his catch, he found it weighted down. With excitement the fisherman tried and tried to pull it up, and eventually managed to drag the net to shore. Yet, in his dismay, he found only the carcass of a donkey inside. He lost all hope, bereft that the efforts he had put into his work had amounted to nothing, and proclaimed there was nothing good left in the world but Allah himself.

He cried out praises to God, and plunged once more into the depths with his net. This time too it became heavy. And, once more, the man hoped it would be filled with fish. Yet, once more, his hopes were dashed. For there in his net lay a huge clay pitcher, filled with nothing but dirt. He prayed to God once more, asking his forgiveness, and tried a third time, throwing his nets into the sea. This time it came back filled with little other than broken pottery and glass.

Then, at last, he beseeched God to fill his nets on his fourth and final throw. Yet the net caught at the bottom of the sea, so the fisherman jumped in after it. This time he found a jar of yellow copper, stoppered with lead, and bearing the seal of King Solomon himself.

The fisherman, realizing its value, planned to sell the jar after cleaning it out. But, when he had prised out the stopper, he found nothing inside but smoke. The smoke poured out of the jar, spiralling up to the heavens until it formed a huge jinni. Recognizing it as an evil spirit, the fisherman was terrified.

The jinni believed he stood before Solomon himself, and begged the fisherman not to kill him. Yet when the man revealed his true identity, a lowly fisherman, the jinni vowed to kill him within an hour. He offered to grant him only one wish: the ability to choose the manner of his death.

The fisherman was taken aback, demanding to know why he must die. The jinni was happy to provide an explanation. He had been trapped in the jar by King Solomon. For a whole century, the jinni told himself that he would enrich his rescuer forever. Yet, then a second century passed, and during this time he vowed to offer endless wealth to anyone who released him from his prison. Over the third century, the jinni pledged three wishes to whoever freed him. By the fourth century, the jinni had grown tired and angry, and pledged that whoever brought him forth from his captivity would be put to death instantly, yet given a choice of how they would be killed.

The man begged for his life, but the jinni would not relent. A plan began to form in the fisherman's mind.

'How did you manage to fit into such a small bottle, anyway?' asked the man with the cunning of a creature facing its end.

The jinni could not resist displaying his magic. He shrank back down into nothing and, in a billow of smoke, disappeared back into the bottle, whereupon the fisherman replaced the stopper.

'Ha!' shouted the fisherman, 'Now I have you! How would you like to be thrown back into the sea for your troubles?'

And this time, it was the jinni who began to plead for forgiveness, offering to reward the man if he would only release him from his prison. In his cunning, the fisherman conceded.

The jinni rose up in a pillar of smoke as before, and this time kicked the jar into the sea. The fisherman was so afraid – and sure of his own imminent death – that it's said to this day that he wet himself in fright!

Yet the jinni was true to his bargain. He led the man through the wilderness, to a mountain pool filled to the brim with the most colourful fish he had ever laid eyes on. The fisherman eagerly cast his net into the waters. On drawing them up he found he had caught four fish, each shining brightly in a different colour.

The jinni decreed that the man should offer each of the fish up to the sultan himself. Yet, before he left to see the world, the jinni warned the man that he should never fish in the pool more than once a day. The man did as the jinni had told him, and set off at once.

The sultan was amazed. He had never seen such wondrous fish, and paid the poor fisherman a good sum of money in return for his troubles.

The fisherman, content to leave the tale here, returned to his wife and children with happiness and riches. Yet the sultan, whose fate is not yet told, ordered that the fish should be cooked immediately.

A slave girl took them, cleaned them, and placed them in a pan to fry. Yet, on turning them to cook the other side, a woman appeared in the midst of the kitchen heat wearing clothes of silk; her fingers were adorned with jewels and on her arms hung great bangles.

With a stick, she prodded at the fish in the pan, crying out, 'Oh fish, oh fish! Are you still true to your covenant?' And this she shouted three times, as the slave girl fainted away to the floor.

Finally, the fish replied, 'Yes! Yes, we are!'

And when the slave girl came back to her senses she saw that the fish were charred black in the pan, and fainted again in horror.

Soon the sultan's man came to investigate why the meal was taking so long to cook. He kicked at the girl until she came to, demanding to know what had happened, and the girl told him.

The sultan's man went to the fisherman, and demanded that he return to the mountain pool to catch four more fish to replace the last. And the fisherman did as he was commanded.

The sultan's man took the fish back to the palace, and ordered that the slave girl cook these four fish as before. This time he would see the marvel for himself. All happened exactly as before: the fish were flipped, the woman appeared, and the fish cried out to her in reply. Amazed, he ran to the sultan, recounting all that he had seen, and the sultan demanded to see the miraculous fish for himself.

The sultan's man went to the fisherman once more, this time with three witnesses, ordering him to catch four more fish. And so the man did.

This time, the king watched as they were frying, when a slave appeared in the kitchen with a branch in his hand, asking of the fish: 'Oh fish, oh fish! Are you still true to your covenant?' And this he shouted three times.

Again, the fish replied, 'Yes! Yes, we are!'

The slave strode over to the fish, toppled the pan to the ground with the branch, and promptly disappeared.

The sultan summoned the fisherman to him, demanding to know where he had caught the fish. A short time later the fisherman soon walked the path to the pool in the mountains once more, this time followed by the sultan and his men. When the sultan saw the wondrous pool, filled with fish of all colours, he was truly amazed. He vowed to uncover the secret of the pool.

The sultan changed his clothes and jewels, and began to march over the mountain. Once he had reached the other side, he began to climb the next mountain, and the next still, despite the heat and his trepidation. Soon, the sultan spotted a black dot in the distance. Convinced this was where the answer to the mystery lay, he set out to reach it.

After a time had passed he reached his destination. There he found a stone palace plated with iron. One door stood open, and the sultan proceeded to knock on it three times, but to no avail. No one answered from within, so the sultan took it upon himself to enter without invitation.

The sultan wandered through each beautiful room, admiring the gold-embellished ornaments and silk-lined walls. He marvelled at four red-gold lion fountains that stood in one courtyard as the palace birds circled freely above. While the sultan was overwhelmed by the beauty and riches of the palace, at the same time he was deeply saddened that there was no one who could tell him the secrets of the mountain pool. Yet, as he sat in his sadness, a voice began chanting from behind him, and the sultan could tell that whoever it belonged to was laden down with grief. He turned and began to trace his way through the palace, intent on finding whoever the voice belonged to.

Soon the sultan came to two heavy doors. Pushing them open, he saw a young man sitting before him, pale in the face with rosy cheeks bearing a small mole, his head adorned with a gem-filled crown. Overjoyed, the sultan ran to him.

Yet the young man did not rise, still overcome with misery.

The sultan beseeched the man to tell him the secrets of the mountain pool and his fishes. And at this the young man, in his sorrow, began to cry.

'But why do you cry?' asked the sultan, dismayed.

To this, the young man raised his silken garments. And instead of living legs, he revealed that his lower body was made entirely of stone.

The sultan's heart melted with compassion for the man. He begged him to tell not only the tale of the fishes, but his own sad story along with it. And so the young man did, by recounting 'The Tale of the Ensorcelled Prince', a tale within a tale, within a tale – as the *One Thousand and One Nights* often does.

The Tale of the Ensorcelled Prince

Once there was a prince who married his lovely cousin. Yet their marriage was far from a happy one. Unknown to the prince, the wife was skilled in sorcery and magic. Each night, the wife would give the prince a potion, and this would make him sleep through the night, while she crept away to her freedom.

One day, he overheard two slaves discussing his wife's night-time sojourns. The next evening, the prince pretended to take the potion, but did not drink it down. Then he followed his wife on her escapades.

And what he found was that his wife was, in fact, being unfaithful to him: with a slave. He immediately flew into a rage, set on killing the man. In his anger, he beat the unfaithful slave severely. Luck was on the slave's side: he lay there, almost at his end, but death still eluded him. Soon, the prince's wife came to the slave, taking him and tending to him. And this she did for the next three years. When he found out the prince was beside himself with rage. He went to his wife, demanding answers, and with every intention of killing her afterwards.

Fate turned its back on the prince. The wife mustered all she could against him, using her powers of sorcery to bind him with a magic spell. At once, the prince began to turn to stone, from his feet upwards. But once he was petrified to his waist, the spell was done. The prince was destined to be half-man, half-stone forever. And not only this, for the wife had yet more magic. She enchanted their entire city, transforming the four islands it was made of into mountains that surrounded a huge mountain pool. And she transformed people of the four faiths into fish: Muslims into white fish, Christians into blue, Jews into yellow, and Zoroastrians into red fish. To make matters worse, the wife would return to her prince each day, and whip him as he stood as still as stone. And now the tale of the sultan's speaking fish makes a lot more sense indeed!

After the tale was told, the sultan pledged to gain freedom for the prince from his plight. He helped the prince take his revenge by killing the slave, throwing his body into a well, then posing as the slave to persuade the wife to free the prince, which indeed she did. The wife then lifted all of her enchantments, restoring the city and the people to their rightful forms. Finally, still believing the sultan's disguise, the woman went to embrace him. At this, he stabbed her through, and then cleft her in half with one blow.

As for the fisherman, he was rewarded well: with a new position for his son at the sultan's palace, and the stone prince taking one of the fishermen's daughters as his wife, with the other marrying the sultan himself. And now we might do well to reflect on what such a tale might teach us: a story of a woman decried a witch, punished for her love of another man, and then murdered in the name of her husband.

Top Tales from Seas Around the World

1 The Arctic Ocean:
Sedna, the Inuit Mother of the Sea

In one version of this Indigenous traditional story, Sedna was said to be a giant with such a great hunger that she attacked her parents one night and began eating their limbs. Outraged, her father took her out in his kayak, and threw her over the side. Yet Sedna refused to die; and as she held on fiercely to the side, her father promptly cut off her fingers and thumbs. Sedna sank down into the depths to rule the Underworld forever, and her severed digits became all the marine animals of the seas.

2 The North Atlantic Ocean:
The Old Woman Arnaquagsaq

In Greenland, the sea goddess is named Arnaquagsaq – the very great or old woman. She sits in her dark dwelling in the depths of the ocean, while a bowl catches the oil that drips down the sides of her only lamp. The Inuit people of Greenland see this lamp as the sun, while the bowl is the great ocean that stretches out beneath it, holding all of the food-animals of the seas. It's said that when times are harsh, and there is little food, Arnaquagsaq is plagued by parasites, and only the spiritual journeying and prayers of the angakok priests can help her. Yet the priests face great challenges in reaching her. First, a priest must pass through Arsissut, the realm of the happy dead, then cross a great abyss containing a constantly turning wheel as slippery as ice. Next, he must pass a boiling kettle with seals in it, until finally arriving at a house protected by fearsome creatures – either seals or dogs. Once inside, the priest must face the final obstacle: a bridge as thin as a knife's edge. The prayers that are offered up are seen as great weather magic, which chase away the storm clouds that often appear later in the season. Only then will Arnaquagsaq release all of the food-animals back to the people, and there is a time of plenty again.

3 The South Atlantic Ocean: Iemanjá, the Candomblé Goddess of the Sea

Known by many names, Iemanjá, Yemanjá or Janaína is an orixá, or goddess, worshipped in the Candomblé and Umbanda religions across Brazil. She is seen as Queen of the Ocean, often depicted as a woman rising from the waves, and associated with the bountiful fertility of the seas. The orixá has power over all things to do with being a woman, including motherhood and children. She is the patron of fishermen, aiding them in their catch, along with those who have survived shipwrecks. Light blue or white are her colours, and her followers often deck themselves in white dresses, throwing white roses into the waters in her honour. Mirrors and combs are her symbols.

Iemanjá is a figure who came to Brazil with the enslaved Africans brought to its shores. In the African Yoruba tradition she is the orisha Yemoja, a mother spirit who rules over waters, rivers and streams, often depicted as a mermaid. Some statues today show Iemanjá herself as a mermaid, yet many, strangely, also depict her as a slender white woman. This is explained easily: when her followers arrived in Brazil they used religious syncretism to help them to continue the worship of their own orishas in the face of suppression; this is when one deity or spirit is amalgamated with another, local version to aid their acceptance. They began to celebrate

Iemanjá on the existing Brazilian saints' days, and today her festival is still held across Brazil on 2 February – the date of the official holiday of Nossa Senhora dos Navegantes (Our Lady of the Naviagtors). The largest of these festivals is held in Salvador, the capital of the state of Bahia, where her statue is carried amidst thronging crowds. Flowers, candles and toy boats are released as offerings into the sea in her honour, carrying wishes and prayers of the supplicants along with them as they move across the waves. Similar festivities happen on 8 December at the Festa da Conceição da Praia (Feast of Our Lady of Conception). During the de-Africanization of Afro-Brazilian culture, the orixás – spirits or forces of nature that do not take human form – became personified in human-like statues. Iemanjá took on a form very similar to the Virgin Mary: slender, dressed in light blue with pale skin. There has been a movement to make the figure more African by giving her a darker skin tone, and a fuller figure to show her links to fertility and womanhood. Many dispute this movement, claiming there is no racism in the syncretized iconography. The debate continues today, as the expression of this religious figure morphs and changes with each person and generation that follow her.

4 The Indian Ocean: The Great Dragon of the Primordial Seas

Naga Padoha is a great dragon that rules the Underworld and primordial sea in Indonesia, and the opponent of the great creator-god, Mula Jadi Na Bolon, who existed before humans were created when the world began. The birth of humanity actually arose when Mula Jadi's granddaughter fled from her lizard-shaped husband in horror, rousing the sympathy of her grandfather, who offered the girl a handful of earth on which to live. This earth was mistakenly spread out near the fearsome sea dragon, who almost destroyed it with his writhing and churning, and the girl could find no peace. Yet armed with her own shrewdness, and the help of her grandfather, the girl overcame the dragon, running him through with a sword and casting him in an iron block. Now, whenever the bound dragon writhes in his prison, an earthquake wreaks havoc on the land.

5 The North Pacific Ocean: Hit, the Octopus Goddess of Micronesia

On the Caroline Islands, Hit is a beautiful goddess that takes octopus form. The most famous tale recounts how Hit's daughter became the mistress of one of the gods. Yet each time the god tried to meet with his mistress, his sky-wife would not be far behind. Hit took it upon herself to dance as a distraction, giving such a wild and erotic performance that the wife was overcome. She fainted with sheer excitement, and was carried back to her home in the sky. So successful was this plan that Hit committed to the show each time her daughter intended to meet her lover, leading to the conception of Olifat, one of the Caroline Island's most beloved folk heroes.

For the Itneg of the Philippines, the sea itself is sentient. At the beginning of time, only the sea and the sky existed. Traditional stories recount how a kite, having no place to settle, caused the sea to wage war against the sky. She threw her waters up towards the sky, which caused the heavens to make a pact of peace with her. Afterwards, the sky decided to enact his revenge: with a great display of power, the sky rained down huge clods of earth on to the waters, which became islands. The sea was subdued, and was never able to rise up against the sky again, and was destined to run only back and forth forever. This is how the world was created. Some people tell a similar tale to explain the movement of the sea; in it the ancient sea god Magindang endlessly lusts after the youthful god of the pale moon, and so each month the waves rise up to catch him.

6 The South Pacific Ocean: Te Māngōroa, the Shark of the Milky Way

For the last 50 years, the Māori of Aotearoa New Zealand have been fighting to reclaim their heritage after facing years of racism and intolerance; this includes their traditional astronomical knowledge of the stars, both for navigating the seas – *tātai arorangi* – yet also of celestial knowledge relating to Creation, the gods and about the seasons and time itself: *Kauwae-runga*. As often happens in oral traditions, this knowledge has been kept and passed down from generation to generation using traditional sayings, songs and stories. These Indigenous tales of the heavens have an unexpected link to the waters of the earth.

The sea is seen as vital in Māori culture, as the source of food, and of life itself. In the Indigenous creation epic, Ranginui is the Sky and Papatūānuku, his consort, is the Earth. They have many children, and among them is Tangaroa, the god of the sea: the sea has been central to Māori life from the very beginning of time.

Sharks are considered sacred guardians to many, and appear in a large number of traditional tales. One *taniwha* – guardian creature or monster – is Ruamano, who is said to take the form of a mako shark. Tales tell how he rescues sailors from overturned canoes – *waka* – taking them to dry land, and safety.

It is said that the traditional hero and demi-god Maui placed the shark, Te Māngōroa, up in the sky, and this became the Milky Way. Today, it is still referred to as Te Ikaroa (the long fish), Te Ikanui (the great fish) and Te Māngōroa (the long mango shark) because of its fish-like shape.

RED SKY AT NIGHT:
Sailor Superstitions from Across the Globe

With the perilous nature of sea voyages and the uncertainties that prevailed when setting off for waters unknown, it comes as no surprise that numerous superstitions and beliefs have grown up among those who lived their lives on the waves. For despite the treacherous nature of the sea, there were many ways a canny sailor could guard against misfortune, and even more actions and mistakes that needed to be avoided at all cost.

Some people were thought to be naturally luckier than others, and protected at sea. Those who were 'born with a caul' – that is, with a portion of tissue or amniotic membrane attached to their head – were said to be safe from death by drowning. Some believed that this immunity only held for that person, while others stated the protection could be transferred – hence a thriving trade in preserved cauls right up until the 20th century. One particular tale tells of how a child born with this protection caused no end of trouble to his mother at bath time – however hard she tried, the air-filled buoyancy of his caul meant that she couldn't keep him long enough under the water to be properly washed. To be born in the caul was to be in good company; among the great and famous reputed to have been born thus are Byron, Freud, James I and Napoleon. Cicero is often cited as stating that those born at the rising of the Dog Star, Sirius – that is, 3 July to 11 August – were never to be drowned, protected by the accident of their birth.

There has been much concern regarding the luck or otherwise of particular days when it comes to setting sail. In England and Scotland, Sundays were seen as a lucky day to do so, and a voyage beginning on that day would go without a hitch. Wednesday and Thursday were likewise lucky according to Norse tradition, being associated with Odin and Thor respectively and thus, it was thought, invoking the protection of the god in question. Friday, on the other hand, has been considered an unlucky day for sea journeys in many cultures. The obvious and most frequent connection made is that of it being the day of Christ's crucifixion, and it has also been suggested by some that, being the day of the Norse goddess Freya, with her association with the much-maligned cat (see below), it was therefore unlucky for those at sea. On the other hand, Friday was said to be an auspicious day to start a voyage in America, due to many positive events in the history of that nation occurring on that day. For Spanish sailors, Tuesday was a bad day to set sail, as outlined in the proverb '*El Martes, ne te casas, ne te embarques, ne de te mujer apartarse*' – 'Tuesday, don't marry, go to sea, or leave your wife'.

Perhaps not surprisingly, the number of things that were seen as unlucky at sea were more numerous than those that brought favour. It was well known that having a woman on board a ship was seen as a sure-fire way to bring bad fortune (both for the ship and no doubt the woman in question) although, conversely, it has been said that a naked woman actually has the opposite effect and could calm a storm from on deck.

Making a wine-glass ring would cause the death of a sailor, and if the glass actually broke, then any number of disasters could occur. Whistling close to the sea could have perilous consequences, as could anything going wrong during the naming of a ship. Although red sky the night before setting sail could be seen as a positive sign, if it happened come morning, that was another matter entirely and the sailor should beware of what might be about to befall him.

Cats were said to be used by witches to cause storms that put the crews of ships in peril, while in Zoroastrian folklore cats are thought to have been created when a woman copulated with a demon, and it is believed that all the fish will die if a cat dares to urinate in the water.

Haunting the Waves:
Ghostly Ships and Skeleton Crews

The sea is calm. The moon shines on the gently bobbing waves. Suddenly, out of nowhere, sails can be seen, ropes heard thrumming in the rising wind. The ghost ship sails into view, onlookers watching in amazement or terror as it rushes towards them, only to vanish once more before their very eyes.

Legends of phantom ships that haunt the seas of the world are widespread across the globe, providing universal appeal and fascination. Some of these ships are purely fictional in origin, with no known historical ship to correspond to the tale that has built up around it. Legends of *The Flying Dutchman*, believed to have originated in the 17th century, are perhaps the most famous of these: the ill-fated vessel doomed to sail the seas for eternity, never able to come into port. Others can be verified as having been a historical vessel, overcome by an unexplained and terrible fate. These ships continue to be sighted long after the untimely demise of their crews, often on the anniversary of the tragedy.

The *Mary Celeste* is one such ship. She was discovered on 5 December 1872 off the Azores in the Atlantic Ocean, in perfect condition but without any sign of her crew or what had become of them; by definition truly a ghost ship – a vessel discovered without its crew. Despite a vast amount of interest and investigation, no satisfactory explanation has ever been found. The *Mary Celeste* has been sighted many times during the following decades, entering folklore and popular culture as 'the greatest maritime mystery of all time'.

New ghost ships continued to enter the existing catalogue of phantom vessels well into the 20th century. According to legend, the SS *Ourang Medan*, a ship of Indonesian origin, met an unknown fate in the Dutch East Indies. In 1947 the ship gave out a distress call, but when help arrived, it was to find everyone on board dead. Not only that, their faces were frozen in expressions of eternal horror. Although there are various explanations, from the mundane to the paranormal, the ultimate fate of the crew is unknown, and even the existence of the ship itself is yet to be satisfactorily proven.

Perhaps one of the most intriguing tales of a ghostly vessel is that of the *Caleuche* – believed to mean to change condition, or to be another – a phantom ship that is a staple of the rich folklore of Chiloé. The series of islands lies off the coast of Chile, and it was here, during the arrival of the Spanish in the mid-16th century, that the first sightings of this mysterious ship were reported.

The *Caleuche* is said to be quite a sight indeed: brightly lit and with music that drifts across the waves, the atmosphere is one of partying, fun and cheer. The crew, however, are no ordinary sailors; the ship is manned by witches and wizards, and also, it is said, by those who have lost their lives to the treacheries of the sea. Those on board are free from the constraints of human illness and the ravages of age do not touch them; as the name of the vessel suggests, the ability to shapeshift is also attributed to those onboard. This has created an almost veneration for sea creatures and birds in the Chilote people, as they could be the souls of the departed. Sightings of the *Caleuche* tend to take place at night near beaches, and there are tales of the ship transporting sailors to other islands, and also of the ship pretending to be another ship before discarding the disguise and vanishing – much to the amazement of onlookers.

There is another, darker, side to the *Caleuche*. To see the ship is to risk one's very existence; those who have witnessed the spectacle might be taken on board to join the eternal party, or find themselves left behind, but without speech or their sanity. There is also a fear that a *Caleuche* sailor can kidnap or kill an onlooker; and, just for catching sight of the ship, an unwary fisherman could be physically altered and taken on board to serve.

As with most ghost ships, various theories have been put forward to try to explain the many sightings of the *Caleuche* that have spanned history and continue to occur to this day. Mirages, glowing marine plant life and UFOs are among those mooted, but there is one of particular note because it is held by the Chilote themselves. It is said that the *Caleuche* stories are an afterlife narrative for those who have lost loved ones to the sea, providing comfort amid their grief that existence continues in some form aboard the eternally partying ship; this is, perhaps, the most satisfying explanation of all.

THE GRAVEYARD OF THE ATLANTIC:
The Mystery of the Bermuda Triangle

The folklore of the seas is full of terrifying creatures and seductive spirits ready to lure the unwary to their doom. Perhaps even more terrifying is the unseen threat that strikes without warning, leaving no trace of those who fall foul of an invisible force.

The Bermuda Triangle, an area in the Atlantic Ocean loosely framed by Miami, Puerto Rico and Bermuda, is well famed for being a place of tragedy. According to legend, ships and planes crossing this area have completely disappeared into thin air, the men, women and children onboard swallowed up by whatever invisible force is at work there.

An article in the *Miami Herald* on 17 September 1950 by E.V.W Jones is the first known source to suggest something strange was occurring in the area now popularly known as the Bermuda Triangle, listing several boats and planes that had seemingly vanished there. It was 14 years later, however, in 1964, that Vincent Gaddis elaborated on this evidence and put forward a concrete theory that strange happenings were occurring in 'The Deadly Bermuda Triangle'. Referring to the 'mysterious menace' that had destroyed 'hundreds' of planes and ships without a trace, Gaddis traced these incidents back to the middle of the 19th century, with the disappearance of the *Rosalie* in 1840 being one of the earliest. Gaddis even went so far as to allege that almost a thousand lives had been claimed by the triangle.

The most famous and often-cited disappearance in the ill-fated triangle is that of the lost patrol or, as it is popularly known, Flight 19. On 5 December 1945, five TBM Avenger torpedo bombers took off from Florida on a routine patrol. The intended flight plan should have taken around 2 hours, but 1 hour 45 minutes after take-off, a startling communication came from the patrol leader. They were off course and could not see land. Furthermore, despite the fact all were experienced pilots, they could not even identify which way west lay, and the sea below looked strange and unfamiliar. The tower listened, helpless, as conversation between the pilots grew steadily more frantic. The last words heard were, 'Tower, we are not certain where we are ... we think we must be about two hundred and twenty-five miles north-east of base. It looks like we are –'. And then, nothing but silence. Not only was the doomed patrol never found, but a Martin Mariner – a weighty vehicle crewed by 13 men that went to their aid – also vanished.

Such tales, repeated and embroidered, have become the steadfast 'facts' of the Bermuda Triangle mystery. There have been numerous criticisms and debunking attempts, however, with critics pointing out several flaws in the seemingly watertight accounts. In 1975, Larry Kusche published *The Bermuda Triangle Mystery: Solved*, in which he highlighted various problems with the work of Gaddis and others. According to Kusche, exaggeration, inaccurate reporting and flat-out fabrication significantly muddied the waters, especially the omission of references to inclement weather conditions at the time of some disappearances. It has also been pointed out by sceptics that, given how busy those waters are, the number of disappearances and accidents is statistically even somewhat on the low side.

Explanations for the supposed mystery of the Bermuda Triangle range from the bizarre to the mundane. Technology left from Atlantis and UFOs (the latter popularized by Charles Berlitz) are among the more outlandish suggestions that have received attention over the years. Natural phenomenon such as compass variations, the effects of the Gulf Stream and violent weather conditions have found popularity among those looking for a more scientific theory, along with the obvious and perhaps most tragic contender, human error.

The fate of Flight 19 and the other planes and vessels that have vanished will likely never be discovered. It is this very uncertainty, along with the prevailing allure of the unknown, that ensures the continuation of the enduring fascination of the Bermuda Triangle.

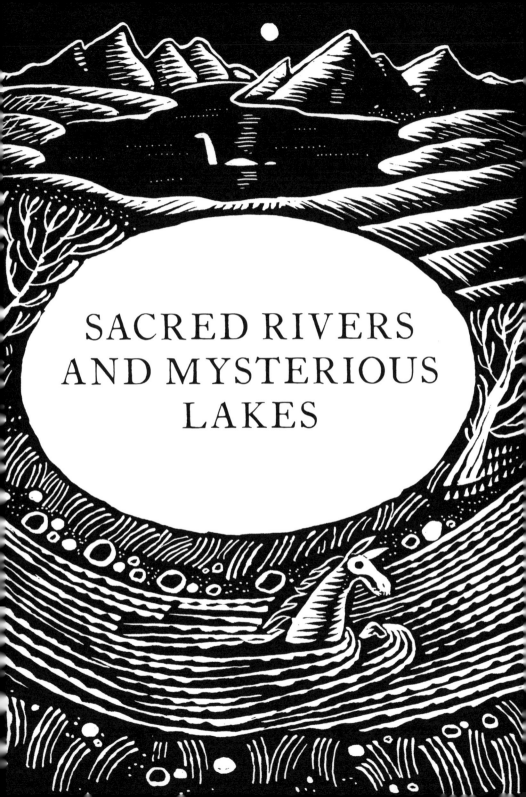

SACRED RIVERS AND MYSTERIOUS LAKES

SACRED RIVERS

Water is a source of life that we cannot live without, so it's no surprise that rivers across the globe have been considered sacred for thousands of years. While many are heavily polluted, pilgrims and the faithful still flock to their banks in countries all over the world to give thanks with votive offerings, to ask for healing, or simply to offer their prayers to the deities that the rivers call their own.

In the 15th century, the Incas saw the great Urubamba River that churns near Machu Picchu as a reflection of the Milky Way, which in itself was seen as a celestial river that draws water from its earthly counterpart. The sacred nature of rivers is no less relevant to many people today: the Whanganui was the first river in the world to be awarded the status of being a legal person by the parliament of New Zealand in 2017, in recognition of the special relationship the Māori in the region have with the river, and reflected in a local saying, 'I am the river, and the river is me.' This means that nature can now be regarded as a person, and have the same right to protection – which can be enforced. In the same year, the Uttarakhand High Court in India declared the Ganges and Yamuna rivers as 'living entities' in the same way. While this decision was reversed a few months later, with the Supreme Court decreeing that the rivers were not in fact living entities, the case highlights that the debate about the nature of rivers and their spirits is at the forefront of people's minds.

While there are seven sacred rivers in Hinduism, the Ganges is the most famous, running through both India and Bangladesh. It's said that chanting the name of the river near the dying allows their souls to pass through the gates of heaven. Bathing in the river is a holy act, which serves to cleanse people from their sins, and liberate them from *samsāra*: the cycle of life, death and rebirth. One of the largest pilgrimages in the world takes place in January when crowds – over a million people in 2017 – gather for the Makar Sankranti festival at Sagar Island, near the Bay of Bengal. This number is only surpassed by the Kumbh Mela, the largest pilgrimage in the world, which appears on UNESCO's Representative List of the Intangible Cultural Heritage of Humanity.

Many rivers are perceived as goddesses, from the Nile in Egypt to the Huang He (Yellow River) and Yangtze in China, and this is also true for the Ganges: there are lots of origin myths for the waters, yet many believe they originated when the goddess Ganga herself came down to earth in the form of a river. The goddess is said to have four arms and three eyes that enable her to see the past, present and future all at once, and she rides a white crocodile. For a river sacred to so many, and integral to life in the region, it's devastating to hear the official figures for river pollution in the Ganges: the E. coli bacteria from human sewage is over 100 times the limit deemed acceptable by the Indian government in some parts. Sadly, the endangered Ganges river dolphin purportedly represents the purity and holiness of the river, as it's said to only be able to survive in pure waters.

RIVERS OF THE UNDERWORLD

For many of us, the Underworld conjures images of echoing caves, cavernous and empty, stalactites drip-dripping into pools where shadows flicker as sea serpents glide in their timeless depths. We will one day join the lines of hopeless souls trudging the well-worn path to the creaking gates that conceal the final mysteries of life, watched over by gatekeepers that reach out to us from millennia of eerie death-tales. All too soon we will see the bejewelled thrones of Hades of Greek myth, or that of Ereshkigal, the Mesopotamian ruler of the land of the dead. We might crouch in fear at the thought of harpies soaring above us, human vultures who carry away souls from the earth to the cold chasm of death. We too might reach down to our pockets, or into our mouths, to check if we have the required coin to pay the ferryman for our final journey.

We are not far wrong with these images, for this is the picture that mythology – many mythologies – teach us: the truths of this chthonic journey into death that haunts us in the dark waking hours of the night, tossing and turning, wondering if maybe we alone can escape the grip of the Underworld like the woeful Persephone.

We see the same images arise in many death tales: that of the Greek hero Orpheus; the Norse Baldr; Hutu who won back his love, Pare, from Hine-nui-te-pō, the Māori goddess of darkness and death. One tale less well-known is that of the twin heroes Xbalanque and Hunahpu, who travelled to Xibalba to defeat the lords of death in the Mayan Underworld – later becoming the Sun and Moon of the heavens in the *Popol Vuh,* the 16th century cultural narrative of the K'iche' people of Guatemala.

Greek

Many myths tell us that we will soon reach a river that encircles the Underworld – or separates it from the realm of the living – on our way to the land of the dead. In Greek mythology, this is the Acheron, the river of pain. It is here that Charon, the ferryman, silently steers his murky craft through the waters for eternity. Virgil describes him as a figure 'terrible in his squalor' with 'unkempt, hoary hair', eyes that are flaming orbs and dressed only in rags that hang from his shoulders. According to Virgil, the soul of the deceased must carry an obol – Charon's obol – under their tongue as payment to the grim ferryman for bearing their souls across the river to the Underworld on his dark ferryboat. Strangely, the *Suda*, a 10th-century Byzantine encyclopaedia, gives a different image of the river: 'Acheron is like a place of healing, not a place of punishment, cleansing and purging the sins of humans.' Once more, we see rivers as a place of purification, even in death.

The Styx is often confused and conflated with the Acheron, and some say that Charon is tied to this river instead. The Styx circles the Underworld seven times and is very different to the Acheron. The *Suda* says it is a dead river, as it is all dried up, while Homer calls it the 'Water of Terror'. Some say it is a river in Arcadia, the northern Peloponnese, a 'down-flowing' river that can cause death to anyone who drinks it, yet with wonderful properties: the water will break anything made from glass, crystal or pottery, and corrode anything made from metal; gold is immune. The only thing strong enough to carry this water is the hoof of a horse. Homer says it is a river in Hades, as well as the name of the goddess Styx, daughter of Oceanus.

Many other rivers snake through the Greek Underworld: the Lethe is the river of oblivion, while the Phlegethon is the river of burning, along which 'those deserving of punishments go away and dwell'. Those deserving of punishment also 'go away' along the Cocytus, the river of lamentations and dirges, which is the opposite of the Phlegethon, and said to be very cold.

Korean

There is also a river that separates the Underworld in a well-known Korean myth from Jeju Island: Chasa Bonpuli. Here, the hero Gangnim Doryeong is tasked with capturing Yeomra, King of the Underworld. He must cross the Henggimot Lake, which is surrounded by spirits who – starved for eras and unable to enter the Underworld – attack him. Gangnim throws himself into the lake to escape, and on emerging he finds he has indeed reached the Yeonchu Gate: the entrance to the Underworld, where he defeats Yeomra's 30,000 soldiers and captures the King of the Underworld with a steel chain.

Norse

There are mutterings of an Underworld river in Norse mythology too. Snorri Sturluson briefly tells us of Gjöll in his *Gylfaginning*, the river closest to the gates of Hel over which the Gjallarbrù bridge stands. In the story of Hermódr rescuing Baldr from Hel, it's said that this bridge is thatched with glittering gold, guarded by the maiden Módgudr, and must be crossed on the way to Hel. The Norwegian ballad *Draumkvæde* tells of the journey of Olav Åsteson into the otherworld. On falling asleep on Christmas Eve, he dreamed of the fate of the dead and their final journey, taking them across the bridge Gjallarbrù – which might seem familiar to those who know the work of Charles Dickens! Here on the steep bridge over the river he found thrusting serpents, biting dogs and an ox that gored and fumed blocking the way. In the *Grímnismál* of the *Poetic Edda,* both the rivers Gjöll and the Leiptr wind through the world of man, but then fall to Hel.

WATERFALL FOLKLORE

Waterfalls churn with beauty and power, so it's unsurprising that many come with their own folklore. Niagara Falls, a group of three waterfalls on the border between Ontario, Canada, and New York state in the USA, is the site of the Indigenous tale: *The Maid of the Mist*.

The Maid of the Mist

This traditional story from the Haudenosaunee (also known as the 'Iroquois', though this is often seen as a derogatory exonym imposed on the group by colonialists) tells that the great Hé-no or Hinon – the spirit of thunder – made his home in a cave behind the veil of water, living there with his assistants who had been given to him by the Great Spirit. One year, a young maiden of Ga'-u-gwa village, above the falls, was betrothed to an old and disagreeable man. As the contract could not be broken, she committed to ending her life by throwing herself from the top of the waterfall. The girl took a great bark canoe, and went bravely to her death. Yet, seeing her fall, the god and his assistants caught the maiden in a blanket, and carried her to their cave behind the falls. Captivated by the girl's beauty, one of the assistants took her hand in marriage. Before this event, the village had been troubled by a great plague, and a year after the marriage the thunder spirit took pity on the girl. He whispered the secret of the illness to her, and the solution, and sent her into the village with this news.

It so happened that a giant snake lurked under the village. Each year, the snake would be overcome with an insatiable hunger, and would feast on the bodies of the dead buried near his lair. He would creep into the village and poison the water to ensure enough people would die to satisfy his hunger. Hé-no advised the people to move their homes to Buffalo

Creek to escape the fiend. Yet the creature was intent on following his prey, and took to the waters, swimming with the current to find their new resting place. As he did, Hé-no sent out a great thunderbolt, which killed the monstrous snake. The creature's body floated downstream, blocking the waters when it stretched from one bank to the other until the land could resist no more. The gushing waters broke through, great chunks of land crumbling into the abyss below.

This is how the great Horseshoe Falls were born. Yet, should any curious wanderer seek to find the great Hé-no's dwelling place today, they will find nothing, for the cave also smashed into the churning waters, and was no more after the thunder god's great act of kindness for the people.

Controversially, a publicity poster by local artist Evelyn Carey, for the 1901 Pan-American Exposition in Buffalo, was released to over 35,000 postmasters across the country, depicting a scantily clad figure, veiled in French Art-Nouveau style. Entitled 'Spirit of Niagara', it is thought by some to be based on the Native American personification of the falls, or the maid from the tale of Hé-no. This would be seen as grossly inappropriate today, and an example of cultural appropriation of a traditional Indigenous story that many people still consider sacred.

A terrible phenomenon has been reported at the falls, whereby the brain sends the signal that one must step back – as the height is too much, and one might fall – yet this is often too quick to interpret correctly, and even today many people feel the urge to throw themselves to their death in the undulating waters below.

The Dragon's Gate

Waterfall lore also links to one of the most popular tattoo symbols: the koi fish of China. Koi fish tattoos are well-known symbols of courage and determination. Many people are unaware of the ancient story behind this symbol when they use it as a design – another example of how traditions can be appropriated by others across the world.

The tale tells that a school of koi were swimming up the Huang He, or Yellow River. Each tiny fish fought against the current, until they all – finally – reached the base of a great waterfall. Seeing the churning waters, many of the fish turned back, flowing downstream with the current. Yet a few of the golden school remained, determined to carry on their journey despite the obstacles. Jumping from deep in the depths of the waters, the koi used all their strength to try to reach the top of the waterfall, but with no success. Unbeknown to them, a group of demons sat in the undergrowth. Mocking and

jeering, they used their demonic powers to make the waterfall even taller. The years passed until they became a century. And on this fateful day, one single golden koi managed to jump the great distance, and reach the top of the waterfall. As a reward for its determination, the gods gathered together and decided to honour the fish for its perseverance. The tiny fish was at once transformed into a great golden dragon, and its destiny was fulfilled.

This place has been named the Dragon Gate ever since, and while people generally attribute this tale to the waterfall in Hunan Province, many places with this name exist across China.

There is a Chinese proverb that goes: 'The carp has leapt through the dragon's gate', historically used when passing the exam to become part of the administration of the Chinese emperor. It now has a more general meaning: that if a person works diligently they will one day be rewarded with success.

Lover's Leap: Suicidal Lovers

The star-crossed lovers motif is a popular one throughout both folklore and literature, from Shakespeare's *Romeo and Juliet* to the tragic tale of 'The Dargle Lovers' who leapt to their deaths in County Wicklow, Ireland. Love – or lack of it – is a constant preoccupation of the human race, but sometimes it can take a dark turn.

The stunning setting of the Huay Kaew Waterfall in Thailand makes it a popular place for lovers to snatch a few moments together. According to legend, during the Second World War, a young woman named Bua Ban – beautiful, kindhearted, the loveliest in her village – fell in love with a soldier from Bangkok. He returned her affections, and the smitten lovers talked of marriage and the happy future they would spend together. When the soldier was called back to Bangkok, Bua Ban did not despair – her lover promised he would return, and they would be together.

Unfortunately for poor Bua Ban, the soldier was already married, and never intended to return, as he had reunited with his true wife. Expecting his child, heartbroken, shamed and alone, the jilted Bua Ban made her way up to the rocky precipice. Devoid of all hope, she threw herself to her death.

She is remembered in local legend in the name of the waterfall: the spot where she fell is known as Wang Bua Ban. It is believed that her spirit frequents the place, providing a place of pilgrimage for lovers hoping for a happier ending than Bua Ban herself. Intriguingly, another tale linked to the Huay Kaew falls tells of a rich young girl who fell in love with a boy beneath her station. Despite their deep attraction to each other, the girl's family forbade their union, arranging instead another match for their daughter. The ill-fated couple continued to meet in secret until the day before the wedding. In desperation, vowing never to be parted, the pair leapt from the top of the waterfall, cheating fate as they met their end together.

THE TOP FIVE RIVER SPIRITS
from Around the World

1 French Melusin

The tale of this French water nymph goes back centuries. The first literary version was written by Jean d'Arras at the end of the 14th century, based on old documents kept at the castle of Lusignan, near Poitiers – yet there are many versions throughout northern and eastern France, as well as Luxembourg. A popular version tells that a youth, Raymond of Poitiers, the son of a count, one day came upon a nymph at a sacred spring in the forest of Coulombiers. The nymph agreed to be his wife, with just a single request: that he should grant her the gift of as much land around the spring as could be covered by a stag's hide, where she could build a castle. The tale tells that this did indeed come to pass, and the castle was named Lusinia, after the nymph herself, becoming the very same castle mentioned in d'Arras' telling of her story.

There was one addendum to this request – that she could come to her castle each Saturday and be entirely undisturbed – or the lovers would be separated forever. Of course, the young man agreed. But, as happens with all promises, the pledge withered as the years went on. One day, Raymond went to the castle after an old clergyman asked about his wife. On finding all but a single door open, he looked through the keyhole. There stood Melusine in her bath, her lower body the tail of a monstrous fish or serpent. In his sorrow, Raymond shared her secret. Melusine left him forever, yet promised to hover over the castle whenever a French king – or indeed any of her descendants – was near his death. It's said that her footprint was visible in the room where she leapt from the window in grief, but one of the last times she was heard was at the command that her castle should be pulled down, when she wailed and cried terribly.

2 Greek Naiades

The naiades were female nymphs of the freshwater rivers, streams and wells in Greek mythology. Many of these spirits had individual names and were associated with specific locations across the world. Worshipped by local cults who made sacrifices to them, people believed many could offer magical healing and cleansing through ritual bathing. They were often seen as vengeful and jealous spirits. A boisterous annual folk festival, celebrated centuries later, was rooted in the tragic myth of one particular Greek naiad and offers a lovely example of how a myth can inspire folk festivals and celebrations in later times. Herodotus tells us that Pallas was the naiad of Lake Tritonis – said to be in Libya in ancient times, but thought by some to be in Boeotia in Greece, or in the south of modern-day Tunisia. Pallas was the child of Triton, a river god and son of Poseidon. Triton raised the young Athena along with Pallas, and taught both girls the art of war. One day they took part in what some say was a mock battle, others a falling-out, hurling spears at one another. Zeus, loath to see Athena lose, distracted Pallas. The spear inflicted a mortal wound, and the naiad breathed her last. In her grief, Athena made a wooden statue of the girl, which became the famous Palladium stolen from Troy by Diomedes and taken to Rome by Aeneas.

It's said that this myth led to a festival celebrated in Libya to honour Athena. Herodotus tells us that the girls would be separated into two groups, then armed with stones and staves to fight each other. The crowd would choose their favourite before the event, and arm them with Corinthian helmets, put them in a chariot and carry them round the lake; any girls dying of their wounds would be given the title 'false virgins'. Charming.

3 Italian Anguane

In the national epic of the Ladin people from the Dolomites of north-eastern Italy – *The Rëgn de Fanes* ('Kingdom of Fanes') – the anguane are sacred lake nymphs who take human form, yet with near-transparent bodies. Helpful to humans, they can offer the gift of fertility and predict the future, often through prophetic dreams. Singing the sweetest songs, they live deep in lakes, or very close to them. They know the secrets of witches and can speak the language of owls. While not immortal, it's said they will live as long as the world lasts.

4 French Fenettes

In French mythology, fenettes are dangerous water fairies that come from the River Rhône, near Lake Geneva. The sweet, sad song of these evil fairies drifts through the reed-covered marshlands, soon becoming a gloomy groaning. It's said that anyone working the land or fishing in the waters withdraws quickly, never turning to look at what pursues them, as sight of the fairies will lead to death within just a year.

5 Norwegian Fossegrim

The fossegrim is a male Norwegian river sprite, famous for playing the fiddle under waterfalls and in millponds. He often plays on dark evenings and will teach anyone who brings him an offering: the student must look away and throw a white kid into a north-flowing waterfall – but only on a Thursday. Grimm says a black lamb is another fitting sacrifice. A lean goat is enough to ensure the learner will be able to tune the instrument, yet a fat goat ensures that the fossegrim will grasp the learner's hand and use it to play the fiddle until the fingers bleed; after this tuition they will play so well even the trees will dance, and waterfalls will stand still.

THE MYSTERIOUS WATERS OF SCOTLAND

Scottish folklore is replete with all manner of strange and terrifying creatures lurking in its rivers and lakes. Perhaps even more disturbing, however, are the spirits reported to lie in wait to prey on the unwary.

The evocatively named shellycoat is one such spirit. As the name implies, a shellycoat's main identifying feature is the shells it wears, these adornments clattering together to make a loud and frightsome noise. Unlike some water spirits, the shellycoat isn't out for blood; the danger with this creature is the penchant it has for trickery and instilling fear into the hearts of unwary travellers for its own amusement. In one tale, two men fell victim to the questionable humour of a shellycoat. On the banks of the River Ettrick, they heard a cry; fearing that some unfortunate person had tumbled into the water and was now battling for survival, they hurried to their aid. It soon became apparent this would not be as easy as first anticipated; not only could they not locate anyone, but the voice moved away, going upriver. The two men followed the pitiful voice throughout the night, the futility of their mission becoming clear when, upon reaching the top of the mountain that the river climbed, instead of finding anyone, the voice started to descend again on the other side! It was, of course, none other than a shellycoat, his satisfied laughter filling their ears as they slunk off on their way.

What then of the boobrie? Said to frequent the highland lochs, the boobrie – or *tarbh boibhre* ('bull cow-giver') – is believed to take its name from its cow-like behaviour. As the belief goes, this spirit wanted to join the cows that drank from the river, and so took on the appearance of a cow or bull to better achieve this aim. It could not entirely conceal its true nature, however; rather than sounding like a cow or bull, it made a noise like a terrifying bird.

Along with these two more common forms, the boobrie was also reported as a water horse, the *each-uisge*. Other forms it could take ranged from a large fly, a serpent bull and an earwig with a penchant for horse blood, the size of a man's little finger. It was believed to actually favour the shape of a bird, so terrible in appearance that it would have to be seen to be believed. This incarnation of the boobrie had a body larger than 17 eagles, a long sharp bill and huge claws on the end of webbed feet. The sound it made was just as terrible as its appearance – like a loud, enraged bull. This creature preyed on calves, lambs and sheep, and otters. The boobrie, in bull form at least, was thought to be not always evil. In one tale, it rescued a woman named Phemie from a rejected suitor who tried to carry her off; after knocking the man down, it took her to safety.

It is thought that the boobrie and ideas of its appearance come from sightings of the bird species the great auk. It is unlikely you would run into one of these creatures today; it was thought to have become extinct by the mid-19th century due to its habitat of heather being burned.

The *bean-nighe*, or the washerwoman at the ford, is believed to be a fairy or otherworldly woman. Found alone by ill-frequented rivers or streams, the bean-nighe is a terrible sight, washing, it is said, the clothes of those soon to die. She is best avoided, the sight of her serving as a death omen. This spirit doesn't cause harm herself, but seals the fate of others if not stopped. They are believed to be spirits of women who died giving birth, leaving life before their time. The bean-nighe is doomed to continue with her thankless task of washing until the day she would have left the earth.

The appearance of this spirit differs from area to area. In Perthshire, the bean-nighe is 'small and round' and wears green. On the Isle of Skye, on the other hand, she is characterized as childlike and squat, small of stature. Other identifying features of the bean–nighe are long dangling breasts. They are so long that she throws them over her shoulders to keep them out of the way, and it is this habit that can be the quick-thinking observer's salvation. If the discoverer can grab one and get it to his mouth to suckle, she becomes his nursing mother, and he her foster child. She will then tell him whatever he wants to know – including who is about to die. There were other ways to gain mastery over this ghostly washerwoman. In some areas, catching the bean-nighe at swordpoint meant she had to tell whoever caught her everything she knew. This could also mean on some occasions that her captor had to tell her everything she asked in return.

WATER HORSES:
Majestic and Malevolent Creatures from the Depths

A lonely and weary traveller finds himself walking beside a river, when suddenly he hears the sound of something moving through the water. The beat of hooves, the flash of a mane, and then, there, a horse: the answer to all his woes. The man mounts without caution, but this is no ordinary steed. He has become the next victim of one of folklore's less friendly creatures: the water horse.

One of the most famous water horses is the Scottish kelpie. However, while the terms are often used interchangeably, water horses and kelpies are two distinct creatures in Scottish folklore, with the latter found in rivers, while water horses such as the each-uisge frequent the still waters of the lakes and lochs.

With the unwary traveller on his back, the kelpie ultimately drags his victims down beneath the water to their death. There were ways to cheat the kelpie, however. In some tales it was possible for the kelpie to be at least seemingly tamed, made to do one's bidding by way of a bridle marked with a cross. This control would prove illusory and fleeting, and the moment the work was done the kelpie would flee back to its watery home, sometimes taking the rider with it. In one story, we learn that it is possible to kill a kelpie, the deed on this occasion carried out using that scourge of so many folkloric creatures: red-hot iron.

The prominence of the kelpie in Scottish folklore is evident from the sculptures located near Falkirk and visible from the M9 motorway. Measuring a staggering 30m (98ft) tall, they have been part of the landscape since 2013, testament to the enduring hold the kelpie has over the Scottish imagination. Another testament to the lasting and far-reaching nature of the legend is the appearance of the kelpie in modern literature, such as the works of Lari Don and an entry in J.K. Rowling's *Fantastic Beasts and Where to Find Them*.

Despite this great fame, interestingly, the kelpie or indeed any variant is not present south of the border in English folklore, with England's lakes and rivers being decidedly lacking in water horses of any kind.

This deficit is redressed in Wales where there are tales of the Ceffyl Dŵr. Still a staple of Welsh folkloric belief into the 19th century, the Ceffyl Dŵr varied in appearance and purpose. In the north of the country, the horse was just one form taken by this spirit that was prone to shapeshifting and violence towards people. In the south, the Ceffyl Dŵr presented consistently as a small horse, enchanting in appearance, that lured people onto its back. Speed is commonly remarked upon in tales of the Ceffyl Dŵr, and they are said to be able to cover huge distances in an impossibly short space of time before vanishing, leaving the hapless rider to drown. One exception to this rule – and an example of denominational equality – was where clergymen were concerned. Clergymen of any creed were said to be able to ride the horse without the rude treatment afforded to others, and there are several tales that relate how a minister reached his destination unscathed, while their accompanying clerk or deacon was left behind or thrown into the water.

The Scandinavian water horse is the *bäckahäst* or 'brook horse'. Most often seen when foggy, the bäckahäst is described as a majestic and luminous being. After beguiling riders into mounting, it plunges back down beneath the water to drown the victim, who is unable to dismount. Frequently in tales of the bäckahäst, those who ride the animal are children, perhaps because they are deemed more foolhardy, or perhaps to increase the sense of peril and impending tragedy in the reader. One popular version is that of a group of boys playing on a winter evening near a frozen river. When a beautiful horse appears, they climb onto it one by one. The last child, marvelling at the sight of his friends all mounted, declares the horse to be amazing, using a colloquial phrase that also happens to rhyme with the words Jesus Christ, which he says instead due to mispronunciation. The horse then disappears, leaving the lads with sore behinds but saved, due to the bäckahäst's hatred of the name of Christ. Despite the terrible predictions, many, or in fact most, tales end with the riders surviving. Like the kelpie, the bäckahäst could also, according to some tales, be put to work, sometimes because the rider had tricked it.

HUMPED SERPENTS AND VICIOUS EELS:
Loch Ness and the World's Most Fearsome Lake Monsters

There is something undeniably compelling about tales of large monsters lurking in the depths of lakes and rivers. Although each individual monster, or type of monster, is firmly rooted in the location associated with it, it might be surprising to note that sightings of such creatures share certain characteristics across different places, times and locations. The reliable, upstanding nature of witnesses cited, the appearance of the monsters themselves – often described as 'humped', or in other cases eel- or serpent-like – and attempts in recent years to photograph the creatures have been key in the development of such tales, further fuelling debate and the continuation of the legends. Here are a few of the most fascinating lake monsters across the world.

Although it is impossible to know when the oral tradition of a monster in Loch Ness began, *An Niseag* – or the Loch Ness Monster as it is more famously known – first entered the historical record in written form in the 6th century. In the *Life of St Columba*, a man is tragically killed by a water beast or monster while out on the River Ness, and the saint successfully saves one of his own companions from the same fate by compelling it to back off in the name of God. There is some dispute as to whether this describes the same creature that in the 20th century became known as Nessie. A 12th-century manuscript by Walter of Bingham, held by the British Library, actually depicts the monster as a large bear-like creature. Despite occasional sightings of something in the loch, they were few and far between until an account by George Spicer was published in the *Inverness Courier* in 1933.

According to Spicer, a creature about 12m (40ft) long with a long neck crossed the road in front of his car, before entering the nearby loch. This sparked a spate of further sightings and reports, including serious scientific studies, and the interest in Nessie remains until this day.

In Lake Lagarfljót in Iceland, a large worm of the same name is said to lurk beneath the waters. Another monster with a long pedigree, it is suggested that the first mention of the Lagarfljót Worm is from the 14th century, when in 1345 a 'wonderful thing' was recorded in the Icelandic annals. No head or tail was seen, but humps were witnessed rising out of the water. Further tantalizing detail is provided in a map from 1585, where the intriguing 'in this lake appears a large serpent' is engraved beside the lake itself. The 'worm' has been witnessed across the centuries that followed, and it is said to be up to 12m (40ft) long. Most popular explanations for these sightings include misidentification of foam floating on the water, bubbles of methane gas, and debris from a nearby forest and mountain.

The horse-headed, serpentesque inkanyamba of South Africa has its origins in both Zulu and Xhosa beliefs and folklore. Said to eat the bodies of those who fall into the water, and to attack those who come too close, this name is given to a group of creatures, though the most famous is the one said to reside in KwaNogqaza (the Place of the Tall One) at Howick Falls, in KwaZulu-Natal Province. These creatures have a wide span of operations, with sightings occurring in several other locations, including the Mkomazi River, nearly 72km (45 miles) away from Howick. Meaning 'tornado' in the Zulu language, the inkanyamba are blamed for violent storms over the summer, a belief also reflected in the Xhosa idea that the creatures take to the skies during those months in order to mate. In the late 20th century journalists recorded a belief among locals that a tornado that struck the village of Impendle was a huge snake. Storms that led to 2,000 people losing their homes were also blamed on the creature's wrath. There continued to be regular sightings, and a reward was offered in 1995 for photographic evidence of the creatures. Unfortunately, the only picture to result was proven to be a hoax. It is believed by many that inkanyamba are actually a form of eel – large, carnivorous and migratory, but not the monsters of legend.

The Banyoles monster was a terrible, dragon-like creature found in Banyoles Lake in Girona, northern Spain. During the 8th century, this dragon struck terror into locals with its penchant for feasting on livestock and people alike. According to the legend, the most powerful army belonging to Charlemagne came to vanquish the beast, but the soldiers' confidence proved misplaced: the army was decimated, the people left more hopeless than ever. Could no one save them? In desperation, some of the villagers visited France, where they sought the advice of a monk, St Emeterio. He drew the creature from the watery depths with prayers and words, and in doing so, either turned it into a peaceful creature, or – according to some versions – discovered that it already was, and that the rumours of its terrible deeds were merely a cover story for the pillaging army. Whichever version you believe, some say the Banyoles monster is still to be found in the lake to this day, where it lives peacefully enjoying a vegetarian diet!

THE FOLKLORE OF
SWAMPS AND MARSHES

Not far from New Orleans, in the swamps of Slidell, Louisiana, there's said to be a monster lurking in the woodlands. Two men, Billy Mills and Harlan Ford, are the first people who claimed to witness the creature in 1963, and said they managed to make a cast of its tracks a decade on. Years later Dana Holyfield, Ford's granddaughter, unearthed alleged footage of the creature, supposedly filmed in the 1970s, featured on Fox News. Now named the Honey Island Swamp Monster, it's said to be a hairy, human-like creature, over 2m (6½ft) high. Online videos and reports with people claiming to have witnessed the monster in recent years abound. Dana Holyfield herself has produced a film documenting the creature and collecting accounts to prove the veracity of her grandfather's story and honour his memory. In a filmed interview another eyewitness, Ted Williams, claimed he saw the creature jump a bayou and watched two of the monsters swimming in a river, stating that they looked human but with arms hanging by their knees. In another recent siting Herman Broom remembered it had a 'face like a man, and a body like an animal'.

Yet monsters that lurk in the Louisiana swamps are not just a modern phenomena. The Létiche is the soul of an unbaptized child that swims in the bayous of Terrebonne Parish, blamed for unsettling the *pirogues* (tree-trunk canoes) that navigate the waterways. Some say that this is a creature from Houma (Native American) legends, and the origin of the Cajun loup-garou. Similar to the European werewolf, the loup-garou is a human-wolf hybrid cursed to drink human blood. The only way to combat the creature is to throw salt over it, at which it will promptly turn to dust.

In Indigenous Australian beliefs, particularly from the Kulin nations and the area around Victoria – still living traditions today – the fearsome bunyip haunts creeks and billabongs. Sometimes said to be a devil or a dreaded water spirit, eyewitness accounts from the Barwon lakes near

Geelong in 1845 say it is over 3.5m (11½ft) tall, sporting an emu-like head with a serrated beak, and the body and legs of an alligator. It has a brightly feathered chest, gigantic claws and lays large blue eggs double the size of those belonging to an emu. It is amphibious, swimming frog-like, and only ventures onto the bank to bask on hot days. It walks upright on its hind legs and kills by hugging people to death. Further reports come from William Buckley, a Cheshire man who lived with the Wathaurong people between 1803 and 1835, who described it as having grey feathers, and being the size of a calf. He said bunyip only venture from the water when the weather is calm, and they have a supernatural power to cause illness and even death. One sign of a bunyip in the lagoon is a massive amount of eels; it's believed that they are specifically there because of the bunyip's presence, for him to feast on. It's thought that the creatures are viewed as supernatural by Indigenous Australians, and anyone killing a bunyip might even forfeit their own life.

Wherever you are in the world, when walking near stagnant waters, remember that they have lain in the land, long undisturbed ... and who knows what might be lurking in the depths.

Sinister Bog Lights:
Will-o'-the-Wisp

The road is long and the traveller weary, though he is not yet near his destination. Suddenly, in the distance, he spots a light, glowing and beckoning, urging him to follow. Thinking it might be a short-cut, some kind soul showing him the way, he steps from the path, deciding it is worth the risk. It is a choice that he might well live to regret, if he is lucky – as the traveller ventures onto the increasingly marshy land, the solid ground he has left so rashly no longer visible, the light is the only thing that can be identified for certain in the gloom. Still optimistic, he continues on, and on, growing wearier with each moment. Suddenly, without warning, the light goes out, just as the traveller feels his foot sink into the water …

That water has posed a danger to travellers across the millennia is indisputable, this very fact is made glaringly apparent by the large number of legends focused on this most treacherous of nature's elements. *Ignis fatuus* – fool's fire – exists in many variations in folklore across the world. Witnessed especially over swamps, marshes and bogs, these atmospheric lights are particularly prevalent across Europe, Norway and areas of the USA. Presenting in varying hues and sizes, these lights are frequently said to lure travellers to a watery fate or, at best, leave them hopelessly lost.

In England, the common name for such lights is will-o'-the-wisp. Derived from 'wisp', the 17th-century word meaning a bundle of hay or straw, and is often said to be someone called Will holding a lighted torch. Will's American counterpart is Jack-o'-lantern, and both are frequently depicted as having malicious or mischievous intent, and these lights are often referred to as spook lights, orbs or ghost lights.

Within European folklore, there are many explanations for these intriguing lights. Some say they are linked to the fairies. Others believe a man named Will or Jack, doomed to haunt the watery marshlands for all eternity due to some terrible deed committed during life, is the source of the lights that bob and dance in the distance. According to Swedish folklore, the lights are the souls of those who have died unbaptized. Ever hopeful, they lead travellers to the water in the hope that they themselves can receive the sacrament of baptism that they missed in life.

The Bengali phenomenon of Aleya – 'marsh ghost light' – appears to fishermen, causing confusion and leading to them becoming lost, sometimes forever, drowned in the marshes. Traditions in West Bengal and Bangladesh hold that the lights are the ghosts of fishermen who lost their lives at their work. They are not always intent on harm, however, some actually leading people away from danger, to escape the fate they met themselves.

The Hessdalen of Norway, Marfa Lights of Texas, and Hobby Lantern of Europe to name but a few, known by different names in different places ... the descriptions of these ghostly lights are intriguingly similar, descriptions across time and place being startlingly consistent.

In the Scottish Highlands, the ghostly lights, known as Spunkie, are common around lochs and have a more human form. Resembling a link boy (children who would illuminate the way for pedestrians with a lighted torch), the Spunkie was well-known for leading those who followed him to a deadly end. There was no end to the mischief caused by this manifestation, also causing ships to be wrecked by luring them onto the rocks, thinking it to be light of the harbour.

In the West Country of England, in Cornwall and Devon, such spirits are known as pixy-light: they are responsible for luring travellers into the dangerous bogs of the area. The swamp-ridden Massachusetts' Bridgewater Triangle in the USA has a history of sightings of ghostly lights. These are not just an historic occurence however – modern sightings are equally plentiful.

Scientific theories to explain these lights have abounded since at least the 16th century, when the lights were attributed to the decay of organic matter. Today, the accepted explanation is that the lights are caused by the oxidation of phosphine, diphosphine and methane.

There is also considerable lore that the lights mark the location of treasure: in Finland, St John's Day was the time to look, as the lights would reveal the location of riches hidden by others.

THE SHAPESHIFTING PINK DOLPHIN OF THE AMAZON RIVER

In Brazil, accounts of the infamous Boto Encantado – or enchanted dolphin – occur as early as the 19th century. As large as a canoe, they swim incredibly fast and move between animal and human form at will. Reputedly shameless creatures that enjoy dancing at parties, they enter houses silently at night to paralyze their victims before taking advantage of them. These creatures seduce unsuspecting women with their passionate embrace, and sire numerous illegitimate children – there are even cases where mothers have legally listed the father of their child as just such a dolphin. Many women are often left bewildered when their Romeo rushes off, dives into the river and swims away after their rendezvous; while others remember nothing afterwards, the visits only becoming apparent when they grow pale and thin after repeated encounters.

In contrast, the female botos are so insatiable that the only way to stop a man engaging with her is to hit him smartly on the leg. Looking into the eyes of such a dolphin – *maulhado de bicho* (the creature's evil eye) – can cause a type of madness, where the afflicted try again and again to jump into the river, as they alone can hear the dolphins calling to them. Despite their reputation, anyone who kills a pink dolphin will be punished with a curse: they can never catch food again, and only a *curador* – a healer – can lift the affliction. Today, the Worldwide Fund for Nature is attempting to tag and study river dolphins throughout Bolivia, Brazil and Columbia, since they are under threat of disappearance due to pollution of their natural habitat; they are classified as 'vulnerable' in some areas.

BE CAREFUL WHERE YOU REST:
The Insatiable Appetite of the Irish Joint Eater

Be very wary indeed if you happen to fall asleep beside a stream. For it is then that the Irish *alp-luachra* – or joint eater – is said to strike. This small, newt-like creature is in reality a bad fairy, a parasite that preys on the slumbering walker or traveller. Slipping unseen down their throat, it sets up camp in the stomach, stealing any food consumed until the victim wastes away and perishes from sheer starvation as loved ones look on helplessly. How to fight the unseen enemy? Some say they can be drawn out by the smell of strong food. They may also reveal themselves if the host eats something salty, then waits by a stream for them to abandon their host in search of water.

Although a very sneaky foe, there are signs that can reveal the parasitical creature. Pain and a huge, insatiable appetite are said to betray the presence of the joint eater, while the victim wastes away even as he gorges himself. While tales of the joint eater are many, perhaps the most sensational of all is that of the man who had a grand total of 13 of these parasitical creatures within him – thankfully, due to the help of a beggar man and a prince, he lived to tell the tale!

Despite their ghastly reputation, these creatures are not all bad; licking an alp-luachra is said to be a good cure for burns.

WELL FOLKLORE

Wells have been used as a source of life-giving water across the world since prehistory, so it's no surprise that myths, tales and legends surrounding them abound in many cultures. They are seen as a source of wisdom, used to highlight stupidity; they are places of deep mystery and unrivalled horrors. At the bottom of the wells in Malta lurk unspeakable terrors: the *belliegħa*, which snatches away unsuspecting children and has the power to make wells dry up or overflow; and the *mnalla*, a giant eel that lurks in the depths and preys on anyone who ventures into its lair.

Wells are often sacred places, with deities, saints or spirits associated with them. In India, *nāgas* are a semi-divine race who are half-human and half-cobra. These beings can shapeshift to either appear as entirely human, or in snake form, sometimes with many heads. Banished to live underground by Brahma, and ordered to only bite truly evil people, the nāgas often reside in wells, lakes and rivers, and are guardians of treasure or doorways; statues of them are often found watching over the entrances of temples. In a contemporary twist to the use of traditional stories in the modern-day media, a public row ensued over 'racist revisionism' after a South Korean actress was cast to play Nagini in the movie *Fantastic Beasts: Crimes of Grindelwald* – a cursed Asian female character subservient to the white, male Voldemort. People complained further when J.K. Rowling made an error on Twitter: that *nāgas* are originally from Indonesian tradition, rather than Hindu.

Well dressing is a tradition practiced throughout Staffordshire and Derbyshire in England, thought to date back to at least the 18th century. Wells are decorated with flowered panels, often depicting scenes from the Bible, from May to September, by local children and community groups. The most famous site for the custom is Tissington in Derbyshire, which some say developed to give thanks for the village being spared from plague in the 14th century due to the waters being so pure, while others believe it's a remnant of ancient practices to honour water spirits. Clootie wells are places of pilgrimage in many Celtic areas, found across Wales, Scotland, Cornwall and Ireland. Munlochy, on the Black Isle in Scotland, is one of the best examples of these wells. Believed to be the site of an ancient church, the remaining spring is dedicated to St Curidan, where sick and disabled children were once left overnight for healing. Here, to this day, strips of cloth called clooties are submerged in the sacred waters, then tied to a nearby tree with a prayer or wish whispered with each ribbon, in the belief or hope they will come to fruition as the cloth disintegrates. Some groups are now trying to raise awareness around such practices due to environmental concerns. They aim to encourage people to only tie clooties made from natural fibres, as cloth containing plastic will never decay. Not only does this mean the folk magic won't work, but it means that the items will remain forever – or at least until someone clears them away. Some have labelled these kinds of offerings 'ritual litter' and are trying to raise awareness of practicing responsible folk magic and rituals in the modern day.

Similar customs are observed in France, for instance at Courbefy, where offerings like coins and flowers are left in the area at three wells dedicated to St Eutrope. *Ex-voto* offerings to ask God for his grace and healing are also given; this type of offering is usually either a strip of cloth, shoe or piece of clothing that has been in contact with the patient's body, providing a magical link to the owner. Yet the most famous curative spring in France has to be that at Lourdes, where it's said that 70 miraculous cures were reported out of the 555 sick who attended in 1879, while this figure doubled the following year. An estimated 2–4 million pilgrims flock for healing each year today.

In Norse mythology, the Well of Urðr is the well of fate that lies beneath the World Tree. From this well come the Norns, three maidens who dictate the fates of humanity and set their laws. Said to represent the past, the present and the future, they are similar to other depictions of the three Fates or Destinies around the world, like the Greek Moirai or Graeae. Other examples include the Sudjenice or Narucnici of Croatian and Bulgarian folklore, who either appear as white maidens or as tall, cheerful old hags shrouded in white veils. Urðr is just one of three wells that lie in the roots of the World Tree: another is Hvergelmir, a bubbling, boiling spring; and the last is called the well of Mímir, guarded by the mysterious Mímir himself – said to be either an Aesir god or a giant. One

shadowy tale from Norse myth tells that Odin once ventured into the depths of the World Tree, following the root that led to the realm of the giants. Here, beneath the root, he came to Mímir's Well. He asked for a drink from the waters, in order to gain knowledge of his fate. Mímir refused until the god offered to sacrifice his eye in return. This is how the infamous Allfather of the Norse gods came to have only one eye.

Yet not all well folklore is so profound. The infamous Nasreddin Hodja (or Nasreddin the Teacher) is a 13th century trickster figure known throughout the Islamic world. He has an interesting encounter with a well in the darkly comic Turkish tale 'Restoring the Moon'.

> *One night, Hodja went to draw water from the well, but on looking down, saw the face of the moon staring right back up at him – it had obviously fallen into the well! Alarmed, he took a rope and hook to pull it back up. Yet the hook, catching on a rock, snapped as he pulled and pulled, making him stumble and injure himself. Lying flat on his back, Hodja noticed the moon sitting back in its sky. Relieved that his efforts hadn't been in vain, and that he had indeed pulled the moon from the well, he exclaimed, 'O praise and glory, I have suffered much pain, but the moon has got to its place again.'*

A tale from Tibet (China) tells of a troop of monkeys with a similar plight, and in this case the leader of the group decided that they should form a chain of monkeys in order to pull the moon from the well – and so they did. Yet, as the monkeys reached and stretched, the branch that they clung to bent and bent, and soon the water became troubled; the branch promptly broke, and the monkeys fell about in a heap. A deity adds a moral to the tale, with the words: 'When the foolish have a foolish leader, they all go to ruin, like the monkeys which wanted to draw the moon up from the well.' A later story can be found in the controversial *Nights with Uncle Remus: Myths and Legends of the Old Plantation*, where Br'er Rabbit and his friends also try to retrieve the moon from a mill pond, to no avail. The tale ends with a little wisdom: You can only catch the moon in the millpond when you use fools for bait!

Strangely, folk tales from the UK mirror these stories. In West Yorkshire, it's said that a bunch of smugglers were caught in the act by the local militia. Loath to be punished for their misdeeds, the men declared that they were attempting to catch the moon from the water. Realizing that the men were talking about the moon's reflection, and concluding they must be a ha'penny short of a shilling, the law enforcement officers laughed, told them to carry on, and went on their way – leaving the men free to carry on their crimes. After this, 'moonraking' passed into local folk language, used to mean smuggling goods. The story is celebrated with the biennial Moonraking Festival in Slaithwaite, West Yorkshire, where locals make lanterns from willow and paper. The festival ends with floating a giant moon down the Huddersfield Narrow Canal on a raft, where – of course – people try to grab it with rakes, after which gnomes in beards rescue it, and parade it round the town, as one might expect! An almost identical tale was recorded in 18th century Wiltshire in the south of England.

The Fountain of Youth

Given the human preoccupation with life and death, the fact that stories exist of waters that defy age and even death itself is to be expected. Today, the Budapest thermal springs are visited frequently for their medicinal and health benefits, while Lake Assal, a salt lake with healing properties in the Danakil Desert of north-east Ethiopia, southern Eritrea, and north-western Djibouti is well known for curing aching muscles and more joint problems. The most well-known throughout folklore and legend is that known as the fountain of youth. These waters take several different forms, variously an actual fountain, river or a spring. The idea is always the same, however: those that bathe in or drink the water have many years stripped from them and regain their youth.

The tale has a long vintage. Although not named specifically, Herodotus, writing in the 5th century, tells of a fountain with magical properties. The King of the Macrobians told of how the minimum age his people lived to was a staggering 120 years. The source of such longevity was the violet-scented waters of the fountain, which left the skin smooth and restored.

Some say that the first origins of the story come from Eurasia, with the 13th century Arabic *Romance of Alexander the Great* being one of the earliest written versions. In this story, Alexander looks on amazed as aged warriors pass through the waters, each emerging 30 years old again. Even more amazingly, men of over 100 years of age bathed there, only to leave the water as youths.

Legend has also linked the fountain with the exploratory voyages of Spaniard Ponce de León, who became Puerto Rico's first governor in 1509. According to the tale, the primary aim of his famed expedition of 1513 was to discover the location of the fountain of youth. However, there is no evidence in the historical record to support the search for the fountain as the main – or indeed any – aim of the voyage. Lack of proof does little to dampen the fervour of legend, however. The Fountain of Youth Archaeological Park, the place in modern-day Florida where Ponce de León was said to have first landed, was established in the mid-19th century, and tales of the fountain continue to excite and entice people even today.

MYTH AND MYSTERY:
The Lady of the Lake

Arthur, that valiant king, noble warrior, had been lucky to escape his last battle with his life. Merlin had put his foe – the tallest knight in the entire land – into an enchanted sleep, and had taken Arthur to have his wounds healed by a skilled hermit. Now physically recovered, the King rode onwards with the wily sorcerer, lamenting his lack of a sword.

'Have patience,' Merlin cautioned, and he was again proved right. As they approached a large lake, an intriguing sight caught Arthur's eye. Out in the glistening water was a mysterious arm, holding aloft a beautiful sword.

'Who is that?' Arthur demanded.

'The Lady of the Lake,' Merlin responded. 'If you wish for the sword to be yours, you must ask her for it – be sure, however, to do so courteously.'

As if sensing his intent, the beautiful woman was gliding towards him over the water, and, as she approached, Arthur seized his chance.

'Who does the sword belong to?' he asked, adding that he had lost his own weapon in battle.

'It is mine,' she replied, 'but I will gift it to you in return for something I will ask you for.'

Arthur agreed, and duly followed her instruction to enter the nearby barge, rowing it towards the sword. He took it with him, not forgetting her injunction to make sure not to leave the scabbard behind. It was the scabbard, Merlin later told him, that was most important, as he would never be injured whilst wearing it.

Viviane, Nimue, Nyneve. Whichever of the various names she is known by, the Lady of the Lake is inextricably connected with that most famous and legendary of English kings: Arthur. Credited with giving the great warrior his famed sword Excalibur, she has exerted a pull on the imaginations of artists, poets and authors across the centuries, and remains a vital character in retellings of the Arthurian tales today.

Aside from her pivotal role in Arthur's destiny, the Lady of the Lake has strong connections with two other prominent figures. According to some tellings, she enchanted Merlin, first by her physical beauty, and then, making it a condition of her capitulation, by the very magic she persuaded him to teach her. Utterly taken with her, Merlin wanted her for his own. The lady, however, had other ideas; she would only acquiesce if Merlin first taught her everything he knew, in effect making her as powerful as he was himself. The smitten sorcerer agreed, despite seeing only too well the fate that would befall him – eternal imprisonment in either a cave or tree.

The other important role played by this mysterious lady is that of fairy or foster-mother figure to Lancelot. Chrétien de Troyes, creator of this favourite knight, has him raised by a fairy in the lake. There is, however, potentially an even older German version with Lancelot raised on an island of thousands of happy maidens after being taken away by a merfeine or water fairy.

Just who was she? Some sources conflate her with Morgan le Fay, Arthur's sister, while another idea is that she was a third child to Uther Pendragon, sister to Arthur and Morgan. There is some argument that she was literally created from Merlin. In that subtle blend and development of language, the Welsh *hwimleian chwyfleian* – meaning a pale-faced wanderer – is said to have been corrupted into 'Viviane' in the French telling of Arthur and his knights. Originally meaning Merlin himself, this morphed into a fair maiden, and over time the mysterious and ethereal lady who entrapped Merlin was born and adopted into the Arthurian canon.

WOODED

WORLDS

WOODLANDS AND FORESTS
Wooded Worlds

Trees are the lifeblood of the earth. Their roots run deep in the soil; they are the veins and arteries of our world, sustaining and nourishing the life of the ground around them. Their very existence replenishes the air we breathe, creating oxygen that sustains most life on our little planet. We are only now beginning to understand the intricate network of trees that cover the land, and how they are able to communicate with each other. Yet the ancients somehow knew this, without the science we have today. They saw how the trees' branches reached up to touch the heavens and gave a home to the birds of the air. How they dug deep into the soil below us, connecting the skies with the land we walk upon; often stretching out as far as the eye could see, fading into horizons, deep and unknown. Since humanity first walked this earth, the trees have provided sustenance, and we have relied on them to provide our food: from the berries and mushrooms that grow in them, to the animals our ancestors hunted from within their midst. They provide fuel for warmth, and timber for our shelters, as well as for the boats that first carried both people and their wares to distant shores.

Strangely, while trees were once a way for us to communicate with both spirits and gods, now, in the modern day, they are used to communicate our words to others and share our ideas across the globe. The book you are now reading was once part of a tree. And still, we forget them. We cut them down. We burn them, and mould them, and shape them again and again. Yet as we do, their stories linger. We carry the essence of trees with us always. Wherever we live in the world, most of us have woodlands – or even a single tree – that we call our own; trees that we have loved since childhood. They might be horse chestnuts that bear the conkers of our childhood games, conjuring images of soaking the leathery brown balls in vinegar to outrank our rivals, rapping the knuckles of children across Britain. Sometimes they are the argan trees of Morocco with goats clamouring in their branches – something that may seem strange to all but those who know the secrets of the traditions that surround them. For some, they are the great firs of the northern forests, with wild boar snuffling in their snow-covered undergrowth. For others, they are the olive groves of southern Italy, with their gnarled, twisting trunks and roots that venture far into the red earth below them. Wherever we are in the world, our relationship with our trees is symbiotic, irreplicable and timeless.

INTO THE
TREES

THE WORLD TREE

For thousands of years people have conjured images of the outermost reaches of the universe they lived within. For many cultures, the cosmos took the shape of a tree, with its branches reaching up to kiss the heavens, and its roots twisting down into the soil of existence. This is what rooted them to their reality and shaped how they saw the world around them. This world tree was at the very core of everything they believed, an indication of how trees have been at the heart of human life since the beginnings of time. We are all creatures of the forests, yet the world trees that span the mythologies of Europe, Mesoamerica and the Near East show how many of us, once, were also people of the trees.

The world tree looks different across the globe, but many similarities exist. Usually, the trees' branches stretch up, extending into the clouds and beyond, often with a bird at the top. The roots delve deep into the earth, or lie in water, and here there is usually an underworld beast lurking in the depths, symbolizing chaos and creation. In the middle exists the world of humankind. The number of realms or planes the tree encompasses often varies, yet one thing is constant: the tree is timeless and connects all of us to each other and the creatures and spirits of the world. It is a thing of gods, spirits and humankind; it is the place where the spiritual, intangible and physical meet. The world tree is part of the concept of the *axis mundi* – the axis or central pivot that the world revolves around. In some mythologies, a mountain or pillar plays a similar role to this tree. In Baltic mythology, the *saules koks* – tree of the sun – is an apple, linden or oak that is entirely silver or gold. Many have searched for it in legends, but no one has ever seen it. In the Batak religion, the banyan tree is seen as bringing the layers of the universe together. Hindu texts also talk of a cosmic tree, a topsy-turvy growing banyan, with the roots in heaven, and branches reaching down to bless the earth.

Yggdrasil

For some, the most famous world tree is Yggdrasil of Norse mythology, said to be an evergreen ash in the poem 'Völusp ' from the *Poetic Edda*. Within it lie the nine worlds of the Norse cosmos; some appear vertically along its trunk, while others are arranged horizontally. The realm of the gods lies at the top, the worlds of humankind and giants at the middle, and the underworld at the bottom. The tree is known by the kennings 'Odin's horse' and 'Odin's gallows', as he sacrificed himself by hanging upon it. Its top is so high that it reaches above the clouds and is snow-capped, while winds tear around its branches.

Three roots delve deep into watery places beneath the tree, and different sources say that they are in different locations. One lies over Mímir's well of wisdom, where the god Odin sacrificed his eye for a drink of the waters. It crosses into the land of the rime giants, which was once where the yawning primordial void of Ginnungagap could be found.

Another root is over the spring Hvergelmir, meaning 'the Cauldron-Roaring'. This is in Niflheim, a place of mist, cold and ice. It is here that Níðhöggr the monstrous serpent gnaws at the tree's roots from the dark mountains of the underworld, and sucking the blood of the slain. Hel lives under this root in her underworld realm of the same name, a place of darkness and the dead, some believe to be underground. Hel is sometimes seen as the goddess of death in Norse mythology, a giantess who rules over the portion of the dead who were not taken off to other realms on their passing. It is said half the warriors who fall in battle go to Valhalla, the 'Hall of the Slain', ruled over by Odin. The other half go to Fólkvangr, the field of the goddess Freyja; women who have faced a noble death can also reside here in the afterlife. The 13th century Icelandic scholar Snorri tells us at one point that those who die of illness or old age are taken by Hel, yet many suggest he often exaggerated original sources of Norse mythology, while others say he invented his own lore. We do know that Hel is the daughter of Loki and Angrboðr the giantess, cast out by the gods with her siblings, Fenrir the wolf, and the Midgard Serpent, Jörmungandr.

The poem 'Grimnismol' tells us that beneath the last root is the land of men, while 'Gylfaginning' tells us one is over the well of Urðr in the heavens among the gods, belonging to the three norns who weave the fate of humanity: Urðr, Verðandi and Skuld – representing the past, the present and the future. It is here that the Æsir gods come each day over the rainbow bridge Bifröst to hold court and conduct their business. At the top of the tree is Hlithskjolf, meaning 'Gate-shelf'. This is Odin's tower, where he sits with his ravens, Huginn (meaning 'thought') and Muninn ('memory' or 'mind'), and watches over all of the nine worlds from the heavens. From here, he sees all – from everything humankind does, to the acts of the gods.

Many animals live among the branches of Yggdrasil. An eagle resides at the top of the tree, and a chattering squirrel, Ratatoskr, runs up and down passing messages between it and Níðhöggr the serpent. The stag Eikþyrnir feeds from the branches of the tree from the top of the hall of Valhalla, the afterlife home of warriors who died in battle. The goat Heiðrún also grazes on its leaves. While both the stag and goat feed from the tree named Læraðr, many identify this as Yggdrasil itself. When the tree shivers and groans it is said that Ragnarok, the end time, is near.

The Sky-High Tree

The Hungarian world tree, *égig éro fa*, is less well known, but just as magical. It's said that it grows from the mountain of the world, connecting the upper, middle and lower realms, and both the sun and moon are held within its branches. Snakes,worms and toads live in the roots, and at the top sits a bird, often the mythical turul, the falcon-like bird of prey often seen as a national symbol of Hungary. The tree itself is thought to grow from an animal: a deer or horse.

Many believe the tree has shamanic overtones, showing how people can travel through different realms, of which there are often seven or nine. The ability to climb the tree is restricted to the chosen folk heroes – namely the *táltosok*, shaman-like figures in Hungarian tradition. A *táltos* is usually marked at birth to follow the path by being born with teeth or a caul (a portion of tissue or amniotic membrane attached to their head) or having an extra finger. Other signs include late weaning, speaking little, and being withdrawn and aloof, yet very strong. In some regions, an individual would have to pass a test, sometimes climbing a ladder in Nagyszalonta (now Salonta, Romania), or a tree in Hajdú-Bihar county in Hungary. It's said that a táltos can reach out to the bird and send it to discover anything they want to know.

Many know it as the 'sky-high tree', or 'tree without a top', and its tales are reminiscent of Enid Blyton's *Magic Faraway Tree* collection; in these, folk-tale characters find small doors and cottages as they climb. The stories about it are often Jack-in-the-Beanstalk-like tales of fairies and castles. One tells of an unlikely hero rescuing a princess from the evil clutches of the dragon who lives above it. Another reveals that both heaven and hell can be seen when climbing the tree. Walking in the sky is a common theme, something people of the past could only dream of.

Trees and Tengriism

In ancient Turkic tradition, each tree had a spirit that was honoured and respected. Tengriism, a belief in an all-powerful sky god, was widespread. It was believed that the Tree of Life stood at the centre of the world, linking the earth to the North Star in the heavens. It was through this tree that babies would come to be born, and god would travel through it.

This is not just a thing of the distant past. Tengriism has seen a revival since the 1990s throughout Mongolia, Kazakhstan and parts of Russia, as well as the surrounding regions. While thought of as the original religion of the Turkic peoples, it is very much a living tradition. In the modern day, too, people believe in this world tree as connecting the day-to-day world with the underworld and upperworld. Today, certain trees are still seen as a sacred symbol of life that protect from evil and must never be felled. They are the centre of worship for many; strips of colourful cloth are tied to their branches, representing prayers, and people are even buried underneath them.

The Yaxche

World trees were common throughout the Mesoamerican cultures of the past. For the pre-Colombian Maya, the *Ya'axché* or *Yaxche* was a great ceiba tree that stood at the centre of the world. Various names exist for the tree depending on the specific Mayan language used. The *Popul Vuh* – the 16th century cultural narrative of the K'iche' people of Guatemala – tells that the gods placed four ceiba trees in each corner of the universe, yet the Yaxche was placed in the middle of all of them, connecting the everyday world to the underworld (Xibalba) and the sky. It represented the four cardinal directions – linked to the Mayan calendars – and was believed to support the entire universe, allowing both humans and gods to travel throughout the realms. Depictions often show the tree with birds in the branches, and a water monster at the roots.

Trees have been central to the region's cultures for centuries. The *Memorial de Sololá*, a 16th century manuscript written by Francisco Hernández Arana Xajilá, chronicles the origin of the Kaqchikel nation. Part of this is their creation epic, which tells how man fed upon the very trees themselves, their wood and leaves, when the Creator first made man from the earth. The power of the sacred Chay Abah, or Obsidian Stone, helped the Creator to make humankind. This was the oracle of the Kaqchikel nation's sorcerers that had come from the underworld and represented the principle of life itself. The ceiba is still the national tree of Guatemala, considered sacred and central to their cultural heritage. The gods must be asked permission before cutting one down, even now. Today, having a ceiba tree in your community is to have a divine presence in your midst; it is the mother tree of the nation. One belief should be noted though: anyone who hugs this tree risks becoming just as obese as the tree itself, so beware!

TREES OF MYTH AND MYSTERY
from Around the World

Over the centuries, trees of all sizes and colours and from all locations have inspired a great wealth of myths, legends and folklore. Whether revered and admired from afar or used for practical purposes, here are some of the most fabulously folkloric trees of the world.

Baobab Trees

Native to the plains regions of Africa and Australia, the very appearance of this giant is as fascinating as the folklore that surrounds it. The baobab – also aptly known as the upside-down tree or the monkey-bread tree – looks, at first glance, as if it is growing upside down. The branches, reaching high and wide, look more like roots to the onlooker, suggesting that they should therefore be reaching down into the earth. Unsurprisingly, there are many tales explaining how the tree came to have such an intriguing appearance.

Many found the sight of the baobab displeasing. The African god Thora, creator of the world, tossed the baobab out of his paradise garden. It fell to earth and started to grow, but it landed upside down. That is why it looks as it does today.

Another folk tale, this one from Namibia, tells how the Creator decided to give a different tree to each animal he had made. The hyena, late and not paying attention, found herself at the very end of the line. When she was given the last remaining tree – the baobab – the hyena was far from impressed and threw the strange-looking sapling away. It was not so easy to get rid of however and, landing upside down, the tree has grown this way ever since.

Another story suggests that the baobab itself was to blame for its upside-down appearance. The tree was said to have been very opinionated, constantly telling the Creator what it thought of his other creations – most often comments of a decidedly negative kind! In a fit of frustration, the Creator lost his temper and tore the chattering tree from the ground. Temper vented, the Creator realized that he did not want the baobab to perish; instead, he shoved it into the earth once more, but with one vital difference: the tree was upside down. If the baobab continues to voice its opinion, to this day, no one is able to hear it!

In some stories, the tree goes on to redeem itself for both its appearance and behaviour. This explains how, despite being so troublesome at its creation, the baobab tree is actually one of the most useful trees out there. Its gifts are manifold: from rope and paper being woven from the fibres of its trunk, to glue from the pollen and a potent tea or beer from the bark. The baobab can grow over 20m (65 ft) in height, holding the honour of being the largest succulent in the world.

It is believed among some of the Indigenous peoples of Southern Africa that spirits live within the flowers of the baobab tree. If anyone is foolish enough to pick them, they will pay a harsh price: the offender will find themselves ripped apart by fierce lions.

Pine Trees

The great pine tree is nowhere revered as much as in the folklore and beliefs of Japan. This tree has long been held as a symbol of longevity and good fortune, constancy and the endless nature of existence. They are often found growing outside the gates of gardens, and lanterns hang from their branches during the Festival of the Dead. They are known for heralding good fortune. The pine remains evergreen, unchanging. The tree rests between the world of the living and that of the dead, said to protect against evil spirits and bad fortune.

Perhaps one of the best-known tales of the pine in Japan is the beautifully evocative story of the twin pine trees: there are several different variations of this story of the spirits of two eternal lovers. In the version related in one of the greatest known Noh dramas, there are two pines planted from the same seed, one at Takasago and the other some distance away in Sumiyoshi. One day a Shinto priest meets an old couple beneath the Takasago pine. They get talking, and the couple tell the priest how the man tends the pine trees in both locations, travelling between the two pines to look after them and to meet his love. As the tale continues, it is revealed that the couple are in fact the spirits of the pine trees, joined together forever.

'The Wind in the Pine Tree' is another version of this story. A pine tree was planted a long time ago by a deity from heaven. A young man left his home for a great journey and, as he travelled over the sea, the sound of enchanting singing reached his ears. Coming ashore, he pushed his boat back into the waves and walked on until he came to the pine tree. Beneath it sat a lovely maiden, her voice being the sound that had drawn him in. They married, and lived for many, many happy years together. Finally, old, wrinkled and happy, the couple left this life, and were received into the branches of the pine tree. They remain there to this day.

Two ancient pines that stand in the grounds of the Takasago shrine today are known as Jo or Joo and Uba – old man and old woman. They are visited frequently by couples who are hoping for a long, happy and healthy life together.

Another tale is that of the 'Silent Pine'. When the Emperor Go-Toba found the noise of the wind blowing through a certain pine displeasing, he ordered it to stay still. The ever-obedient pine tree stopped moving and remained so from that moment onwards. Awed by such a display of compliance, the wind was never able to stir the tree again.

During wedding feasts, both male and female pine cones are displayed on tables to bring the couple a long and happy life.

Yew Trees

This tree comes with darker connections, as the yew, perhaps more than any other tree, is first and foremost associated with death and dying to our modern minds. This is not a new connotation, but one that goes back many, many years: in Celtic mythology, the yew is explicitly linked with the otherworld.

Of all the trees, the yew is, perhaps fittingly, most often to be found growing in or beside graveyards. It was once believed that the tree's roots would grow down through the eyes of the dead buried there and keep them in their place, so they would not escape. Another burial custom associated with the yew is referenced in Shakespeare's *Twelfth Night*: that of placing a sprig of yew in the shroud before burial.

One reason for this link with death is the toxic nature of the yew; its poisonous qualities are greatly attested. Again, we turn to literature to find evidence of the yew's history, where a potion made from it is referred to as 'juice of cursed hebenon' in *Hamlet*, and 'juice of hebon' by Christopher Marlowe in *The Jew of Malta*. Hebon and variants of the word were well-known names for yew during the 16th century.

The yew tree has been a staple of the British landscape since before the last ice age. Yew wood was the wood of choice for longbows in medieval England. In Yorkshire, in the north of the country, a legend tells how a young maiden who did not pay attention to the addresses of the local priest met a terrible end when the slighted cleric decapitated her. To conceal his crime, the priest hid the girl's head within a yew tree. In the years that followed this awful deed, the tree took on a holy significance, attracting pilgrims who collected branches from it to take with them. The reason? The 'hairs' between bark and wood were said to be those of the murdered maiden.

In Dibden, Hampshire, a large yew was prominent in the churchyard there until the early 19th century. The tree was known as Lady Lisle's yew, due to the fact that the ill-fated noblewoman, wanted for treason, was said to have been taken prisoner as she tried to conceal herself within its branches. Her attempts were to no avail: she was captured and executed in Winchester marketplace on 2 September 1685. In the 19th century it was believed her spirit remained at the yew, two hundred years after her death – it was said that she drove four headless horses around the tree when the moon was covered.

In Nevern, Wales, the churchyard is home to some yews with a mysterious history. Lining the path to the front of the church, these trees are said to be around seven hundred years old. One of these is known as the Bleeding Yew, after the blood-red sap that is seen to seep from it. There are many explanations and stories that try to explain this strange sight, the most common being that the tree bleeds in sympathy with the crucified Christ.

Another famous example is the Fortingall Yew in Scotland. According to legend, this tree has links to Pontius Pilate, the Roman governor who washed his hands of Jesus and sentenced him to death. Depending on which version you listen to, Pilate was either born beneath the yew itself, or enjoyed many a playtime in its branches as a small child. Or perhaps both!

Dragon's Blood Trees

The *Dracaena* or dragon genus – believed to contain upwards of one hundred species – is as fascinating as its name suggests. Named after the blood-red sap that is seen when the tree is scratched or injured, certain trees within the genus are known as the dragon tree or dragon's blood tree, inspiring legends and having many uses since ancient times. Their shape resembles an umbrella.

Found exclusively in Yemen, in the Socotra archipelago, the species *Dracaena cinnabari* has a long history. Resin from these trees, a valued commodity, was traded by Rome from at least the 1st century. The famed resin was also mentioned by Pliny. Today, small amounts of their berries are fed to livestock for health purposes. Socotra itself has a rich wealth of folklore attached, and it is known as the 'island of the phoenix' and the 'island abode of bliss'.

Another dragon tree, the *Dracaena draco*, is found on the Spanish island of Tenerife growing in semi-desert areas. Tenerife is home to the largest-known dragon tree in existence: El Drago Milenario, 'The Thousand-Year-Old Dragon', in north-west Tenerife. There has been considerable confusion and debate regarding the exact age of this tree: although estimated to be several thousand years old in the late 19th century, it was later concluded that the oldest dragon trees in Tenerife were in fact no older than three hundred years. It is now thought that the tree, and its fellow dragon trees, could be anything from three hundred years old to a thousand. Indigenous Guanches used the sap from dragon trees to embalm the dead and worshipped them specifically.

In Greek mythology, the existence of the dragon tree is explained. Hera set the serpent-like dragon Ladon to guard the golden apples of Hesperides that she had given to Zeus as a wedding gift. All went well until Heracles – or Hercules as he is sometimes better known – came along. Of the twelve labours he was tasked to carry out, the penultimate was to steal the sacred apples that Ladon guarded so carefully. Unfortunately for Hera and the dragon, Hercules was successful: finding Ladon curled around the tree he slayed the guardian, spilling his blood all over the ground. As it flowed and flowed, trees sprang up where the blood touched, and these were the very first dragon trees. The vanquished Ladon was rewarded with a place in the skies, becoming the constellation Draco. In the Roman telling of the tale, it is Juno – likewise queen of the gods and also mother of Mars – who was given the apples by her mother, Gaia, upon her marriage. Ladon goes to the stars in both accounts.

The interest in the dragon tree does not end with legends, and the tree was highly valued from ancient times for a variety of uses. In his 1640 work, *Theatre of Plants*, English botanist John Parkinson listed treatment of burns, urinary issues, watery eyes, gonorrhoea and fastening loose teeth as among its uses. Throughout history it has also been used as a dye, medicinally for rheumatism, as an abortifacient, and as an ingredient in toothpaste. Today, the Socotra people use it for a variety of things, from decorating pottery to dyeing wool and curing gastric sores.

Cedar Trees

This list would not be complete without mention of the mighty cedar. Sacred to many First Nations and Native American groups, particularly the Indigenous peoples of coastal British Columbia, the Coast Salish, the cedar tree is prominent in their beliefs, stories and everyday use.

The two types of cedar that feature most are the red and yellow varieties. Red cedar, due to the fact that it is lightweight and doesn't rot easily, is especially suited to architecture and canoes. These giants can reach as high as 70m (230 ft) and are known for their longevity. The bush-like yellow cedar, on the other hand, has a fibrous and pliable texture, which makes it well-suited for making clothing and mats.

The cedar features in a creation story of the Coast Salish. There was once a good man, who thought more of others than himself, and never hesitated to give to others, whether that be food or his own belongings. This goodness did not go without notice, and the Creator, seeing how selfless the man was, pledged to honour it. He said that on the man's death, the red cedar would grow where his body was buried: the tree would be of great help to everyone, just like the man himself. In this way, the man would continue to provide for others, even after death.

Yellow cedar had a different origin. Raven – both creator and trickster – chanced upon three young women. They were drying salmon on the beach, and Raven decided to try his luck to get some food from them. He questioned the women as to whether they were afraid, being as they were alone. Raven listed various threatening creatures – wolves, bears and others – and each time the women denied being afraid. 'What about owls?' Raven asked finally. He had struck gold, as it transpired that all three were terrified of them. Armed with this knowledge, Raven took himself to hide in the trees, where he made owl calls loud enough for the women to hear. In terror, they ran and ran, never stopping until they were halfway up the mountainside. There they stopped, never to move again. The women transformed into the yellow cedar that is known today, found on the high slopes of the mountains. Their long slender shape, smooth trunks and soft hairlike inner bark are said to be reminders of the origin of the yellow cedar.

To the Coast Salish, and other coastal First Nations groups, cedar is a very useful and helpful tree; practically all of it can be used for something or other. Cedar has life and spirit within, a living spiritual force and being. Because of this, ritual is observed before harvesting takes place; a prayer is said to the spirit of the tree, and thanks given. The importance of regeneration is observed, and sustainable methods are used. The tree must be harvested with care: if the tree is killed, then the person who committed the act would be cursed by the remaining cedars. Cedar is also one of the most important plants for ceremonial use. Used in sweat-lodge ceremonies, it symbolizes providence and generosity. It is also used for healing; the bark of the yellow cedar has anti-inflammatory properties and can be applied as a dressing.

In the tradition of the Potawatomi, there is the story of 'The Men Who Visited the Sun'. In this story, as you might imagine, there were six men who decided they wanted to visit the sun. With the blessing of their tribe, they set off on a journey, venturing to where the sun started. As it rose, they caught on to it and climbed on top of it so they could talk. They told the sun they believed it to be the Great Spirit and that they wanted to take its power back to their people so they would be happy.

They each asked for something from the sun. One man told the sun that he did not want to die, that he wanted to live on and be of use and aid to his people until the earth itself was no more. The sun, listening, told the man that on his return journey he would find himself transformed into something that would never die – the cedar tree. He would be forever with all nations and all people and would be the first to be used in feasts, considered sacred by all. Sure enough, before reaching the end of the return journey to their tribe, the man came to a halt and declared that was where he must stay. His companions looked back to see he was transformed into a great cedar tree.

There is also a belief that pregnant women shouldn't braid baskets made with cedar, as it could lead to the umbilical cord being twined around the baby's neck. It is not always linked to bad things; some Coast Salish groups place the afterbirth in a large cedar stump to ensure long life for the child.

Perhaps confusingly, some juniper trees are also referred to as cedar. At Hat Point near Grand Portage Ojibwe Reservation harbour in northeastern Minnesota there is a great tree, believed to be at least 400 years old. Known as Manido Giizhigance, Little Cedar Tree Spirit, the tree is sacred to the Ojibwe people. In a disturbing display of cultural ignorance, the tree is often disrespectfully referred to as the 'Witch Tree' and has been the victim of vandalism in the past. Today, those who wish to visit it must be accompanied by a member of the Ojibwe, and permission to do so is granted infrequently.

North Carolina folklore has several beliefs about cedar, mainly surrounding death. Planting a cedar would mean that a family member was going to die, a belief that potentially stems from the fact that cedars are often found in graveyards. Another variation is that if you plant a cedar, when it grows big enough to shade your grave, you will yourself die. Cutting a cedar was also risky business; if someone were to cut twelve inches (30cm) from the top of a cedar, they were sure to die before those inches grew back.

Cedars also feature in the mythology of Mesopotamia. In the 'Epic of Gilgamesh', the titular hero comes across The Cedar Forest, guarded by Humbaba the demigod. At the behest of Enkidu, his travelling companion – who plays on Gilgamesh's desire for fame – Gilgamesh slays the guardian, before cutting down the great cedar trees. Gilgamesh decides to use the greatest of all these trees to make a gate for the temple of Enlil in Nippur. Gilgamesh and Enkidu build a raft from the wood and use it to travel home down the Euphrates river.

In a Chinese tradition, there was once a king who deeply desired the wife of one of his most faithful subjects. Intent on having her at whatever cost, the king had the man thrown into prison on a trumped-up charge, getting him out of the way. It seemed the king would be successful, as the husband died from a broken heart, leaving the way clear. But the object of his desires had other ideas and threw herself from a great height. Buried apart as they had died, the couple's love prevailed: a cedar tree grew from each grave, and as time went on, the branches and roots of these great tall trees twined together, victorious in their reproof of the king and his evil intentions. They were known as 'the trees of the faithful loves'.

Banyan Trees

Is there any tree more greatly revered and admired throughout history than the majestic banyan tree? This noble member of the fig family has been sacred to many for over two thousand years and is particularly revered in India. What is so special about this giant among trees that has led to them being venerated by the great and humble alike?

Today, the term banyan is used to refer to one of the many – and there are 750 – types of known fig tree. Originally, however, the banyan referred to a specific species found in India, the *Ficus benghalensis*. Under these giants, Hindu traders called *baniyas* carried out their business, and it was from them that the banyan is said to have got its name.

Upon seeing a banyan tree from a distance, you might be forgiven for thinking that a whole forest stands before you. This is due to the huge size that banyans grow to: they hold the record for broadness above all other trees; the area they cover knows no equal. (Where overall volume is concerned they are pipped at the post by another giant, the sequoia tree.) This illusion is also magnified by the manner in which a banyan grows and spreads. Unlike most plants, the banyan grows from the top downwards; seeds landing on the canopy of trees send out tendrils towards the ground. These roots, in time, each grow as thick as a trunk, anchoring the banyan to the ground and smothering the host tree in the process. There is a reason the banyan belongs to the subset of fig trees known as strangler figs!

The sacred banyan is, in India, a symbol of stability and immortality, and some believe the banyan itself to be immortal. They do indeed live for an impressive length: the Thimmamma Marrimanu banyan tree, located in Anantapur near Andhra Pradesh, India, is over five hundred years old. The legend goes that the tree came into being in the year 1434, when the recently widowed Thimmamma threw herself on her husband's funeral pyre, ending her own life in the process. The tree grew in that location, and worship of it is still going strong today; there is a temple on the site. This banyan is also linked to fertility, with the belief that it will ensure a healthy child for those who believe and

worship there. Around 20,000
people are said to be able to
shelter beneath it. Another
famous banyan is the Great
Banyan Tree at Howrah, near
Kolkata (the former Calcutta),
India. More than 250 years
old, the tree reaches over 450m
(1,475ft) wide, and is believed
to be one of the widest trees in
the world.

Alexander the Great is
credited with being the first
European to witness the majesty
of the mighty banyan. When
he and his troops reached India
in 326 BCE, the naturalists
travelling with him marvelled at
the sight. It was also under the
branches of a giant banyan tree
that the crucial moment when Buddha first obtained enlightenment
took place. In Hindu belief, Krishna was said to have delivered the
Bhagavad Gita from under a banyan. The world tree of Hindu belief is
said to be a banyan.

There are several stories that explain how the first fig came into being.
One is that it happened when Gaia opened her own chest in order to save
her son, Sykeus, from the wrath of the gods after an attempted coup by
Sykeus and his siblings against the inhabitants of Olympus went terribly
wrong. Sykeus, safely hidden inside his mother's chest, was transformed
into a fig tree.

Another popular tale regarding the banyan is that of Savitri and
the Banyan tree. When a man named Satyavan died beneath a banyan
tree, his wife, Savitri, refused to let him go. Instead, she went head-
to-head with Yama, god of death, arguing and winning back the life
of her husband, bringing him back from the dead. In memory of this

remarkable pair, the festival of the banyan takes place in India each year during Jyeshtha (May/June). In Uttar Pradesh, and other places, on the day of the new moon, women worship the banyan in memory of Savitri and her story.

Unsurprisingly, it is considered sacrilege in some cultures to harm the banyan in any way, including chopping it down, although this is not such a prevalent belief as it once was. This is the belief among some Odia tribes; even if the act of chopping it down is done by accident, a goat must be sacrificed to the tree gods in order to make amends. The banyan is sacred to the Jains too, as the first Tirthankera of the Jaina religion received his knowledge beneath a banyan tree. The banyan is also known as the Vata-vriksha, meaning wish or meditation tree.

In Hindu belief, banyans are, importantly, linked with death, often to be found growing near crematoriums. They are also connected to Shiva, the god of destruction. In the south-facing form of this god – the direction of death and change – he is depicted sitting beneath a banyan tree. This can often be seen on the south-facing walls of temples in southern India. Banyans are also linked with the end of the world itself. We have already seen the link between banyans and the god of death, Yama, but they are linked with Vishnu too: at the end of the world, the *pralaya*, when flood waters cover the earth and everything is dissolved and swept away, Vishnu – or sometimes his form Krishna – is there as a baby on a banyan leaf.

Modern banyan trees are not confined to India. Today, there are examples in Florida and Maui, Hawaii. The strangler fig features on the coats of arms of Indonesia and Barbados.

There is a further dark side to the banyan and its history. Many sacred banyan trees were desecrated by English troops in India, and rebels were executed there, hanged from their branches, over a hundred men at a time hanged from just one tree. *Kinnaras*, half-human, half-animal, are said to live in the banyan, as are *yakshas* – tree spirits. It is a foolhardy person who sleeps under a banyan tree at night, as it is well known that they are filled with spirits; ghosts and demons are said to dwell there.

THE MARVELLOUS
MUSHROOMS
of the Forest Floor

Mushrooms, we are often told, are neither animal nor plant – a living creature somewhere in between. Others say this isn't true, and instead suggest that the only answer to questions about their animal-versus-plant nature is this: the things belonging to the fungi kingdom are so strange that they are almost unexplainable to non-scientists. Some people love them, weaving their way through old woodlands to forage them from the forest floor, braving ticks, wild boars and other predators of the trees. Others hate them. Some suffer a phobia called mycophobia: the irrational fear of fungus. The poem 'Mushrooms', by Sylvia Plath, conjures this dread perfectly, revealing them as an unseen, creeping force, biding their time before taking over the mundane realities of the human world – believed by many to be a metaphor for the quietly rising women's revolution of the time.

Mesmerizing folk names are bestowed on different types of fungi across the world. To the Mapuche of Santiago de Chile, the changle mushroom is known as 'little feet of a rat'. *Xylaria polymorpha* is a fungus more commonly known as 'dead man's fingers', because it does indeed resemble corpse-like digits reaching up through the soil from the grave. Many are linked with folkloric creatures: they are the saddles of witches, elves (*Helvella*) and dryads (*Polyporus squamosus*) alike. Others, thought to be aphrodisiacs, were named 'Devil's horn' – pun certainly intended. St John's Eve, on 23 June, is a night famous for magic, and associated with a mushroom named 'troll's butter' – so-called since it is said to reveal trolls have been nearby. In Sweden, people used to light bonfires made from nine types of wood at crossroads on this night, casting the mushroom into the flames to stop evil spirits wandering the land.

Across the world, mushrooms and fungus have been used as food, in curious folk remedies galore, as fabric dyes and even tinder. Yet the beliefs and superstitions that have arisen around them are as mysterious and varied as mushrooms themselves. In Ozark traditions from the US, mushrooms can only be gathered under a full moon or they will be unpalatable, and might even be poisonous – although it's also believed that mushrooms growing in an apple orchard in bloom can always be eaten. Don't try this at home, though! It is thought rain is sure to follow within twelve hours if mushrooms appear suddenly. Often, mushrooms are believed to hold the souls of the dead. In Siberia, the Orotch believe that those who have died are reborn as mushrooms on the moon. Mushrooms are linked to astral phenomena across many cultures; some are said to sprout from the landing sites of shooting stars, or the place where lightning strikes.

Of course, any child knows that mushrooms are things of the fairy folk. Indeed, we might expect any self-respecting fairy-tale illustration to feature at least one bulbous mushroom – replete with shiny red cap and white spots – with a fairy, or at least a toad, sitting on top. In California, particularly in Irish tradition, it is believed that 'the little people' – namely leprechauns, shoemakers who dress in green and are passionate dancers – live in an array of natural places, including under mushrooms and toadstools. Yet in Illinois, fairy rings – with or without mushrooms or flowers – were thought to be created by dancing fairies. Fairy rings are often said to be made when fairies join hands and dance in a ring, usually resulting in a circular mark in the grass, or a circle of mushrooms growing there.

As entrances to Fairyland, anyone who steps into one will have the power to see the fairy folk and their possessions. In some Welsh tales, people taken into a fairy ring tell of hearing seductive music nearby, and then feeling no hunger once inside them. Such bewitched people are made to dance forever or are transported to Fairyland for years at a time while believing that only days have passed; they fall down stone dead as soon as they eat mortal food once more. On the Isle of Skye, some

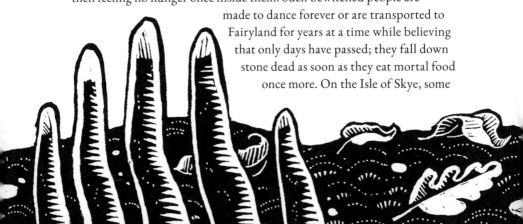

say anyone stepping into a fairy ring becomes invisible to those standing outside of it. Yet in York, fairies can be seen if someone runs around a fairy ring a magical number of times – usually either three or nine.

People are often wary of fairy rings. At the end of the 19th century, Shropshire folk were still loath to bury their dead where such rings appeared. In Wales, it was believed that misfortune would follow anyone who dared step foot in one. And an English rhyme from mid-19th century Berwickshire tells of the ill fortune to be faced by any who disturbs a fairy ring:

> *He who tills the fairies' green,*
> *Nae luck again shall hae;*
> *And he who spoils the fairies' ring,*
> *Betide him want and woe;*
> *For weirdless days and weary nights*
> *Are his til his dying day.*

Some modern fiction sees a toadstool circle's magic slightly differently, in that it actually protects *against* fairy folk. A giant ring of mushrooms appears in the 2008 film *The Spiderwick Chronicles*, based on the book series of the same name by Holly Black and Tony DiTerlizzi. It is used as a protective circle to keep the inhabitants of the house safe from murderous goblins, intent on reclaiming a magic book that will help their ogre master with his nefarious deeds. The magic only works if they stay inside the ring, since – we are told – no fairies can enter into it. The book itself contains information on how to destroy the circle, at which point the mushroom ring will lose its magic.

Whatever you believe, you would do well to stay away from any mushroom circles you might happen upon when strolling through the woodlands. Do remember to watch where you tread, for there may be a fairy tea party happening right under the toadstool beneath your feet.

THE TREES OF
CHRISTMAS

O Christmas tree, O Christmas tree! Throughout the millennia, people the world over have marked and celebrated the time around the winter solstice with a variety of customs. Across Europe, however, to the modern imagination, there is little that sticks in the mind more than the trees and branches used in decoration and commemoration of this magical time, when the nights are dark and the days short, and the year is drawing its final breaths before preparing for the renewal of another year.

Although decorated trees were a familiar sight in continental Europe, the iconic Christmas tree itself is a relatively recent import to Britain and the US, coming from Germany to England with Prince Albert, Queen Victoria's beloved consort in the 1840s. It is certain, though, that this was only the latest development in an array of long traditions in such countries that involved trees and the festive period. In what other ways, then, have trees been used to mark this important time of year? Let us take a look at the varied customs of the Yule log, the festive tradition of apple wassailing, and what happens when the Tió de Nadal is beaten on Christmas Day...

Charring the Old Wife and Other Customs: The Magic of the Yule Log

These days, a Yule log conjures up images of chocolate-covered cake, filled with cream or butter icing, topped perhaps with icing sugar, plastic holly leaves and a robin. But what are the roots of this festive treat?

The tradition of the Yule log can be traced across the United Kingdom, Europe and North America. A log – often of a specific type, such as birch or ash – was selected, brought into the house, and burned in the hearth over a specified period, with various beliefs and practices attached to this long-lived custom.

There is a great deal of discussion regarding the origins for the tradition of the Yule log and Yule itself, and it is believed that they originated with the Germanic peoples. Although both traditions without doubt date back to pre-Christian times, it is difficult (nigh-on impossible in some cases) to be certain of the exact origins and original practices.

The selected Yule log for the year would be burnt over the period of the midwinter festival known as Yule, though the exact dates varied between time and location; common dates run from 21 December until 5 January, Old Christmas Eve. There was good incentive to select a log of considerable size; in many areas, including Scotland and Norfolk, 'good' alcohol would only flow to servants while the Yule log continued to burn.

The idea that it was lucky to keep a piece of the Yule log until the following year was also a common belief in many areas. This remnant

of the old log was used to light the next year's log and continue the good luck associated with it. Keeping it under the bed would, it was believed, protect a household from lightning and fire. In Somerset, this practice was said to prevent chilblains. In Scotland, it was believed the ash from the log would not only bring good luck but would offer a household protection from witches.

The length of time the Yule log needed to burn for also varied. In some places, twelve hours was enough to ensure good luck for the year to come. In others, it had to burn consistently from Christmas Eve until 5 January.

A Yorkshire tradition from the first quarter of the 20th century saw the Yule log still very much in use. Just prior to supper on Christmas Eve, after those assembled enjoyed games and stories around the lighted Yule log, two candles would be lit from the flames. While this was taking place, absolute silence was to prevail, as those gathered made wishes. With the candles lit and placed on the table, the silence could be broken, but the wishes had to remain secret to ensure they would come true.

The Yule log has been known by many different names throughout history and across different locations. In Scotland, it is known as the *Cailleach Nollich*, Christmas Old Wife or Lady. The name came from the chalking of the figure of a woman on it; this was burnt away as the log was consumed, known as 'charring the old wife'. Similarly, Ireland has its *Bloc na Nollaig*, *Yeel Carline*, or Christmas Oldwife. In Wales, Yule was celebrated with the *Boncyff Nadolig* or *Blocyn y Gwyliau*, Christmas or festive log or block.

Until 1937 in Stromness, Orkney, the Southenders and Northenders of the town would battle over who would gain possession of the largest Yule log, and thus the luck for the year. A massive tug of war ensued, the winning team being the one that managed to drag the log to their side of town. The act of cutting down a tree for this purpose was banned by the Town Council in 1933, and the tug of war itself was last recorded in 1937, until a revival of the event in 2017.

In France, there is the legend that the confectionary Yule log, or *Bûche de Noël*, originated after Napoleon banned the traditional style of Yule log; refusing to be downtrodden, the inhabitants of Paris created one out of cake instead, around which they continued to gather and make merry.

Tió de Nadal:
The Defecating Christmas Log

Caga tió, caga torró,
Avellanes i mató,
Si no cagues bé
Et daré un cop de bastó.
Caga tió!

Poop log, poop nougats,
Hazelnuts and mató cheese,
If you don't poop well,
I'll hit you with a stick,
Poop log

A Catalan tradition similar to that of the Yule log is the Tió de Nadal. Loosely translating as 'Christmas log', 'Tió' is a log or piece of wood about 30cm (1 ft) long that plays a very special part in the lead-up to the Spanish Christmas in Catalonia, and also some regions of Aragon.

Starting on 8 December, the Feast of the Immaculate Conception, the careful looking-after of Tió begins. On this date, Tió is fed with a small amount of food, a practice that continues nightly until Christmas Eve. It is very important that Tió iswell looked after, and he is sometimes wrapped in a blanket and put to bed to make sure he has all the comfort he needs. For on Christmas Day, Tió has a very special role to perform.

Tió is placed in the fireplace, where the command is given for the log to defecate. The children of the household then leave the room and either pray or wish for Tió to bring them gifts. Upon returning, Tió is then beaten, and a special song sung, of which there are many variations. Although larger presents are said to be delivered by the Three Wise Men, Tió defecates sweets, nuts and small toys for those who have looked after him throughout the lead-up to Christmas.

Although originally a simple piece of wood, the modern Tió has taken on a more lifelike appearance, with eyes, legs, a smile and a red sock hat on his head.

WOODLAND
CREATURES

WHO'S AFRAID OF THE BIG BAD WOLF?

The wolf is one of the world's most alluring creatures: dangerous, threatening, majestic and powerful, a danger to humans and animals alike. The wolf skulks through the forests of our history, lurking in the shadows, waiting to strike when least expected. Denizens of the forest since antiquity, stalking us from the pages of folklore, fairy tale and myth, the heady blend of fear and fascination inspired by the wolf ensures they have never been forgotten.

In Turkic tradition, the wolf is revered, considered to be one of the ancestors from which Turkic peoples are descended. In the legend of Asena, in northern China, a baby was left behind after soldiers raided a Turkic village. Asena, a she-wolf with a blue mane, found the child and cared for him. The she-wolf went on to birth half-human, half-wolf children, the ancestors of the Turkic people.

In Inuit folklore there is Amarok, the monstrous wolf who will devour those out hunting alone at night. In one tale, the Amarok, which is said to be all-seeing, scented out a man who was hiding from him, destroying him and taking the very soul from his body.

A Mongol legend says that a woman, thrown out of her master's house because she was pregnant but not married, gave birth to her child in a cave. She left the child there and went in search of food; when she returned with help to find her baby, a crow flew and a wolf came running out of the cave. Certain that the child must have been devoured, the woman entered the cave, only to find the baby unharmed, with milk on its lips as if it had just suckled. In related Mongol lore, the wolf and crow are inextricably linked, in tales as they are in nature.

An intriguing Scottish story tells how the wolf lost his tail. When out with the fox one day, the pair stole a dish of crowdie (porridge or cheese), and the wolf ate much more than his share. To punish the wolf, the fox tricked him into lying down on the ice with his tail over the reflection of the moon, which he told his gullible companion was a nice ripe cheese. The wolf stayed there so long his tail froze to the ice, only for the fox to suddenly call for the farmer, alerting him to the wolf's presence. The wolf ran for his life: he escaped, but left his tail behind, leaving the wolf with a lesser tail than the fox ever since.

Wolves likewise feature in First Nations and Native American tales, some of which contain the theme of a wolf gotten the better of, such as 'Fox Tricks Wolf', a Menominee legend, and a series of trickster tales of the Potawatomi where a raccoon constantly bests a wolf. The wolf is a popular animal in these cultures, however, with loyalty, strength and courage being their main attributes. Wolves feature in the creation stories of several Indigenous groups and are also common clan animals.

It is not surprising to discover that the wolf is mentioned in the Bible. Here, the wolf is a negative creature, the enemy of both flocks of sheep and men, there to lead the faithful astray. Wolves are used to illustrate the danger of lustful and dishonest men and are often a metaphor for the Devil himself. Perhaps the most well-known warning is that of Matthew 7:15: 'Beware of false prophets, which come to you in sheep's clothing, but inwardly they are ravening wolves.'

What of the Norse Fenrir, son of the trickster god, Loki? This terrible wolf was himself tricked and bound with a dwarf-made fetter, Gleipnir, made from six impossible things: the sound of a cat's footfall; the beard of a woman; the roots of a mountain; the sinews of a bear; the breath of a fish, and the spittle of a bird. The heavens were spared from being consumed by him. He remains chained and will continue to do so until Sköll and Hati, the wolves that chase the sun and moon across the sky, finally catch their quarry; then the world will be covered in darkness. When this happens, Fenrir will finally break his chains and spring free, resulting in Ragnarok, where he will fight and devour Odin, and then the destruction of the world will follow.

According to Japanese lore, the wolf is a largely positive creature. Among other things, the hair from the wolf's eyebrow is said to be imbued with magical properties. Food offerings were left near wolf dens in return for protection of crops against other wild animals, while wolves were also worshipped at shrines.

One Slavic tale that closely resembles the selkie stories of Orkney tells of a she-wolf that haunted an enchanted mill. One night, a soldier decided to stay there, where he saw a wondrous sight. Not realizing he was there, the she-wolf appeared and cast off her skin, revealing a beautiful maiden. While she slept, the soldier took the wolf skin, nailing it to the mill wheel. The maiden woke, distraught when she could not find her skin, unable to transform back to her wolf form. The maiden and the soldier were married and had two children, and after a time the mother's secret became known to the oldest son. He questioned her, and she denied everything. He then asked his father, who confirmed that his mother was indeed a wolf and showed him where her skin was to prove it. The child returned to his mother who, in turn, quizzed him as to where the skin was – when the child told her she immediately took it, turned back into wolf form, and was never seen again.

There are many tales of human children being raised by animals, so-called feral children who spent their formative years with animals rather than humans, thus lacking the basic socialization that we take for granted. It is hardly surprising to hear that, along with being raised by dogs, goats, bears, monkeys and even ostriches, children have often been said to have been raised by wolves. Perhaps the most well-known wolf-raised children of myth and legend are Romulus and Remus, the founders of Rome. Twins born to vestal virgin Rhea Silvia and the god Mars, the king ordered their death as punishment for their mother's transgression. Thanks to a merciful servant, the babes were instead abandoned on the bank of the River Tiber: according to the legend, a she-wolf discovered them there and took them to raise as her own. The boys lived happily with the wolf family until, a few years later, they were found by the shepherd Faustulus, and they grew to adulthood in his family.

In these and similar stories, the children have minimal difficulty adjusting to life in human society, whereas real feral children are often recorded to have much more trouble, including difficulties with speech, movement and social interaction. Although such tales are popular due to their often-sensational nature, such as the case of the Lobo wolf girl of Devil's River in 1845, these cases are often proven to be fakes. A good example is the case of Amala and Kamala from Bengal, India. In 1920, missionary and orphanage director Rev. Singh claimed the girls were discovered in the wild having been living with wolves; after much publicity and investigation, however, it was determined that the story had been fabricated.

THE STORY OF GELERT

In the 13th century, Llywelyn the Great of Wales had a dog named Gelert, the most trusted, faithful hound a man could wish for. One day when he was out hunting, he left his four-legged friend at home, confident that no harm would befall those there in his absence. Upon his return home, though, Llywelyn discovered a gruesome scene: the cradle which held his baby son was upended, the child nowhere to be seen. Then he spied Gelert, blood plainly visible around the dog's mouth. With a cry of anguish, Llywelyn drew his sword and killed Gelert, believing he had slaughtered his son. Too late, the sound of another cry reached the distraught father's ears. Barely daring to believe, Llywelyn lifted the fallen cradle, discovering the babe alive, safe and well. Beside him was a dead wolf, the real villain of the piece. The wolf, Llywelyn realizes, attacked the child, and Gelert in turn, faithful to the end, had killed the wolf, protecting the child as he had been charged to. The poor wronged Gelert was buried with great honour, the sound of the creature's last yelp staying with Llywelyn until his own dying day. It is said that he never smiled again.

There are few who can read the tale without shedding a tear, and the legend of Gelert has inspired several poems and other mentions throughout the years. Gelert's burial site is said to be in the Welsh village of Beddgelert – literally meaning 'Gelert's grave' – and visitors are treated to a sight of the mound that covers his remains, along with a memorial that tells the story.

It might come as a surprise and disappointment for fans of Gelert to learn that he is most certainly fictional. Beddgelert itself is named after a saint – named Celert or Kilart – rather than the legendary hound. What of the grave? It is little more than a cunning piece of tourist advertising created by the 18th-century landlord of the Goat Hotel, David Pritchard, who saw an opportunity to draw people to the village. It worked: people visit the grave to this day, where they can read the legend in English and Welsh. Intriguingly, there are similar tales told in many areas of the world, including India, Malaysia and the Alps.

Little Red Riding Hood

The tale of the little girl in red who ventured into the woods, unknowing and innocent, is one we all find familiar and it needs no retelling. We see her skip into the trees, only to be pursued by a big, bad wolf who kills her ageing grandmother, disguises itself in her clothes, and then lies patiently in wait for the child in the old woman's bed. There are many different endings to the tale. Stories of this ilk, and the themes contained in them, have spread across the world like tree roots from Asia to Europe – and, some argue, even further a field.

The most famous version of this fairy tale is certainly Charles Perrault's 1697 French story, 'Le Petit Chaperon Rouge', thought to have been inspired by earlier tales from French oral tradition. The Brothers Grimm collected and rewrote several variants of the tale in Germany in the 19th century. Certainly, versions of the story exist all across Europe. While the most common ending to these is that both grandmother and girl are eaten up by the evildoer, the fates that unfold before us can be as grisly as they are numerous. Often, the pair are rescued and jump alive from the wolf's belly after it is slit open by a woodcutter or huntsman. In some, the wolf's tummy is filled with rocks, and he drops down dead from the weight, or is put off-balance and falls into a well and drowns. In others from across the world the girl uses her own wits to escape and, in some, to also kill her adversary – by drowning, or with boiling oil.

Sometimes, the villain is not a wolf at all. In an Italian tale from the Abruzzo region, 'La Finta Nonna' (The False Grandmother), the villain is an ogress, rather than a wolf. Here, the grandmother is gobbled up completely – apart from her teeth, which are put on to stew in a small pan, and her ears, which the little girl finds sizzling away in a frying pan. These are later offered up for the child's supper when she complains she is hungry; the teeth as 'beans', and the ears as 'fritters'. Luckily, she does not fall foul of cannibalism and refuses the macabre meal, saying the teeth are too hard to eat, and the fritters not crispy enough. In some versions from France, Italy and Austria, the villain is an ogre or *bzou* (werewolf), and the child does indeed drink the grandmother's blood and eat her flesh, which the wolf neatly stores in the larder for the girl's delectation once the grisly murder is complete. One story even details how the old woman's intestine is put up as a latch string, obviously installed by the thoughtful wolf as a way for the child to open the door and let herself into the cottage.

East Asia has many similar tales too; one from China is 'Grandmother Wolf'. The evildoer is a tiger in the variants 'The Grandmother Tiger' or 'Grand-aunt Tiger' – hailing from Japan, Korea and China. Some believe the tale may have roots in classical Greek and Roman legends where wolves or wolf-men often play the villain. Some believe the tale of 'Little Red Riding Hood' goes back to an 11th-century poem by Egbert de Liège, 'The little girl spared by the wolf cubs' (*De puella a lupellis seruata*), yet this is still widely debated by scholars. This story tells of a little girl, wearing a red dress gifted by her godfather, who is chased into the deep, wild forest by a wolf and offered up to its cubs as prey. Yet, in an unexpected twist, the cubs refuse to tear the child into pieces, and instead caress her head. At this point, she forbids them from tearing her garment since it was a gift for her baptism, and it seems divine intervention tames the cubs' savagery, as if the red dress itself is a form of protective amulet against their wild natures. It seems that here too, like in the *hulder* and *fossegrim* tales of Scandinavia, Christian belief separates humans from their own wild nature, and the Christian God alone can avert the ferocity of the creatures of the forest in yet another European tale. In folk and fairy tales the wolf is often seen by many as a creature that represents both our love and fear of the wilderness.

This fairy tale has been retold by Disney and Angela Carter alike, and even inspired the poem 'Little Red Cap' by Carol Ann Duffy, the first female and LGBT+ poet laureate of the UK. Layer upon layer of meaning has been pulled from it like pieces of thread, as people – especially women – have tried for centuries to unwind the tale.

In many European versions the girl enters the dwelling, then is soon told to undress and get into bed with the wolf. Many consider this part as having erotic undertones; either underlying hints of sexual predation or coming of age and female sexuality. Some suggest her red cap or hood can be likened to the red menstrual blood of puberty, set against the white snow of the forest floor. The predators that lurk both without and

within ourselves are themes explored in many readings of this tale, as we learn what it really means to be predator or prey, and our misfortune to be either – or both. As psychologist Clarissa Pinkola Estés says in her best-selling *Women Who Run with the Wolves*, a child – who is not sufficiently taught to identify the predators around them – will only learn once having confronted this danger for themselves. She takes this further, saying that they must also confront the innate predator that lurks in the reaches of their own subconscious, a destructive force that needs to be understood and restrained. Fairy tales help us to do just that, in a safe space that is outside of everyday life, and not governed by our normal social rules and constraints. It is interesting that scholars like Jack Zipes suggest that the wolf might represent natural urges and the refusal to conform to social norms and niceties – in essence, that part of ourselves that is wild and animalistic, and can't be bound by culture.

In *The Bloody Chamber and Other Stories*, Angela Carter explores the Red Riding Hood story in a series of wolf-tales, retellings rife with symbolism drawn from the original tale and reinterpreted for modern life. In 'The Werewolf', the girl does not shy away from the monstrous predator chasing her, and instead cuts off its paw and takes it as a trophy. The end of the tale reveals that her pursuer was not the expected wild animal, but instead the girl's very own grandmother in werewolf form, as if the real monsters in our lives are already well known to us and are not strangers at all. In 'The Company of Wolves', the forest takes on a life of its own, and the path through the woodlands alone will keep a human safe; anyone who strays from it can expect to belong to the things of the wild. In this story, a pubescent girl hands her only weapon, a carving knife, over to a dashing huntsman who offers to carry the burden of her basket for her, and – despite her initial wariness – leads her away from the safety of the path into the trees.Relying on his compass to guide them, the girl steers away from her own inner strength, and surrenders this to the man also. Soon, the girl is challenged to a race to her grandmother's house and ends up making her way through the forest alone and unarmed. Of course, the dashing huntsman is far from her saviour, and is really the wolflike predator. Yet there is a twist to the original tale to be found – some might say a reclaiming of the tale from the predator and the fear that comes with it. The girl takes back her own power: resisting being reduced to just meat, she stares her fear straight in the face. She refuses to be devoured, and instead uncovers her own wild nature, joining with the wolf in a feast of animalistic desire. 'The Company of Wolves' was later developed into a 1984 film of the same name. 'Wolf-Alice' is the least like the original tale. Here, the girl is herself raised by wolves, and takes on their likeness, becoming the thing that was originally feared. By exploring the nature of the beast from within, we see there is nothing to be feared in our own animalism. The story is an exploration of her own animal body, and the onset of her bleeding and womanhood.

The meaning of the Red Riding Hood story is often said to be that young girls should be wary of strangers. Perrault himself tells us the moral at the heart of his own story: 'Children, especially attractive, well-bred young ladies, should never talk to strangers, for if they should do so, they may well provide dinner for a wolf.'

Yet we are still wrangling with the age-old question at the heart of this tale today by retelling and rewriting the ending, putting the emphasis on how Little Red Riding Hood herself should have behaved. In daring to speak to a stranger and revealing her frail grandmother is alone in the forest to the deceitful wolf, was Red Riding Hood's own rash courage the true reason for their gruesome fate? Or was she, in her innocence, a true victim of the predators of the forest and thoroughly without blame? This question is one that still raises its ferocious head in women's rights debates across the world today, be it via lawsuits, honour killings and female genital mutilation, for instance. The grisly tale of women and power over their own sexuality continues, and where this version of the story will lead no one yet knows.

Creatures of the Night:
The Curse of the Werewolf

The woods are still and quiet as the weary traveller hurries on, the moon high above the trees to light his way. This brings little comfort, however, and he glances behind him and around, eyes wide with terror at the thought of what might lurk, waiting to pounce. He is right to be afraid: in the distance comes the unmistakable howl that strikes fear into the hearts of all who hear it. For it belongs to a fierce creature, born of darkness, that knows no mercy: the werewolf.

Fearsome as the wolf was thought to be, the threat of the humble *lupus* pales before the sinister shadow of the werewolf. Meaning quite literally 'man who can transform into a wolf', werewolves have been prominent in the history and folklore of Europe for centuries. These creatures were greatly feared: possessed of tremendous strength, they were said to lust after human blood and terrorize villages, people and livestock. These cursed creatures are also found in folklore across the world, in Asia, America and Africa.

Far from a modern invention, werewolves are mentioned well back into antiquity. In the 2nd century, we hear of King Lycaon who, after angering the gods, was transformed into a wolf as punishment. Belief in such creatures continued unwaning through the Middle Ages and became linked inextricably with the witches and witch trials of the 15th to 17th centuries. Werewolves were accused, tried and condemned in the same manner as their witch counterparts. Today, werewolves continue to captivate and stir fear, featuring in films, books and television shows. There were various tell-tale signs that gave away the identity of a werewolf if you knew what to look for. Perhaps a person's eyebrows met suspiciously in the middle, or their fingernails curved in a manner reminiscent of claws. They might have a distinctive, loping gait, or ears set lower on the head than usual. If you were brave enough, cutting the skin to reveal the fur beneath was also a manner of identification. After

turning back into a human, werewolves were known to be lethargic, drained of energy, so anyone who was in that state come morning might be considered suspect.

When in wolf form, there were likewise ways to tell a werewolf from a normal wolf. In Russia a werewolf was said to have bristles under the tongue, and in Sweden the werewolf was known to run on three legs, holding the fourth out behind to mimic a tail.

How did someone become a werewolf? The most commonly reported method of transformation was the use of a wolf belt – a belt made of wolf skin – that was tied around the body. The use of a salve, imbued with magical properties and rubbed into the skin, was also said to lead to an individual turning into a wolf. Sleeping outside in the summertime when the moon was full was also fraught with danger – if the moon shone directly onto your face, you ran the risk of becoming a werewolf. You were likewise in danger if you happened to drink water from the footprint of another werewolf. Sharing a beer with someone who was already a werewolf was another way, but only if they knew the spell to recite at the same time. In France, where the *loup-garou* roamed, it was still believed well into the mid-19th century that some men were fated to be werewolves, and turned with the full moon. After leaving their house by jumping from a window, the ill-fated individual would leap into the nearest fountain – this submersion in the water aided the transformation and they would emerge covered in fur. They would then go on a rampage through the woods and streets, causing mayhem, biting any they met. In Russia, to become a werewolf – or *oborot* – one had to go to a forest and find a tree that had been cut down, stab it with a small knife made of copper and then walk round the tree reciting an incantation. Upon leaping three times over the tree, the transformation would occur, and the person would run into the forest as a werewolf.

Although the fate of a werewolf was a terrible one, all hope was not lost; there were ways of breaking the curse and setting the sufferer free. These methods, however, were far from foolproof and involved varying levels of danger. Sometimes, just calling the werewolf by its given name or scolding it were considered enough to break the curse. One Danish woman broke the curse on her husband when she saw him in wolf form, exclaiming, 'Good Lord, man, why, thou art a were-wolf!' Wearing the person into exhaustion was another method that provided very little risk. The Middle Eastern solution of piercing the sufferer's hands with nails or striking their forehead with a knife was a little more extreme.

In the 16th century, the work of Sebastien Münster mentioned 'witch women' and sorcerers who confessed that they became wolves, going on to attack anyone in their path.

At Christmastime, werewolves of Livonia, Lithuania and Prussia gathered together in order to attack people and animals. They also met annually on the border between Lithuania and Curonia where, among other things, they competed to see who could jump over the wall there. Woe betide those who couldn't manage it – they were whipped by the leader.

A common theme in werewolf stories is the way in which the identity of the werewolf preying on a local community is discovered. There are many tales relating how a werewolf is injured in wolf form, only for a man to display a corresponding injury the next time he is seen. For instance, there is the tale of a woodcutter who was working with his brother in the forest one day; the brother left him, but shortly afterwards a wolf appeared and tried to attack him. The woodcutter managed to get a blow in, cutting the wolf's right front leg with his axe. Later that day when he returned home, he found his brother in bed – his right arm wounded.

BEARS, GODS
AND HEROES

So far on our journey into the trees we have heard tales of women and their woodlands, of wolves and wolf-men – as this is where the trail into the folkloric forests leads. The werewolves and their kin show a wild, masculine side to the trees; they are both the predator that lurks outside between the dark branches as we peer out from our cosy cottages, yet they are also the wildness within ourselves. What we likewise find, as we delve further into our forest fables, is that bears – and their bearlike counterparts – are more usually male in folklore. Bears are the ferocious, lordly kings of the forest, and their tales are as complex and varied as these exquisite, lumbering creatures of the woods themselves are.

Bears are often both heroes and villains in myth cycles and national epics. Jambavana is the King of Bears who helps Rama – a major deity of Hinduism – defeat the antagonist Ravana in the *Ramayana*, one of the two major Sanskrit epics of ancient India. He is sometimes also depicted as a monkey. Yet Jelping-Ja-Oyka, whose name some say means 'bear spirit', is the antagonist of the culture hero Mir-Susne-Hum in the tradition of the Indigenous people of Siberia.

Jean de l'Ours – or John the Bear – is a famous hero in French folklore. Legend tells that his mother was once carried off by a bear to his den; yet it was said that he was not the bear's son at all, despite his bearlike form. Many told tales of how she was already with child at her capture, and the boy was transformed by some magic while in her belly, just by being near to the bear. This half-man, half-bear hero is described as a naughty but strong child, as if his wild nature could not be suppressed, who was later trained as a blacksmith. He is famous for rescuing three princesses from a castle with the help of his companions.

Deities and demi-gods are often bears or bearlike. Veles or Volos is a Slavic cattle god linked to the underworld, some say with the form of a bear. In Norse mythology, both Odin and Thor were gods who regularly disguised themselves as bears. Many say the Norse warrior bands known

as berserkers – who acted as a king's special guards – were part of a bear cult and known for wearing bearskin garments. The 'ber' in their name is said to mean 'bear', and their leaders were often known as Björn, also meaning 'bear'. J.R.R. Tolkien features the character Beorn in *The Hobbit*, a 'skin-changer' that could take the shape of a black bear.

Disguise is not the only function of the bear in myth and folklore: princes and lords alike are renowned for transforming into bears when enchanted. In Norse folklore, the *Saga of Hrólf Kraki* – dating to around 1000 CE – tells of Bjorn, the son of a king, who is enchanted by his troll-stepmother in retribution for refusing her advances while his father is away. He is cursed to take the form of a bear during the day for eternity, but a man by night. Bjorn goes to live in a cave, yet is one day followed by Bera, a freeman's daughter – who follows him after recognizing his eyes. Here, he takes on the form of a man once more, and the girl stays with him, soon becoming pregnant. Fate turns, and the 'bear' predicts he will be killed for hunting his own father's livestock. He tells Bera that when this happens she is to go to the king and ask or the ring under his (Bjorn's) left shoulder.

Bjorn's death soon comes to pass, and Bera does as he asked and retrieves the ring from his body. During the bear's meat feast that follows the hunt, the stepmother presents Bera with some of Bjorn's flesh to eat. He had warned her that this would happen, and that she should refuse, as their children would be marked if she did. Yet the troll-queen forces Bera to eat two morsels of the bear flesh. When she births three sons, two take a monstrous form because of it, one with the lower quarters of an elk, the other with dog's feet; only the youngest, Bothvar, or Bödvar Bjarki, is perfectly human. Before his death, Bjorn told Bera of a chest with three bottoms, engraved with runes that showed each boy the inheritance that Bjorn had bequeathed on him: one of three weapons embedded into the rock for each. The youngest is heir to a sword, wedged into a stone in the cave, which his brothers before him tried to pull free, yet in vain – since each son could only retrieve that which was intended for him alone. You will be glad to know that the troll-queen also received a just fate. Bera revealed her crime to the king, using the ring as proof, and Bödvar dragged her through the streets with a bag over her head, beating her, and sent her all the way to Hel. Soon the old king died, and Bödvar ruled the kingdom until he became bored, so legend tells. Some may feel this is a familiar tale, reminiscent of the British King Arthur, and the 'Sword in the Stone'. Yet others suggest that Bödvar Bjarki is a very similar character to Beowulf, and the two might be the very same; many others disagree.

Bear Worship

Bears do not just appear in myth and fairy tales, they also play a central role in folk rituals and customs today from North America to Asia and Europe, as they have done for centuries.

Bear worship has a long history, and some have even proposed that a bear cult existed in prehistory based on rock art from southern Europe. Many have disputed the evidence for this, yet it has captured the imaginations of people across the world. Jean M. Auel's bestselling fictional book series, *Earth's Children* – beginning with *Clan of the Cave Bear* – follows the story of a Neanderthal tribe and touches on their tribal bear worship. It should be noted that there was a backlash against the novels by scientists and archaeologists, who called them both 'bad science' and racist.

We do see worship of the Romano-Celtic bear goddess Artio in the Iron Age, specifically around Bern, Switzerland, and the Moselle river running near the French-German border. A similar male god was patron of bears, Mercury Artaius, from eastern France and Switzerland, a Romanized version of an earlier local bear god.

The *Kalevala* is considered the national epic of Karelia and Finland, compiled from smaller pieces of folklore by Elias Lönnrot in the 19th century. Here, the bear is depicted as a woodland god. He can never be named directly, so he is only ever alluded to indirectly by names like 'King of the Forest', and 'Honeypalm'. One ritual song tells how the celestial bear was cast from the heavens after breaking the taboo of looking at the earth – a thing forbidden by the ruler of heaven – and was thus let down from the heavens in a golden cradle on a silver chain, becoming the guardian of the forest and its animals.

While most evidence dates from the 1600s, the bear festival of the Finns could be witnessed even in the 20th century. Parts of the legend of Väinämöinen – the folk hero and shaman – reflect these rituals. In poem 46 of the *Kalevala*, 'Otso the Honey-Eater', Väinämöinen takes on a quest to slay Otso the bear. He kills the creature, and then returns for a feast of its flesh, singing songs and telling the story of how the bear was created:

The myth begins that Honey-paw was born in the Moon-land, with the daughters of creation. Through the ether a young woman, clad in purple stockings and golden sandals, walked on the red-tinted clouds on the edge of the heavens. In one hand she carried a box of hair. On her shoulder she carried a box of wool. When she reached the ocean, she threw the wool onto it; and the hair she threw into the rivers. Buffeted by the wind and waves, they soon reached the sandy shores of land, surrounded by woodlands on a forest-covered island. Mielikki, forest-hostess and daughter of the glen, took the wool and hair, and sewed them together and placed them in her birch-bark basket. She took chains of gold and bound it to the top of a pine tree. And there she sat, rocking it, until she had rocked life into this strange child, swaddled in the pine needles. And so Otso was born, in the branches of the honey-tree in the middle of a forest.

Soon the bear grew, with his velvet fur-robe, wide mouth and short nose. Mielikki promised the bear teeth and claws – if he, in turn, promised never to use them for ill. The bear fell to his knees, swearing he would never do such a thing. Mielikki went to a great pine, and here she gathered silver branches and golden cones, and from them she fashioned teeth and claws, and set them in Otso's jaws and feet. After this, she set the bear free to roam the forests in his fur-robes.

After he had recounted this tale, it's said that Väinämöinen took the body of the bear back to the place of his silken cradle, at the top of his pine tree, where the branches would rock him into endless sleep.

The bear-hunting ritual reflects this tale of Väinämöinen and Otso, and an early description of the custom comes from the *Viitasaari Text*, dating to the end of the 17th or beginning of the 18th century. The ritual had three parts. First a bear would be hunted and slain. This was a highly symbolic thing, and not taken lightly. A hibernating bear must always be woken, in case its soul was journeying in the spirit world, separate from the body, in which case the rituals would not work, and the bear would be stuck in the otherworld and able to seek its revenge. Also, the hunters must never say aloud that they had killed the bear, but instead say that it had died accidentally, by falling or the like, to avoid other bears coming to avenge its death. Secondly there would be a feast in honour of the bear. Called *peijaiset*, this would take the form of a wedding feast, yet it also acted like a wake. The bear would be greeted as an esteemed guest and led into the house with traditional wedding songs. A young boy and girl were chosen as the symbolic bride and groom, and the group would feast on the sacred bear's flesh. Here, sorcerers would cause the bear's teeth to fall from the head with just the power of their words, and each hunter would take his share of the teeth as amulets, and then eat the head to take on the powers and attributes of the bear. Lastly, the bear's bones would be returned to its forest home and buried in the tree roots, with its head placed on top of the same pine or spruce, known as 'the skull tree'. The bear would be close to its home in the stars once more, the origin of all bear souls, and then be able to reincarnate and return to the earth. With this resurrection, humans were perpetuating the cycle of life by hunting and honouring the bear. Killing it was not a malicious act; the hunters were instead ensuring the cycle of eternal life. With this, many suggest this ritual might have represented the constant struggle between life and death. People would visit this skull tree and leave offerings for the spirit of the bear for some time to come.

Another source of folklore and mythology of the people is their famous collection of 'magic songs of the Finns'. These teach that one way of stopping a bear preying upon your livestock is to pray to him; if this doesn't work, a foolproof method is to put a mushroom up one of the bear's nostrils and an apple up the other, so the bear cannot smell the cows. Do let us know if this works.

We do not need to delve deep into the past to find evidence of the animal's sacred nature; bear worship can still be seen all around us today. The bear is seen as a symbol of Russia even now and was the mascot for the 1980 Moscow Olympic Games. In Bulgaria, St Andrew's Day is also Bear's Day, Mechkinden – the beginning of winter. It is celebrated by boiling grains, and the mixture should be thrown up the chimney to ensure a plentiful harvest. It is believed that if the grain is offered up to the bear for it to eat, it won't eat the townspeople instead!

VIRGINS, HUNTSMEN AND JESUS CHRIST:
The Quest for the Unicorn

Alone in a woodland glade, a young woman sits, seemingly alone, eyes fixed demurely on her hands in her lap. Suddenly from the trees sounds a rustling, and a moment later out steps that icon of chastity, virtue and strength: the unicorn. The majestic creature approaches and lays its head in her lap, her only movement to raise her hand to stroke it until it falls into a peaceful sleep. The tender scene is soon disrupted, however, as a huntsman bursts from his cover; the unicorn is swiftly captured and taken to the king so the hunter can gain his reward.

Popular throughout history in folklore, literature, film and art, and even on coats of arms, the unicorn has fascinated and intrigued mankind since antiquity. Today, when we think of a unicorn, the image that springs to mind is that of a breathtakingly beautiful white horse, sometimes winged, with a single, shining horn in the middle of its forehead. In our modern imaginings, the unicorn is also often capable of magical feats that know no bounds. This image of the unicorn, though, is a relatively new one, and the unicorn of antiquity looked quite different. An early and influential account of the unicorn comes from 398 BCE with Ctesias, court physician to Darius II of Persia. In his work on India, *Indica*, Ctesias intriguingly describes a creature like a wild ass, but roughly the size of a horse. These animals had white bodies, dark red heads, and eyes of a dark blue. Most strikingly, they had a horn on their forehead, measuring about 45cm (18 inches) long. Ctesias goes on to describe the horn in detail: white at the base, black in the middle and bright crimson on the end.

Following from Ctesias, Aristotle, writing in the 4th century, mentions several creatures with a single horn, including the oryx and

Indian ass, both of which had a horn in the centre of their forehead. Strabo in turn relates how there was a creature in the Caucasus that resembled a horse with the head of a deer and one horn. Pliny the Elder, in the 1st century, mentions the monoceros. This fierce creature sounded like a most wondrous animal indeed: with the body of a horse and a stag's head, the monoceros had a boar's tail, and elephant feet finished off the strange sight. The monoceros had a single horn: black, and two cubits long (around 90cm). According to the age-old writers, the unicorn was nigh-on impossible to capture.

What were people really seeing when they reported on these ancient unicorns? Candidates for the true identity of the unicorn are varied, with debate raging over the issue. There were five creatures reported in early texts to have had single horns that were potential contenders: the oryx, the monoceros, the Indian ass, the single-horned ox and the horse.

One of the oldest surviving physical depictions of the unicorn comes from the Indus Valley, where the image has been discovered on Bronze Age seals unearthed in the mid-19th century. Used to mark goods ready for market, the seals showed a variety of animal images. Many are known to us today as actual creatures: the bull, elephant, crocodile and rhino. The unicorn stands out as being the only legendary creature among them, a tantalizing fact that has led archaeologists to suggest that they may have had mythical or religious symbolism; yet this meaning is now lost to time. The unicorn motif is the most common to appear on such seals, showing the symbol had unparalleled importance.

The unicorn also makes an appearance in the Bible, and in the King James Version of the Old Testament there are seven references to the animal. There is no suggestion that the writers saw the unicorn as a supernatural or mythical creature. This is shown as it is mentioned along with other verifiably real animals, such as the bullock or lion. The unicorn's magical properties likewise have a long pedigree. According to Ctesias, a potion of dust from a filed unicorn horn offers protection from drugs, and drinking from the horn itself protects the drinker against poison. Drinking out of a unicorn horn can also protect against epilepsy and convulsions.

Unicorns also make an appearance in the European bestiaries. These fascinating volumes, a collection of stories where the animals were used to illustrate moral points, contained all manner of creatures, both real and fictional. In line with previous writers, the unicorn was fierce, immune to capture by traditional hunting methods, and had a single horn on its head. Unlike in the works of Ctesias and those who followed him, however, the unicorn of the bestiaries is described as being much smaller, the size of a kid, with a fierce temperament. Indeed, the unicorn of the medieval period was small enough to curl up in the lap of a virgin.

According to the bestiaries, there were ways that a unicorn could be captured. The Physiologus tells us that the creature could be captured if lured by a virgin. The virgin was to sit alone in a place where the unicorn was said to frequent, with the hunters waiting nearby. According to the story, the unicorn would approach, put his head in her lap and then fall asleep there as she stroked it. The hunters would then emerge and capture the animal, taking their prize to the king.

In the bestiaries, and the works that were inspired by their version of the unicorn, it was sometimes said that the creature stood for Christ, the virgin represented the Virgin Mary herself, and the hunter was the Holy Spirit, the whole capture narrative taken as representing the Incarnation of Christ. In the Provençal Bestiary, there is a distinct variation to this,

with the unicorn representing not Christ but the Devil. In this instance, the virgin, representing virtue, provides the only way to overcome evil, the Devil. Another variation is the assertion that the unicorn is able to determine whether someone is truly a virgin or not. Woe betide the false maiden, for it is said that the unicorn will kill her when the deception is discovered! Other writers stated that there would be a greater chance of succeeding in its capture if the virgin was both beautiful and naked.

One of the best-known pieces of unicorn lore is its reputed and long-standing feud with the lion. According to legend, this represents the historic rivalry between Scotland (the unicorn) and England (the lion). This conflict between the two beasts, however, is believed to be much older, stretching back into antiquity. The unicorn was also said to be the adversary of the elephant, and that it would always beat it.

Although belief in the unicorn started to wane in the 18th century, it was not until 1825 that its existence appeared to be ruled out scientifically when Baron Georges Cuvier, a French naturalist sometimes called the founding father of palaeontology, argued that an animal with a cloven hoof must have a cloven skull, therefore making it impossible for such a creature to have a single horn on its forehead. This was, however, later disproven.

JACKALOPES AND WOLPERTINGERS:
Creating a Legend

As we have already seen, there are many weird and wonderful creatures and spirits associated with the forests and woodlands of the world, some almost too fantastical for words. But there are some creatures that are made of a mix of animals already familiar to us: combining animal features and characteristics to form some of the most outlandish creations known to folklore.

Many such hybrids have been created in physical form by individuals – quite literally, from the parts of two other forest-dwelling animals – turning previously existing legends into reality. They may have been created for personal amusement, entertainment or financial gain, and have often become part of local lore, used to trick tourists and visitors. Some of the most famous of these creatures – folklore in their own right – are explored below.

The North American jackalope is perhaps the most famous of all the 'forest fakes' out there to date. This legendary critter is a hybrid creature with the body of a jackrabbit and the horns of an antelope. The jackalope is understood as part of the 'tall tale' genre, prevalent in American culture and beyond. Although it may have existed in oral folklore before this point, the jackalope first leapt to fame in 1934. Brothers Douglas and Ralph Herrick of Douglas, Wyoming, who had studied taxidermy via post, created the first 'real' jackalope quite by accident. Late for dinner one night, they threw down a rabbit they had acquired on the floor of their taxidermy shop. As fate would have it, the rabbit just so happened to land next to a pair of antlers. Upon seeing it on their return, the brothers decided to mount the creature, with Douglas exclaiming, 'Let's mount it the way it is!' Thus, according to local legend, the jackalope was born.

The pair did a roaring trade, and the jackalope brought many curious visitors to Douglas in search of the 'legendary' creature. To date, tens

of thousands of stuffed and mounted jackalopes have been sold. The
original jackalope to be created was bought by Roy Ball, the owner of
Hotel LaBonte; it was stolen, however, and its fate is currently unknown.

Today, it is possible to buy a licence that permits you to hunt
jackalope. Be aware though that this is under the strictest conditions –
hunting can only take place on 31 June, between sunrise and sunset. In
addition, the hunter has to have an IQ of between 50 and 72. Despite the
obvious joke at the expense of wannabe jackalope hunters, these 'licences'
do a roaring trade. Some of the other products associated with jackalopes
have not been quite so successful – jackalope milk, in particular, never
quite took off.

The jackalope continues to hold a firm place in the history and
culture of the town of Douglas: the official website for the town sports
the tagline 'Home of the Jackalope: We Know Jack'. Not only does the
town sport a larger-than-life-size statue of the creature, the image of
the jackalope can be seen in various forms throughout the town to this
day, with an annual celebration of the creature on Jackalope Day, and
countless themed souvenirs available to tourists who flock to Douglas

for their jackalope fix. This roaring trade provides ample opportunity for locals to sport with unsuspecting visitors: the aforementioned licences are just the tip of the iceberg!

Jackalopes are complex creatures. Said to be particularly fond of whiskey, they are notoriously dangerous if cornered. They do, however, have lovely singing voices, and one legend attached to them is their habit of joining in with cowboys singing around their campfires. The jackalope has inspired many, and reached much further than its native Wyoming, featuring in movies, video games, children's books and even on beer branding and as the name of a London pub.

Although clearly a creature of fable, there is actually a possible scientific explanation for the jackalope and stories of similar creatures. The Shope papilloma virus (SPV) – which causes tumours that resemble horns on the suffering rabbit – has been suggested as a cause of alleged jackalope sightings.

The wolpertinger, an inhabitant of southern Germany, is said to haunt the alpine forests of Bavaria and Baden-Württemberg. These creatures are the size of small mammals: with the body of either a squirrel, rabbit or deer, they sport bird feet, deer antlers, feathered wings and fangs. The wolpertinger is seen as kin to the various horned mammals that exist in the folklore of Germany, but is much more elaborate, with the appendages of several different creatures. Generally shy and not harmful to humans, these creatures are thought to have been the creation of Bavarian taxidermists in the 19th century.

Various tall tales are attached to the wolpertinger, used to fool tourists. Such elaborate legends include the belief that if the saliva of the wolpertinger touches human skin, thick hair will quickly grow there, impossible to remove.

How do you catch a wolpertinger? Women with exceptional beauty are said to have the best chance of catching one of these elusive creatures. According to legend, venturing forth into the forest on the night of a full moon with a beautiful woman should ensure the wolpertinger shows itself: if she exposes her breasts, the creature will fall into a stupor and thus be able to be captured. The decidedly questionable morality behind this particular piece of folklore is another matter entirely!

The German Hunting and Fishing Museum was known for displaying specimens of the wolpertinger, and to this day has an exhibition there on these elusive creatures.

The wolpertinger's name has various potential origins. It has been suggested that it comes from a corruption of the name of the town, Wolterdingen, near which the creatures are said to be seen. It is likewise said to originate from the word *Walpurgisnacht*, night of the witches, which falls on 30 April.

The rasselbock is another rabbit/deer hybrid, with the body and head of a rabbit and the antlers of a deer, similar in appearance to the jackalope. This mythical creature is said to inhabit the Thuringian Forest of Germany and is also associated with the Harz Mountains.

Although strikingly similar to jackalope tales, one variation in the rasselbock legend is that it is sometimes depicted with doglike teeth, giving the creature a fanged appearance, a marked departure from the usual rabbit/hare form. In the *Encyclopedia of Beasts and Monsters in Myth, Legend and Folklore*, the rasselbock is listed simply as a variation of the wolpertinger.

You will be hard-pressed to see rasselbock, as they are shy creatures, preferring to venture forth at night when humans are asleep, unfazed by the darkness. Despite its cautious nature, there are ways to spot a rasselbock and know if one has been near: if you believe the tales, its footprints are sometimes spied in the snow, giving away the fact it has passed by.

The Sitzendorfer Museum sports several supposedly stuffed specimens of the rasselbock, and on 1 May every year the annual rasselbock festival takes place, with much merriment, culminating in a hunt for the creature.

'Would you like to go and catch rasselbock?' This question is used to insult the old or learned during a conversation!

WHAT LURKS IN THE LUMBERWOODS:
The Most Fearsome of Critters

In the 19th century lumber camps of North America, the nights were long and entertainment scarce. Talking and yarn-telling were practised almost as an art form, with tales spun to amuse the old hands and to tease and fool those greener loggers who were not so used to camp ways. It was thus that tales of the fearsome creatures said to frequent the forests were formed, growing and mutating as they spread from camp to camp.

The Splinter Cat

One ferocious North American critter was the splinter cat. This creature was of a very strange appearance indeed. The splinter cat was of huge size, comparable to an elephant. It had the body of a cat – with wide black stripes from head to tail – and in that regard was considered a good-looking animal. When you got to his head, however, it was another story altogether. His head was large and made of stone, the very instrument used to cause the destruction that gives this creature its name.

Living on wild bees and raccoons, the splinter cat obtained its food by quite literally splintering open trees to search for its sustenance – the racoons, and bees with their honey, living within the trees. He thus went from tree to tree, smashing each one open until he found what he was looking for. How was this destruction achieved? The splinter cat was said to climb a tree, right up to the top branches. From there, it bounded downwards, in the direction of another tree that was its chosen target, which he bashed with his stone-hard head.

The result was battered and shattered trees as far as the eye could see – although it is clear to those in the know that the culprit was the splinter cat, those who didn't know of him often mistakenly believed such damage to be caused by storms! They could be forgiven for this misunderstanding: every time the splinter cat struck a blow, a flash of lightning issued forth, followed by a rumble of thunder.

There are those who say they have witnessed first-hand the activity of the splinter cat. In the mid-20th century, T.H. Sherrard and Dee Wright, both of the Oregon Forest Service, claimed to have heard a splinter cat while on a camping trip. The resultant destruction was witnessed the next morning by the pair.

The splinter cat is commemorated by Splintercat Creek – a tributary to the Roaring River – in the Cascade Range mountains in Oregon. Named thus by Sherrard to redress the balance he felt was due the much-neglected splinter cat, the name of the creek has been taken in turn as proof of the creature's existence. After all, as it is often pointed out, just because no one has ever seen this elusive creature, that is not evidence that it does not exist.

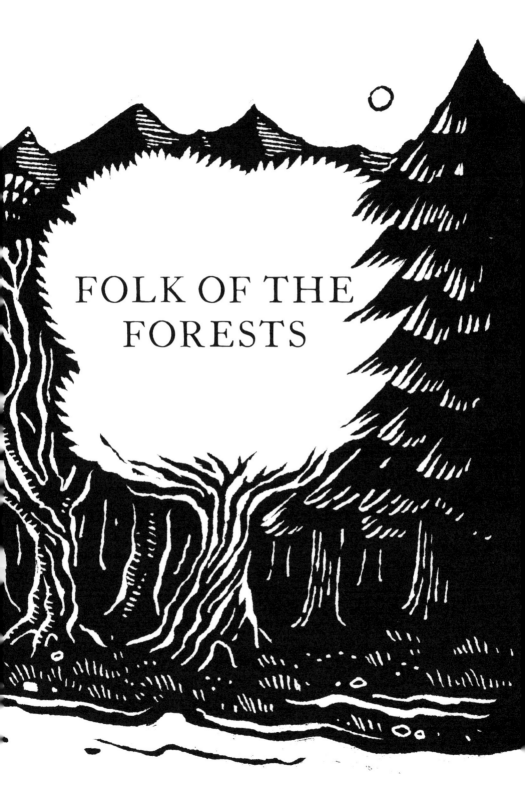

FOLK OF THE
FORESTS

A GIANT AMONG LUMBERJACKS:
Paul Bunyan and the North American Lumber Camps

There is no better-known figure in North American and Canadian lumberjack folklore than Paul Bunyan. According to the huge wealth of lore and legend that exists about this larger-than-life figure, Bunyan was the greatest man to ever run the late 19th century lumber camps of North America, with no deed too great, no feat too fantastical to be attached to his name. Originating in these lumber camps, his tales moved from area to area with the loggers. Paul Bunyan was known of in Oregon, Washington and British Columbia, and many places in between.

These days, there are some facts that are generally accepted as gospel truth where Bunyan was concerned: 2m (7ft) tall, with a stride that matched his prodigious height, the famed lumberjack could not be matched either for strength or the ability to hold his drink. How did this man call his men for dinner across the vast camp? Why, through a hollow tree, of course, the weight as nothing in his large, capable hands. It is debatable whether Bunyan needed such an instrument; it was said that his voice alone was loud enough to make branches fall from nearby trees.

There was just one issue for this giant of a man. Bunyan was, according to the tales, unable to write. This did not deter him, however, and the problem was easily solved by Bunyan's much-noted ingenuity. When ordering supplies, the camp leader simply drew pictures of what he required, the goods arriving as requested on all but one memorable occasion. Bunyan had ordered grindstones, but instead received a delivery of several round cheeses. This caused consternation for only a moment before Bunyan realized that the error was his: he had forgotten to include the holes in the stones in his drawing!

There are several staples in the Bunyan canon. The 'Winter of the Blue Snow', either in 1862 or 1865, was a particularly famous time in Bunyan's operations, and many of the best-known stories associated with him were said to have taken place at this time. This was when Bunyan and his crew were stationed on the Big Onion River, the crew so large that it was split into three gangs. Another popular location for tales was Round River, where Bunyan and his crew spent another winter filled with adventures and great derring-do.

The lumberjack's inseparable companion, the ox, features in many of the Bunyan tales. Babe was as renowned for his size and strength as Bunyan himself. As strong as nine horses, Babe weighed, at the very least, 2,250kg (5,000lb). Across his horns, he measured 2m (7ft). How did Babe come to be blue? That happened during the Winter of the Blue Snow; with the snow lasting seven days and nights, the ox was stained from lying in the snow, and could not be returned to his original bright white afterwards.

According to the wide wealth of legend that grew up around him, Bunyan was responsible for the formation of several of the now famous geographical landmarks across the northern United States and into Canada. The Mississippi River owes its existence to an accident of Bunyan's, when his ox slipped and caused a giant water tank to overturn. The Grand Canyon was formed when Bunyan dragged his axe behind him in the midst of a storm while looking for firewood. The Great Lakes were made by Bunyan as a solution to the problem of having nowhere for his animals to water. In a potentially more modern addition to the Bunyan canon, Niagara Falls supposedly owes its existence to the time Bunyan needed to wash his notoriously energetic – and equally large – young children in the Niagara River.

So where did the tales originate? Paul Bunyan was first mentioned in print in 1893, but tales of the famed lumberjack were part of oral tradition for much longer. A lot of what is accepted as Bunyan folklore today actually originated outside of the lumber camps. There were two main routes by which Bunyan and the tales that came to be associated with him entered the public view. William Laughead heard of the lumberjack hero in 1901 when staying in a north-west logging camp. He was told of Bunyan's exploits and later, in 1914, when he was public relations manager for the Red River Lumber Company, Laughead produced a brochure called 'Introducing Mr Paul Bunyan of Westwood, California', a mixture of the products for sale by the company and Bunyan tales. Due to the fame of Bunyan not having spread outside of the lumber camps he originated in, the pamphlet had little impact, but a later attempt, 'Tales About Paul Bunyan, Vol II', did better, largely due to Laughead linking the Red River Lumber Company products with Bunyan in a large advertising campaign. It was Laughead who gave a name to Bunyan's favourite blue ox, who before had remained nameless.

Although Laughead has been credited with bringing tales of Bunyan to the public eye, the versions he used were not, it is generally accepted, that faithful to the original oral tales told by the logging community. In 1912, K. Bernice Stewart from the University of Wisconsin had started collating tales from the lumberjacks and those who worked with them directly. She and her English professor, Homer Watt, interviewed those from the lumber community and recorded the tales, and it is generally believed that their results were truer to the 'original' Bunyan canon. Their results were published in 1916. From that point on, Bunyan-fever began, and the legendary lumberjack hero became the focus of countless collections, stories, plays and songs, his name familiar to households across the United States.

Bunyan was said to have been incredibly wily, a fact illustrated in another popular tale about him. Finding himself broke when spring rolled round, and unable to pay his crew their wages for the time they had worked, he fixed upon a plan. The king of theatrics, Bunyan ran into the camp, shouting at the top of his prodigious voice that they had inadvertently been cutting down pine that belonged to the government and that arrest was about to follow. At such alarming news the lumberjacks panicked; grabbing whatever they could lay their hands on, they fled in every direction, leaving the camp deserted. By this subterfuge, Bunyan avoided paying anyone for their hard labour, and cleared his camp in the process.

It is to be noted that the tales surrounding the legendary Bunyan are without doubt a product of their time and location. Several references to the 'coloured' helpers who assisted Bunyan's cooks are made, with their often-horrible fates used for comedic value in a way that is utterly unacceptable today. Rather than expunge this from history, it should be highlighted as a prime example of the bias and degradation such prejudices have inflicted on millions of people over the centuries.

Was Paul Bunyan real? Bunyan was perhaps the biggest in-joke of the lumber community. It was tacitly and overtly accepted that all lumberjacks believed Bunyan had been a real flesh-and-blood man, and it was standard for those of a certain age to profess to having even worked with the great man himself. Several authors over the years have proposed theories and evidence that support the idea that Paul Bunyan was based on a real person. Others view him as an invention, or 'fakelore', with a literary origin rather than originating in true lore of the lumber camps, brought to the attention of the public by the tales later created about him.

Arguments for or against his existence aside Bunyan's reputation continues to bring him fame and acknowledgement, long after the lumber camps that spawned his legend are no more than a distant memory.

LORDS OF THE WILD

Lordly spirits and creatures of the forests and jungles abound the world over. Some are malevolent creatures, living alone in the woodlands, wreaking havoc, leaving naught but destruction in their wake. Others are protective wild men, looking after the creatures of the forests and the trees within them. Here we take a look at some of these lords of the wild, uncovering their true faces as we brush away the leaves that hide them in the shadows.

The Forest God Tapio, Finnish

Tapio – also known as Metsähine, or Hiisi – is the Finnish king of the forest realm. He is tall, thin, with a coat of either ermine fur or moss, and his head is capped with a hat. Like the green man or foliate heads of Europe, he peers out from underneath bushy eyebrows of moss and lichen, usually with a great beard – sometimes of straggling black hair. Similar to the hulder or other female spirits of Scandinavia, he is said to look thoroughly human from the front, but with the back of a gnarled tree. It's said he is as tall as a tree and is both the personification and the protector of the forest. In the past, hunters had to ask for his blessing before their chase, to ensure a good hunt, pledging to respect the ways of the woods, that they would be respectful of the land and creatures, hunting quietly, and disrupting no one and nothing. It was believed Tapio was lord of all creatures of the forest, and could ensure a hunter a plentiful haul, or curse him to leave empty-handed. The Estonian equivalent of the god is similar, yet, like the Norse god Odin, has only one eye.

Like many gods of the Finns, Tapio has a family. His wife is named Mielikki when she is benevolent, and Kuurikki when she is not; their son, Nyrikki, is said to help hunters by making marks for them to find their way through the trees. Tulikki, their daughter, helps those in the forest by directing prey towards them.

The Leshy, Slavic

The *leshy, leshii* or *lyeshy* is a Slavic tutelary spirit of the woods, and a protector of the trees and animals; in Ukraine he is guardian of wolves above all other animals, while others say he is only servant to his favourite animal, the bear. Like bears, the leshy hibernates in winter. Known by many different names, all usually show these creatures to belong to the forests, and as being ruled by either the woodsman or the Devil. Many liken them to Greek satyrs, human from above the waist but sporting horns, claws and a bushy beard that some report as forest green, while others say they are entirely covered in moss. They are shapeshifting creatures, changing size and form at will: they are able to grow taller than a tree, or as short as a blade of grass. Some say they appear huge from a distance but are tiny up close. Leshies can disguise themselves as any familiar human, animal or plant of the forest. When appearing in human form they can be identified easily in that they never have eyelashes or brows, they might wear their shoes on the wrong feet; in Yaroslavl Province in Russia they will have their skirt or kaftan wrapped in the opposite way to the local fashion. Some have only one eye, but all are covered in wild hair, with the cloven feet of the fauns – or the Devil himself. In some regions they have wings and a tail with black fur; in others they wear white and always have swollen eyes.

Their bellowing whips up great winds when they charge through the forest surveying their territory, and all the creatures flee in terror. If people encroaching on their forests uninvited do not flee when warned by the leshy's shrieking laughter, clapping or howling, they will often be lost to the wilds by morning, after the leshy has confused them, lured them from the path and changed their surroundings about them, and they are never seen again. As with other fabled creatures of the forest, leshies are trickster figures, able to alter their voices to mimic others, enticing people towards them, where they can, apparently, tickle their victims to death. Their voices can also sound like creaking branches or rustling leaves. Illness can befall those who cross a leshy, and they abduct women to marry – or otherwise – and often take children found wandering in the forest or those cursed by their parents. The creatures

were famous for inflicting their wrath and cursing entire farms, sucking the milk from the herd; in response, famers from the Olonetsky District of Russia used to sacrifice a cow to them annually to ensure the welfare of their cattle. Those who say a prayer before entering the forest, or leave offerings of bread, tobacco and the like, are safe from their wrath.

It is believed that leshies live either alone or with their wives – the *lesovikha* – and their children, sometimes in a hut in the middle of the woodlands. It seems they are not above battling their own kind, often carrying clubs to wage war, ripping up trees as they go. One leshy from Vologda District was said to frequent local taverns while driving his wolf pack, guzzling down a whole bucket of vodka before venturing back out into the night. They are notorious gamblers, usually bargaining with squirrels instead of money. Playing cards is a favourite pastime – although only using card decks without clubs, since they resemble the Christian cross too closely for their liking.

Like with fae folk across the world, one way of ensuring your safety against leshies is to turn your shirt inside out and put your shoes on the wrong feet; this is said to make them laugh, which returns you immediately to the rightful path you recognize. The method in some areas is quite specific: strip down until you're naked, and then put all your clothes back on, yet backwards. Another way to make them laugh is to swear at them remorselessly, which will make them leave at once. Making the sign of the cross is a less fun way of banishing them. However, if you would like to summon a leshy, the method is simple: go into the forest and cut down a number of young trees – birch is best. Place these in a circle on the ground, tops touching in the middle. Stand in the centre, making sure to wear no Christian symbols, call out to the grandfather of the forest, and he will come.

Herne the Hunter, English

For many, Herne the Hunter is a horned god likened to Cernunnos or Pan, who acts as ruler of the woodlands: the master and protector of the animals. People often visualize him as a vegetal deity, covered in leaves and vines just like the image of the green man. In reality, this is a relatively new image of him, and the story behind this figure is very different. He is traditionally a ghost who haunts Windsor Forest in Berkshire, England – now called Windsor Great Park. His spirit charges through the forest on his steed with his pack of dogs, head topped with tattered, staglike antlers, rattling chains and bedevilling cattle as he goes.

The earliest known mention of Herne is in Shakespeare's *The Merry Wives of Windsor*, from 1597. No one can be certain if the character was grounded in local legend before this. Shakespeare tells that the shadowy spectre, the ghost of one of the keepers of Windsor Forest, could be glimpsed walking round the trunk of his favourite oak in the forest, particularly on a winter's night as the clock strikes twelve. He blasts trees, shakes chains hideously, and even curses dairy cows to fill their pails with blood instead of milk. A 1604 version adds the details that he takes the form of a stag as he roams.

We then hear little of the spectre until the 18th century, when his tale takes on a life of its own. The story goes that the gamekeeper had committed a crime, then took his own life, hanging himself from the branches of a tree – an act which, in folklore and history, curses the soul to walk the world forever, unable to enter heaven. Later, a novel elaborates his backstory to include him being gored by a stag, yet saved by the Devil, only for him to sprout antlers as a mark of this deal – a sign of his nefarious affiliation. Others believe the antlers are an indicator of his bestial nature or a punishment for his crimes. Some say he was secretly a poacher, or that he was falsely accused of this, and was unable to live with the legacy of his reputation. By the 20th century, seeing Herne had become an omen of impending doom and destruction.

Sadly, two trees – both rumoured to be Herne's Oak – were lost in the 18th and 19th centuries respectively, one being cut down and the other uprooted in a storm. One great tree still standing, which was planted in 1906, still bears the name.

However, some suggest that Herne is much older, a character from pre-Christian myth that has morphed over the centuries into a local version of an older mythic figure. Many revere him as the male aspect of nature in some Neo-Pagan religious paths, giving thanks to him as an embodiment of the Horned God, and the spirit of the forest. Some 20th century Pagan writers like Gerald Gardner believed he was an ancient god of the witches, as he is today for many. Margaret Murray says that Cernunnos, a horned god of Romano-Celtic Gaul, was sometimes known as Herne or 'Old Horne'. Many believe Cernunnos is the antlered figure on the famous Gundestrup Cauldron, which dates back to the Iron Age. Others believe Herne may have originated in the Germanic god Wotan, the leader of the Wild Hunt, the ethereal chase across the sky by a wild huntsman and his hellish entourage, aiming to catch mortals to kill or add their soul to their numbers. Little evidence exists to support these ideas of an older myth, and it's interesting to see that the accompanying horse and ghostly dogs make no appearance at all. It is believed that many of the details that have become enshrined in the Herne legend are actually taken from Wild Hunt tales and fictional novels. For instance, his cavorting pack of dogs that accompany him when galloping in the forest are reminiscent of the hounds of the Welsh lord of the otherworld, the Cŵn Annwn, and similar hellhounds that attend the gods of the Wild Hunt. The Herne stories tell that he is tied either only to his tree or to the forest itself; while the hunt takes place in the sky, and can appear wherever it likes.

Is Herne the Hunter the restless spirit of a man cursed to wander the earth for eternity because he took his own life, or was he more than this, a lingering echo of an ancient god? We'll never know for sure.

Papa Bois, Caribbean

Papa Bois or Bwa is the father of the forest in St Lucia and Trinidad & Tobago. As guardian of the animals, he is able to release creatures from hunters' traps and cure creatures of any illness, as well as sounding his horn to warn them when hunters enter their woods. Folk tales tell how he hates his forests to be disturbed by hunters, chasing them away or luring them into the trees, causing them to lose their way. Some stories tell that he is a human, yet a shapeshifter, and can take the form of any creature he wishes, often a monkey, lappe (a large rodent) or stag, to lure hunters to their doom. Papa Bois is said to be short and muscular, with a body that is half-human and half-animal, and a beard of leaves. Covered in donkey-like fur, his left foot is a hoof, and he is so fast he can outrun a deer. As with the leshy, if you meet him in the forest just take off all of your clothes, then put them back on, making sure to turn them inside out, and you will be safe. His counterpart is Mama D'Leau, guardian of the river creatures.

AT ONE WITH THE TREES:
Tree Nymphs and Spirits

The folklore and myths of many different countries and cultures tell of spirits or nymphs that are linked to specific trees within the forest and beyond. These beings are not only part of the tree; their connection is such that their life-force and that of the tree is inextricably entwined. From the dryads of Ancient Greece to the edible penghou of China, here are some of the most fascinating tree spirits from across the globe.

Penghou

The Chinese tree spirit known as penghou is a strange one by all accounts. Penghou sightings are said to be rare, but when they do come to light they are in the form of a black, tailless dog, with the face of a human. The penghou dwells happily within its tree, often a camphor tree, and is usually only discovered when someone cuts into the tree with a view to felling it. The two sources that mention the penghou, the 3rd century *Bái Zé Tú* ('Diagrams of the White Marsh') and 4th century *Soushenji* ('In Search of the Supernatural') both agree that the spirit is edible and, when cooked, tastes like dog meat. This fact might explain why it chooses to remain hidden within its tree!

Dryads and Hamadryads

Perhaps the best-known tree nymphs are the dryads of Greek mythology. Although *drys* refers to the oak in particular, dryads were linked to a variety of trees according to the Greeks. The Epimelides or Meliades, for example, were nymphs of fruit trees, such as apple, whereas the Meliae were associated with the ash tree, and Daphnaie with the laurel.

Hamadryads, in turn, are a particular type of dryad and, unlike the dryads, more intrinsically connected to, and a part of, the tree that is their home. The bond is so strong that if harm befalls the tree the hamadryad is also harmed, in extreme cases leading to their death. Sometimes, it is said that the hamadryad and the tree are one and the same being, with no differentiation between them.

Woe betide the foolish person who harmed a tree with a dryad or hamadryad residing within: both the gods and the nymphs themselves would seek to punish the perpetrator severely.

Eight particular hamadryads were named as the children of Hamadryas the nymph, fathered, according to legend, by Oxylos, her brother, a nature spirit. Their names were often, for obvious reasons, close to that of the tree itself, such as Morea of the mulberry tree or *Morus*, reinforcing the co-existing nature of the relationship between the hamadryads and the tree to which they were associated. Syke was the hamadryad of fig trees, Ampelos of vines, Ptelea of elm, Aigeiros of the poplar (especially black poplar), Morea for mulberry, Kraneia of dogwood, Balanos for oak and Karya for nut trees.

According to some sources, hamadryads lived the longest of all mortal beings; ten times longer than the legendary phoenix, that was itself said to live for at least five hundred years. Dryads and hamadryads have been popular in fiction, and are referenced by Keats, Milton, Edgar Allan Poe and Sylvia Plath.

Moss People

In the forests of Germany, you might come across those variously known as moss people, or moss, wood or forest folk. These dwarf or elf like beings are said to come under the classification of fairy folk and are often described as being of diminutive size and stature.

Jacob Grimm gives details of these wood-dwelling people in his *Deutsche Mythologie* or *Teutonic Mythology*, describing several different types of moss or wood people. Along with often being small, they are sometimes old, hairy and are clad in moss. These beings very often live together in groups, and the males are said to be grumpier than the females.

The females, known as wood-wives, are known to beg food from those cutting wood in the forest. This is not a one-way process, however, and the wood-wife gives something in return, whether that be advice, help with washing or in the kitchen, or a different food. Moss people are sometimes said to be linked to the particular tree they come from. This has perilous consequences: if the trunk of a tree is twisted until the bark comes off, a wood-wife dies.

Wood-wives are also to be found when baking is taking place, and they ask for an extra loaf to be baked for them. The person is asked to leave it at the instructed place, but if they do so they are not left empty-handed. Make sure that you take their return offering, as the wood-wives take great offence if their gift is rejected. Wood-wives also have a hearty dislike of caraway seeds – never offer one caraway bread, unless you want to be guilty of causing great offence!

In general, wood-wives are keen to reward those who help them. A woman who fed a wood-child who was crying at its mother's breast was given a piece of the bark cradle by the grateful mother. Glad to have helped, and thinking nothing of it, the woman took the splinter of bark with her, only to discover it had turned to gold when she arrived home.

The moss folk fear and are popular targets of the Wild Hunt, the supernatural force that chases above the forest in pursuit of its quarry. A tale tells of a peasant who was busy cutting trees when the hunt went past; although he called out to join in, he was left behind. The following morning, however, the gruesome offering of a quarter of a moss woman was found hanging in his stable – his share of the hunt that he had witnessed.

There is also talk of moss people taking human children, akin to changeling myths associated with fairies.

Kodama

The Japanese kodama is another nymph-like spirit. In ancient Japan, the word had several meanings: the etymology of the name comes originally from *ko* = old; *da* = many; *ma* = 10,000. This meaning has altered over time and nowadays, *ko* = tree, and *dama* = soul or spirit. Since the Edo period, kodama have been seen as *Yo ̄kai* – supernatural creatures in Japanese folklore – rather than gods.

The spirit was not always attached to the tree and could move throughout the forest at will. Some, however, were actually in the form of trees themselves, their lives attached to the tree that they were part of. They cursed those who cut into them, making them bleed. It was important to know whether a kodama lived in a tree or not, and this information was passed on to the following generation.

These nymphs are possessed of a supernatural power. They are the spirits, the essence, of the tree they inhabit. The term kodama is also used to refer to the tree itself, highlighting the connection between the tree and the spirit.

The appearance of a kodama can vary, being either a man or woman of ancient appearance; sometimes they are invisible altogether. When the tree dies, everything it knows is passed on to the kodama within it, which it will then take to its new tree. It is still considered the height of bad luck today to cut down a tree containing a kodama.

They have been featured in 'Kodama: The Tree Spirits' board game and have also been made well known by the Studio Ghibli production *Princess Mononoke*, where the spirits are depicted as pale, small, bobble-headed creatures.

Hulder and Skogsrå

The spirits of the Scandinavian forests are both seductive and dangerous. Such beings have the power to shapeshift into different forms, taking on the appearance of a specific person, or animal, or even a tree, and they can even be invisible then appear at will.

It was once argued that the Swedish *skogsrå* were spirits of trees themselves that are able to take human form – so-called 'tree-souls' – but experts no longer believe this was ever the case, nor were they spirits that lived within a specific tree. It is now believed that these seductive spirits of the woodlands were thought of more as rulers and guardians of the forest than wood sprites, and such creatures are believed to personify the forest itself, and its powers.

Like the Scottish *baobhan sith* – vampiric succubi who have deer hooves – the skogsrå can be part-hoofed and are often dressed in green, sometimes with the tail of a horse, cow or fox. They can also appear naked, or in the form of an old woman. In Norway, such female spirits are called *hulder,* or *huldra* when talking about just one. Hulder are sometimes described as 'troll maidens'. They often appear in the forests wearing national dress and look like perfect young maids – that is, until you notice their cow's tail peeking out from underneath their skirts! Some reportedly have furry legs and hooves to boot. Such sultry Scandinavian spirits appear as beautiful maidens from the front, yet some are said to have backs that look hollow or resemble rotten tree trunks. Some accounts tell how these luscious ladies have incredibly long, dangling breasts, and – like the Scottish *bean-nighe* – they are able to fling these over their shoulders.

Both skogsrå and hulder are famous for being a danger to those who wander in the forests – particularly men out hunting or burning charcoal – luring them away to get lost between the leaves, or even snatching away humans entirely to their dwelling places among the trees. Sometimes, the unfortunate individual is driven completely insane. Seduction is usually the motive in such instances, and the skogsrå employs a common technique – raising her skirt to flash her undercarriage at a prospective mate, before relentlessly pursuing him. It was believed that pliability towards such advances would be rewarded with plentiful hunting. Many wives might put this down simply to the idle minds of men out working alone in the woods, and their wishful thinking for the lust of a winsome maiden. Tales do tell of women and children also spirited away by the creatures while out picking berries and other gifts of the forest, yet there are fewer undercarriages in these recollections, you might be less than surprised to learn. Conversely, some tales reveal that the forest spirits can indeed be helpful, leading the lost home in the form of a lamb or bird.

Their mischief, as with other creatures of the forests, can be foiled by turning your clothes inside out, among other methods such as using Christian symbols against them, prayer, or even just saying the name of Jesus. Or, of course, with a complex ritual that includes washing yourself down with your own urine. Delightful.

Nang Tani

Last, but definitely not least, comes the *Nang Tani* of Thai folklore. This spirit – also known as *Phrai Tani* (Nymph of Tani) and *Phi Tani* (Ghost of Tani), is said to haunt wild banana trees. She takes the form of a beautiful young woman, with long, thick black hair, green-tinged skin and deep red lips. She wears traditional Thai costume, again in green.

Nang Tani prefers to remain in her trees, but if you want to catch a glimpse of this captivating spirit, the night of the full moon is the best time to see her. When she appears, you might get a shock however, as Nang Tani hovers, her feet a little distance above the ground.

Should you fear for your life around the Nang Tani? She is generally seen as a harmless, benevolent spirit, but some say that she can turn dangerous, especially towards men who have mistreated women.

Nang Tani is a very popular spirit, with many amulets produced featuring her form. She also appears in fiction and in comic books, in Thai films, including the 1967 classic Nang Phrai Tani, and even in the computer game *Ragnarok Online* as Lady Tanee.

FOREST HAGS FROM AROUND THE WORLD

Forest hags reside in woodlands the world over. These are old women, cast as witches and sorceresses – and their evilness is said to be reflected in their haggard appearance. In many societies, men are seen to gain wisdom as they age, and become more debonair and powerful. The inverse is true of women, however. While older women were once keepers of wisdom and seen as caring grandmothers who would pass on their knowledge to the women of the group and nurture the young, they are now castigated as useless: the power of their sexual allure gone, they are thought to have no use or function in our society. Thankfully, this perception is slowly changing, and women are reclaiming their power.

Much folklore still reflects this outdated idea, though; the forests of the world are populated with evil hags, intent not on looking after the young in their innocence, but instead abducting them, even cannibalizing them; for if a woman is old and ugly, surely all that is left for her is to become monstrous?

Cannibals, Demons and Witches: Top Five Forest Hags

1 Yama-uba, Japanese

This hag haunts the forests and mountains of Japan, often living in an old hut or cave. Some call her 'fairy of the mountains', and it's said she has looked after them since the world began, capping them with snow each winter, and flowers in spring. Tales tell that these women were once real humans who were soon transformed into fearsome monsters. Looking just like regular old ladies, they lure weary travellers with their offers of a bed and sustenance. Yet beware – once their guest falls soundly asleep, these monstrous hags take on their true form: witches with horns or fangs who try to eat their victims. Some stories describe them as having a sharp-toothed mouth hidden under their straggling white hair, the tangled tendrils of which can turn into snakes that reach out to catch little children to eat. Yet, *yama-uba* are less fearsome in some places, like in Shizuoka Prefecture, where they are said to go from house to house to borrow cauldrons to boil their rice, while dressed in tree bark. For some, yama-uba are thought to offer good fortune to humans, and sometimes even appear as beautiful young women instead of monstrous old hags.

2 Batibat, Iloko

The *batibat* is a demon from Philippine tradition that often takes the form of a fat old woman. Similar to the *nang ta-khian* of Thailand, it lives inside large trees and can reside in the wood even after the tree is cut down, and then live in whatever it is made into, including a house. These spirits often dwell in a hidden cavity and can creep out through any knot in the wood. Batibat don't usually come into contact with humans until this happens, and when it does, they have one rule: no one must sleep near their lair. If someone is unfortunate enough to fall asleep near their log, they will come out and take on their real, nightmarish form. One traditional tale tells of just that.

One day, a boy was sleeping in front of a post that housed a batibat. Deep in slumber, he was cursed with the nightmares that the batibat often bring. He dreamed that – like the nightmarish *mara* or *mare* of German and Slavic lore – the creature climbed on to his chest, sitting there until he could not breathe. Like in many such tales, he was unable to utter a word to shout for help. Yet, in this story, the boy was able to move, and managed to bite his thumb to wake himself up. This, or wiggling your toes, is the only way to escape inevitable death.

3 Likho, Russian

Another cannibalistic crone, Likho is a famous one-eyed hag from Slavic fairy tales who lures travellers to her home. (For others, Likho is a male forest goblin, renowned for his evil deeds – in this instance, a different creature entirely to the hag.) Likho's presence means misfortune is always near, and she/he is associated with both grief, and being cheated. One tale tells how two men, a tailor and a blacksmith, went out into the world to find Evil itself. They soon took shelter with the hag, who threatened to eat them up – it seems they had indeed found

Evil. First, she ate the tailor, picking his bones clean. The blacksmith, however, cheated the old woman out of her meal by promising to forge her a new eye. There was one condition to this agreement: that the crone allow herself to be bound so as not to distract him from the work with any sudden movements. To this, the witch agreed. As such tales often do, this one ends in the woman's undoing. After she was securely bound, the blacksmith took a red-hot poker and put out her one remaining eye. Likho fought and fought, and eventually broke her bonds. Yet, while we might expect a grizzly end to befall the man, his immediate fate was only to be kept in the hut overnight – along with Likho and her sheep. The next morning, blind as never before, she felt each animal as it left the hut for grazing. The blacksmith cleverly thought to turn his own sheepskin coat inside out – something that confounds otherworldly creatures in tales across the globe – and disguise himself as one of the sheep. Winning his freedom, the man laughed at the old woman before running away through the forests.

Yet the tale does not end there. Soon, he came upon a golden axe stuck, Excalibur-like, in a tree stump. Wanting the marvellous thing for his own, he of course tried to pry it from the wood, but to no avail. And more than that, his own hand became stuck to the axe. Soon he heard Likho coming, for the axe belonged to her. In panic, he took his knife and cut off his hand to escape her clutches. The moral to the tale is that Evil might be easy to find, yet very difficult to escape once you are within its grasp!

4 Muma Pădurii, Romanian

This shapeshifting mother of the woods is a hag who lives deep in the Romanian forest in a spooky house, all alone. She is protector of the trees and all creatures that dwell within her realm, offering herbal remedies and potions to any animal in need of her help. Yet beware: while benevolent to the plants and animals, she will wreak havoc and revenge on anyone who dares injure her woodlands. This ugly forest spirit is renowned for catching children to devour; but one Hansel-and-Gretel-like tale tells how she is outsmarted by two siblings and is pushed into her own oven after trying to boil the girl alive in soup. She has the ability to send anyone who trespasses into her forest completely mad. Some liken her to the Slavic Baba Yaga.

5 Baba Yaga, Slavic

Baba Yaga famously lives in a hut with chicken's legs in the heart of the forest, flying about in a mortar, hitting it with a pestle, and sweeping away any tracks she may leave with a broom. Her hut has a fence, made up of posts gruesomely topped by skulls that burn brightly with fire each night. Her stories are not for the faint-hearted. Like Muma Pădurii, she can be both benevolent and beastly, depending on who she is confronted with. She, too, is known for eating a child or two with her iron teeth – usually just the bad children, while the good ones get away safely.

For many, Baba Yaga, who is often disregarded as a nefarious old witch, has a truth at the heart of her story that teaches the real value of older women, particularly in the passing on of deep knowledge to the younger generation that follow her. Feminist scholar Dr Clarissa Pinkola Estés, in her ever-popular book *Women Who Run with the Wolves*, describes her as 'the old Wild Hag', and an old woman of death, who helps the younger generation find their way in the world, and move from a state of subservience to self-sufficiency.

One of the most famous tales featuring Baba Yaga is that of 'Vasilisa the Beautiful', a Russian folk tale retold by Alexander Afanasyev in his collection of almost 600 fairy tales in the 19th century.

VASILISA THE BEAUTIFUL

When Vasilisa was small, her mother called the child to her deathbed, as she lay there facing the journey into the next world.

'Here is a gift for you,' she said. She pulled a small wooden doll from under the covers and gave it to the child.

The mother leaned in and whispered: 'This doll is like no other in the world, so treat it as the precious thing it is, and keep it close to you always. Whenever you feel sad or threatened, go somewhere quiet where no one can see you, and give it something to eat and drink. Then, afterwards, you can tell all your troubles to the little thing and ask for it to guide you. The doll will give you advice whenever you need it.'

And with this blessing went the mother's last breath, and she fell into the endless sleep.

For many years, Vasilisa and her father lived in their grief. Yet the girl remembered her mother's dying words all through this time. Each night, when she felt overcome with sadness, this is exactly what she did, keeping her word of secrecy and feeding the tiny doll with wheat bread and kvass – a drink made from fermented black bread. And, each time, the small doll's eyes would light up like fireflies, and it would start to shine with life. The doll would tell the girl to sleep, and that by morning her grief would melt away when the light of the day came again.

Time rolled on, Vasilisa's father remarried and – as in many such stories – the orphaned girl gained a stepmother and two new sisters. In this Cinderella-like tale, the evil women mistreated the girl, commanding her to do all the harsh tasks around the house that they could think of to exhaust her and make her waste away to nothing but skin and bones from her toil. Yet of course – like all good heroines in fairy tales such as this one – Vasilisa never complained, and still secretly confided her problems to the doll each night when the house was silent, and all were asleep in their beds. Each night, as Vasilisa slept, the doll would set about all of the chores meant for the girl. As the sun crept through the windows, Vasilisa would rise and go to sit in the fields, gathering flowers in the sun, knowing her work was all complete.

One day, Vasilisa's father went away on a trip to a distant Tsardom, leaving the girl alone with her stepmother and stepsisters. One night soon after, the stepmother went up to bed, first extinguishing all the fires in the house, all but one candle by which the girls could finish their day's work. Yet this too soon went out, and the three girls were plunged into darkness. The first of the stepsisters said she did not need a light, as she could see the steel pins for her lacemaking just fine. The second agreed, saying that her silver needles for making the hose gave sufficient light. At once, the stepsisters decided that Vasilisa alone must go into the forest to retrieve a light, for she had neither steel pins nor silver needles to help her own task of spinning the flax. They demanded she go to the nearest place in the forest: the home of Baba Yaga, a cannibalistic witch.

And, being a brave yet obedient child, so she did. Yet of course, Vasilisa had her mother's doll tucked away to help her. She brought out the doll, fed it and quenched its thirst. The doll's eyes shone brightly and came alive, telling Vasilisa to be brave, and go and fetch the light from the witch, and not a hair on her head would be harmed. Terribly afraid, Vasilisa ventured into the darkness alone. On the way, a horseman dressed all in white galloped past her, and with this day began to break; then a second came, dressed all in red, and the sun rose into the sky.

Eventually, after searching the forest all night and through the following day, she came to Baba Yaga's dwelling place. There before her, stood a dingy hut balanced on hen's legs, surrounded by a fence of bones, with human skulls glaring with empty eyes from the top of each post. And there in the wall was a gate, with hinges of human foot bones, and locks of jaws and teeth. As the girl stood there in horror, a third horseman galloped past her, clad all in black, and night fell. Through the darkness, the eyes of each skull shone bright with gleaming fire. Vasilisa was terrified, as we all might well be.

And then, with a rustling from the forest, Baba Yaga herself tore through the trees, riding in a huge iron mortar, with the great pestle in her hand. She swept her tracks from behind her with her broom as she went.

First, she smelled the girl; then she spotted her, demanding to know who she was and what she wanted.

Vasilisa mustered her courage, and drew herself up, facing the old woman. 'It is I, Vasilisa. I have come here to fetch a light for our fire.'

'Well then,' said the old woman, her grin all teeth, sharp and crooked. 'Let us strike a bargain. I will give you a light for your fire, but in return you must work for me a little to pay for it. And if you don't, I shall eat you all up for dinner.' The old woman smiled a smile of ages.

So there Vasilisa stayed – behind the locked door of the house on hen's legs –preparing meals for the old witch, sweeping the floors, clearing the yard and sorting the wheat. Yet, when Baba Yaga fell soundly asleep, the girl did as she always had: bringing out the doll, feeding her a little of her meal, and then pouring out her troubles to the tiny thing, knowing all would be well by morning.

The next day, Baba Yaga went out of the house like a whirlwind, and disappeared into the rasping trees. Vasilisa found that, like always, the little doll had completed each of the tasks set for her, and all that was left was to cook the witch's dinner.

On her return, the witch was angry that every task she had set the girl was complete. She clapped and shouted, and three pairs of hands appeared to grind the wheat the doll had prepared. And with that, the witch sat down to her meal.

The next day passed, just like the first. Tasks were set, the witch slept, and the doll completed all before morning. The old woman returned, and summoned her miraculous helping hands with anger, then began to eat her meal – bones and all.

Yet, after this meal, the witch decreed that Vasilisa could ask her any questions she liked. And so she did. She asked who the three men were who had galloped past her. Baba Yaga replied that the one in white was her Day, the one in red her Sun, and the last, in black, her Night. Before she could ask about the strange hands, the doll shivered in her pocket, and the girl stayed quiet.

'Do you not want to know about the hands, too?' asked the witch, smiling slyly.

'No, thank you,' replied the girl. 'I know all I need to.'

'That's good,' said the witch, 'For if you had asked, I would have eaten you – it's not good to ask too much.'

Then the witch asked her a question in return: How could the girl complete so much work in such a short time?

Knowing all too well that the secret of her doll must be kept, Vasilisa replied only, 'Through my mother's blessing.'

This, of course, sent the old witch into a rage, and she took Vasilisa by the scruff of the neck and threw her outside with no apology. After her, she threw a flaming skull.

'There! There is your light! Take it, for I will have no blessings in my house!'

Vasilisa grabbed the skull and fled into the trees.

By the next evening, her own house stood before her, dark as night with no light coming from the windows, no fire gleaming in the hearth.

On opening the door, Vasilisa saw that no flame would catch since she had left, no matter how good the tinder. Each candle the family had brought from a neighbour had gone out as soon as it reached the house. The three women had not eaten a thing in the past days, and welcomed the girl like they had never done before!

Yet, as they drew Vasilisa and her skull inside, the flaming eyes raged, and followed their every move. It became hotter, then hotter still, and finally burned up the two wicked sisters and their mother into ashes.

Yet our story does not end there.

Vasilisa, gaining her freedom from her wretched stepfamily, buried the skull in the garden, locked up the house and went to stay with an old widow in a nearby village to wait for her father to come home.

She waited and waited, and still he did not return. Soon she became bored and begged some flax from the old woman for something to do. The girl spun and spun, and soon the flax was the finest thread she had ever seen. First, she tried to weave it on one frame, then another, then the next; but she soon learned that the thread was so fine that no frame could be found to weave it.

Vasilisa went to her little wooden doll, feeding it and giving it a little to drink, and asked if it could make her a frame good enough to weave the fine thread. She brought everything the doll needed to make it, and awoke the next morning to find the frame fully built beside her.

The girl wove and wove, all through the winter, and soon produced a fabric so thin it could pass through the eye of a needle, and whiter than any snow. She begged the old woman to sell it and keep the money for her room and board. The woman said she knew of only one person who would buy such an extraordinary fabric: the Tsar himself. The next day she set out to the palace to sell it to him.

The Tsar was amazed, and demanded to know the price, as he wanted to buy all of it. The old woman replied that it was not for sale, but was a gift for him, and him alone. He received it gladly and rewarded her with gift upon gift. Calling his seamstresses to him, he asked them to make him as many shirts as they could from the fabric. Surprisingly to him, yet maybe unsurprisingly to us, he soon found that none were able to work such a fine fabric, and he called the old woman to him once more, asking her if she was able to make the shirts herself. Being an honest woman, she said she could not, but knew a girl who could: her own adopted daughter, Vasilisa.

And so Vasilisa did. She washed her hands and face and prepared the twelve fine shirts for the Tsar.

As soon as the man set eyes on her, he of course fell deeply in love. Neatly packaged, as such tales often are, the Tsar married Vasilisa, the girl's father returned, and the old woman lived in riches at the palace with them. And the little wooden doll stayed safely in Vasilisa's pocket until her final days. The moral of the tale of Vasilisa has two parts: that first is that things always seem better in the morning, whether it is missing a loved one in a faraway land, or fear of a cannibalistic witch; the second is that if we face our fears, and enter the dark woodlands, we often retrieve wisdom and a light that shines through the darkness. This is a theme carried through many myths: like Odin's quest into the darkness to retrieve the wisdom of the runes, and many other heroes' journeys through the depths of the underworld to retrieve wisdom, loved ones, or even one's own life.

Some argue that this is a story about trusting our intuition, gaining independence, and coming to terms with our own wild natures – here, characterized by the old wise woman, the witch Baba Yaga, who is sometimes fierce and terrifying to behold, yet also someone who is at peace with death and the fire of life that burns within it. Clarissa Pinkola Estés argues that there are different stages of this initiation, and tasks that must be completed to progress through it. First, the acceptance of the death of the girl's mother in childhood, and learning to look after herself, symbolically allowing those things to die that need to die, and the ability to let go of things in life that no longer help us or serve a purpose. Next comes adolescence, where we confront our shadow selves – the in-between times, when the old self is dying, and the new one is yet to emerge. This is the time when we learn to be ourselves, in spite of what others expect of us, to stand strong in the face of failure. The next stage is where we are able to face up to the dark forest, confront the unknown, and trust in our own faculties to not just survive, but thrive. Here the little wooden doll Vasilisa carries in her pocket represents our own skills, and our intuition that guides us when we have the confidence to trust our own knowing. Like the doll, this inner sense of self, our inner courage and strength, also needs continual attention and nourishment if it is to flourish – and this is not something that should be trusted to others, just as the doll remains Vasilisa's secret and responsibility alone. Finally, we must confront the thing we most fear, and learn to live with it, to live wholly and fully in spite of it. The tale contains all of these elements and leads us through a journey with the wild hag, Baba Yaga.

Yet modern readers might be left with a question after the tale: whether they would prefer the prize of a rich man vain enough to marry a woman purely for her beauty and weaving skills, or the witch's prize of a flaming skull with the ability to burn her enemies into ashes. But then we must also ask another question: Would the flaming skull be a weapon to wield your own hard-won power, or would it be a destructive force that eventually burns you up also? Only you know which you would choose as your own, and what you would choose to do with it.

FEARLESSNESS IN THE FORESTS

While our forests are often filled with terrifying creatures lurking in their midst, they do, of course, also tell of those brave enough to venture between the branches without fear. In fact, the stories of those who walk fearlessly into the trees uncover a different side to our woodlands. In these tales, the trees offer shelter, sanctuary and – in turn – hope to those who ask for it.

The Women Who Turn into Trees

In the Galleria Borghese, Rome, we find the image of a woman fleeing her pursuer, her plight encased in cold white Carrara marble for eternity. This Baroque statue, carved by Bernini in the 17th century, shows Daphne, a nymph of Artemis, slowly transforming into a tree, fingers and hair sprouting leaves, as if her female form is her betrayer, and only by morphing into an arboreal likeness will she be safe from harassment. This is not the only place this story has been immortalized in art; Handel wrote an 18th century cantata dedicated to the pair, *Apollo e Dafne*. Here, as in our fairy tales, we find that trees and their woodlands become a sanctuary for women – and others – trying to escape maltreatment, abuse, and even murderous intent.

Greco-Roman mythology tells that Apollo, emboldened after killing the great dragon Python, meets Cupid, the winged god of love, and begins mocking him for his archery skills – the mythological equivalent of trash-talking your sports rival, with Apollo as the proverbial locker-room youth. This is the point where their good-natured jesting took a darker turn. Cupid drew two arrows from his quiver, one of gold, one of lead. Shooting Apollo with the gold arrow of love, he next shot the nymph Daphne with the lead arrow, intended to instil hate in the receiver. With this, Apollo set his sights intently on the nymph, and pursued her ardently. Daphne, both in her hate of Apollo from the lead arrow, and because she had pledged to remain a virgin all her life as a follower of Artemis, rejected the god, and fled through the trees. In this race of predator and prey they were well matched, and Daphne, a strong woman skilled in woodland sports, held her own. That is, until Cupid gave Apollo an unfair advantage, and helped him overtake the nymph. Seeing at once that she would never escape the god, she called to her father, the river god, for help, to destroy the beauty that had injured her, and the body that had destroyed her life. Her father gave her aid in a way we might consider slightly odd today. Daphne's running slowed, and her limbs became heavy. Soon bark began to grow at her chest, and her hair turned into twisting twigs and leaves; her arms became two great reaching branches, as her feet rooted into the ground beneath them. Daphne's lithe form was now a towering laurel tree.

Apollo, ever the persistent youth, disturbingly, still wouldn't take no for an answer. He embraced the tree, melding his form with hers. Still, the wood that had been her body shrank back from him. He then made a pledge to honour her for eternity and make the laurel his very own tree. The god endowed her with the gift of eternal youth, and this is the reason that a laurel tree's leaves are evergreen. And there the girl-tree stood for evermore, never to grow old and decay, yet never to wander her beloved woods again, nor frolic in the trees with her animals, playing her woodland games. Each translation of the ending is worded differently, with some saying the tree bent its head, as if offering its consent, while others saying that it only appeared so to Apollo. We will let you decide which ending you prefer.

Nymphs are not the only females that tales tell of turning into trees. Witches across folklore are said to go through similar transformations, the world over. One story from Syresham in Northamptonshire, England, tells that a man cut a stick for his child from a tree, some say an elder or oak, only to see the wound gush with blood. Soon after, they spotted a woman with a bandaged arm – it was deduced that the woman must in fact be a witch who had disguised herself as that tree. She was later swum to test her guilt, and found wanting. In Wales, it was a common

19th century belief that elder trees would bleed if they were cut, while some in Staffordshire say it will raise the Devil himself if elder is burned. The elder is also believed to house a tree spirit called the 'Old Lady' or 'Old Girl' in Britain, and known as the 'Hyldemoer' or 'Elder-mother' in Denmark. Permission must be sought to take a branch from the tree before it is cut, else the spirit will wreak her revenge. This idea may be why witches are rumoured to turn into trees.

The Handless Maiden

Astrange tale of the miraculous things that happen under the leaves of the forest is 'The Girl Without Hands'. The earliest version recorded was told by Marie Hassenpflug to the Brothers Grimm, published in their 1812 book, *Children's and Household Tales*.

One day, a poor miller went to the forest to chop wood. Soon, an old man appeared, who offered him riches beyond his wildest dreams – on one condition: that the miller would promise to hand over in three years' time whatever stood behind his mill when he got home.

The miller, knowing that all that stood behind the mill was an apple tree, agreed wholeheartedly.

Yet, on returning home, the miller was appalled to see that there, alongside the apple tree, stood his very own daughter. And with this, the miller knew that in just a few short years the girl would be handed over to the man – who the miller's wife astutely perceived to be the Devil himself.

The years passed. The girl became a young woman of clever and cunning. On the day the Devil was to come to her, she drew a chalk circle around her feet, and had washed until she was spotlessly clean. For, as everyone knows, this is the folk magic that keeps the Devil at bay.

On seeing this, the Devil demanded that the miller keep the girl away from any water, so that she could not purify herself, and he would take her the next day instead.

The next day, when the Devil arrived, there the girl sat sparkling clean once more. Turning her wit to the problem, she had cried into her hands, and washed herself in her own tears.

In a rage now, the Devil demanded the most infernal thing of the miller: 'Miller! You will chop off your daughter's hands, because I will come again tomorrow, and this time I will take her for my own. And if you refuse, I will take you instead!'

With that, he whirled away.

So by the time the Devil came for the third time, the miller had begged forgiveness of his daughter, but had done just that, and cut off her hands entirely. There the girl sat, waiting for him, with her handless stumps on her lap for the world and its Devil to see. Yet, once again, she had cried so much she had wept herself clean, and the Devil could not lay a finger on her, and went on his way.

Although the miller beseeched the child to stay with her family, and enjoy the riches her sacrifice had brought, the girl refused.

'I must leave this place,' the girl decreed. 'There are kind folks in the world that will help me survive.' And so she did.

As the morning sun rose, the girl made herself ready. With a rope of string, she bound her two severed hands together and slung them over her back. And there she took the first step of the journey into her future, and by evening-tide, her feet had carried her as far as the king's garden.

She clambered her way through a gap in the hedge and made her way inside. There she found a tree filled with apples, and shook it until the ground was covered in the fruit. She ate her fill, and did so for two full days. Yet the third time was her undoing. She was caught by a guard and thrown into jail for theft of the king's fruit.

At her sentencing, the king decreed she should be banished. Yet his son, the young prince, came up with a better idea: that the girl should instead look after the chickens at the palace. This was decided. And each day the prince would watch the girl, and soon began to fall in love with her. When it was time for him to marry, he asked that he should be allowed to marry the girl, saying he would agree to no other woman. With the finality of this oath, the king allowed the match. The weeks turned to months, and the months turned to years, and soon the old king died. The happy pair reigned over the kingdom together as the new king and queen.

Until, that is, a dark day dawned – as dark days often do. War swept the land, and the new king had to go to fight, leaving his pregnant wife alone at their castle. The days were kind to her: she gave birth to a healthy baby, and at once sent a letter to her husband with the news.

Yet her fateful past caught up with the miller's daughter. The Devil himself was still seething at the loss of the girl and switched the letter in the messenger's sack as he slept. This new letter announced the news to the unknowing husband that his wife had indeed given birth to a child; yet that this child was a changeling. The king, who loved his wife and any child they were lucky enough to have, wrote back that it mattered not a jot, and to keep their baby safe until his return.

But the Devil – trickster that he is – once more exchanged the letter, and in its place went the message that the queen and her child should be cast out of the kingdom the very same day.

And so they were, with weeping and sorrow, for the people loved them dearly.

But the girl, with resilience added to her cleverness over the years, stood strong in the face of fate. 'I never asked to be queen,' she said. 'I make my own luck, and I will find more of it out in the world than I have here.' And as she had done before, she tied all that she held dear to her back and carried her child out into the world to see what was there to be found.

As the sun set red in the sky, she came to a forest thick with branches. Under the trees ran a spring, and next to it sat a grizzled old man.

'Could you help hold my baby to my breast, so that I might nurse him – for I have no hands to do it myself.' And she held out her stumps in front of her, to show her predicament.

He was a kind old man, and did as she asked, afterwards telling her, 'Good luck will come to you if you wrap your arms around that special tree there.'

Trusting his word, the girl did just that. And in one fell swoop, as quickly as her hands had been cleft from her body, there they grew back with the help of the tree's magic.

Then, through the trees, the old man pointed to a house. 'You can live there and be safe. Yet remember: you must never go outside, and you must only ever open the door to someone if they ask three times, for God's sake.'

The girl agreed wholeheartedly, thanking the old man for his kindness.

The days began to pass, and the girl remained in her cottage, safe from the world and its wickedness. Yet, what she did not know was that her husband had returned to their kingdom and uncovered the foul deeds that had been committed against them. He set out right away to find his wife and their child, and soon came to the forest that she was living in.

As darkness fell over the trees, the king's servant spotted a light through the branches. Seeking somewhere to take shelter for the night, he begged the king that they set out to reach it. Wanting only to find his beloved, the king refused until the servant complained he could go on no longer. A kind man, the king relented and set out to find the cottage.

And so they did. And the king saw his own wife's face peering out from the window into the night. Yet, on noticing the woman's hands, the king knew it to be false hope; it could not be his wife. Sadly, he had the servant ask for shelter, but this the woman refused, and the servant turned back.

The king himself strode forward, begging, 'For God's sake, let us in from the darkness of the night, and offer us shelter, please.'

But the woman warned that she could not, until he had asked three times. And so he did.

On entering the cottage, he saw his wife's face clearly now, and recognized her at once. Taking her in his arms he marvelled at her hands, asking all that had befallen her. Then he looked at his little son, and knew he was no changeling child.

As the sun rose the next morning, the family set out on the journey back to their kingdom. And the little house that had sheltered the queen and her son? Of course, it disappeared from the forest, as if it had never existed at all.

Much of the nature of forests in our myths and fairy tales can be unearthed from the story of 'The Girl Without Hands'. Here, the Devil first lurks in the woodlands, a place of trickery and changing realities. Later, our heroine is cast out of the place where she at first finds safety; yet, she manages to find solace and healing in the forest, and become her whole self once more, despite the atrocity that was inflicted upon her. Here, she learns of her own power and ability to survive, her fortunes are restored, and all that was once her own comes back to her with the help of the healing power of trees.

Forests are filled with miraculous wonders in fairy tales. They are places of healing and safety, yet also of concealment, trickery and hidden things. In a later version of the tale, expanded to add details given by Dorothea Viehmann among others, it is an angel who helps the girl when she is in need, after each time falling to her knees to pray to God. In this version, the king has a pair of silver hands made for his bride. Here, the girl is left in the care of the king's mother. The switched-out letter that the king sends to the palace tells how she should kill the girl and child yet take her tongue and both her eyes as evidence that she has been murdered. Instead, the king's mother plucks the tongue from a doe, then one eye, then the next, and offers these as proof of the girl's death instead. This echoes the story of 'Snow White'. In this tale, the dark-haired, red-lipped heroine is taken into the forest to be murdered, yet the huntsman takes pity on her. The forest becomes a place of deception and shifting realities, for the killing never takes place; the huntsman takes an animal's heart to Snow White's queen as proof of the murder, instead of her own. Snow White herself flees into the forest, which becomes her protector, concealing her from those who wish her harm. Within lies the home of the seven dwarves, and – like the handless maiden's cottage – it is a retreat from all that threatens her; a place of safety. In a later version of 'The Girl Without Hands', it is the girl's own piety that allows her hands to grow back. The earlier telling, however, uncovers the true power of the forest: for here, it is a miraculous tree that allows the girl to recover what she has lost.

The forest offers healing, solace and protection from the evils of the world outside – from the human world itself. Though it is filled with wild things, it offers sanctuary within its wilderness for those who seek it, helping them to move through their journey from young victim, to a level of maturity where they understand that we all control our own fate. And when they leave this wilderness, they return to the world having gained great things: wisdom, friendship, and an affinity with the wild.

STARRY

SKIES

STARS AND SKIES
A Journey through the Skies

Who has not paused for at least one moment in their lives to gaze upwards in awe at the great vastness of the skies above? Whether it is to marvel at a rainbow, seek out the familiar pattern of a well-known constellation or to check whether rain is on the way. For that brief pause in our busy lives, we are at one with the cosmos, linked to every other being that has done the same since time began. During the day, the sun shines its life-giving light down upon us, while at night we are treated to the shimmering spectacle of the stars and the light of the moon. As we look upwards in awe and perhaps a little fear, we find ourselves unwittingly linked with every other person who is doing or has ever done likewise – whether in our own times or many thousands of years ago.

The resplendent canopy of the skies and heavens has been of monumental importance to humankind since time immemorial. First, the stars: guiding people as they travel on their way, pinpointing their location in the vastness of the sea or desert in the earliest of navigational systems. Then there is the weather: the power of the elements determining whether we have access to food and water supplies and, in the extreme of storms and blizzards, threatening our very existence. Our gods and goddesses have likewise resided in the skies in their heavenly splendour: the complex beauty of the cosmos cannot, we think, have been by accident. The constellations must have been placed and designed; there can be no other explanation in our minds, for how could something so intricate have happened by coincidence?

Tales and stories, legends and myths, sayings and superstitions have poured forth from hundreds of different cultures, belief systems and ideas, blending into a melting pot of folklore not unlike the swirling symphony of the universe itself. It is through these tales and ideas that we try to answer the all-consuming questions such as: where does the sun come from? How did the Milky Way come to be? Who are we, and what is our place is this vast, great universe? Too great to comprehend, we could spend a lifetime trying to make sense of it all and still only grasp a fragment of what is out there: through these stories and ideas we have woven ourselves a rich legacy that perfectly bears testament to the splendour of the skies.

Leave the safety of solid ground behind, and take a journey upwards to soar through the wonders that are above us. From frightening creatures and battling gods to shooting stars, constellations and brilliantly dancing lights, prepare to enter the great unknown. And as we explore this celestial realm, listen for the whispers of our ancestors, the sayings and superstitions we still follow today, the origin stories; perhaps long-forgotten, but remembered each time we follow and share them, part of us and our shared cultural heritage forever.

It would be impossible to cover every piece of folklore related to the stars and skies in one volume, and to attempt to do so would be to do a great injustice to both source material and readers alike. Regrettably, therefore, many fascinating pieces of information and stories have not made it to these pages; what you will find, however, is a carefully selected, painstakingly researched and lovingly presented selection of tales and beliefs that illuminate once again how folklore is truly the tie that binds us together across time and space.

STARS
AND
HEAVENS

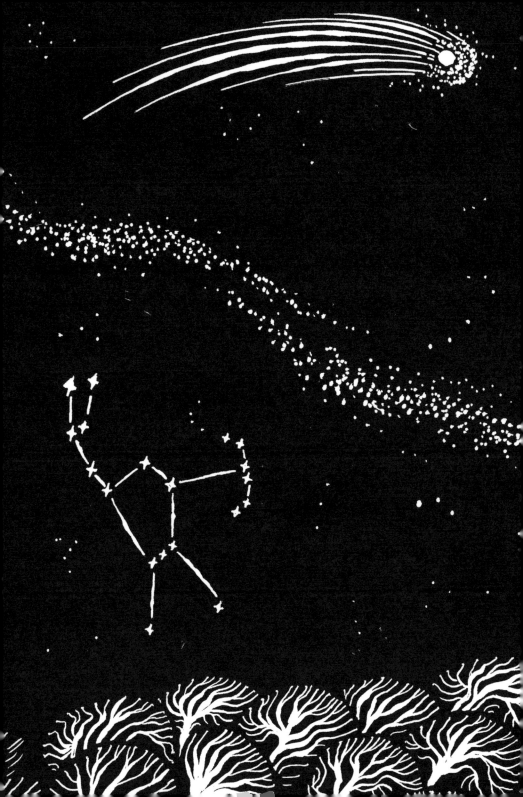

SOLAR DEITIES:
Gods and Goddesses of the Sun

The largest object in our solar system, the sun is the source of all life on earth, looked upon with awe and fear by humankind throughout the ages. Common across many of the world's cultures is the belief in a sun god or goddess, in some cases a personification of the fiery giant around which we orbit. From Japan's Amaterasu to the Lithuanian Saule, here are a few of the most fascinating solar deities from communities around the world.

Amaterasu

Great Divinity Illuminating Heaven, Amaterasu or, to give the goddess her full name, Amaterasu-Omikami, is one of the most important deities in the Japanese Shinto pantheon. Goddess of the rising sun, she is inextricably linked with the Shinto state and imperial family.

Amaterasu was born of Izanagi, the Japanese creator kami or god. When his wife, Izanami, died giving birth to the fire god Kagutsuchi, the grieving Izanagi journeyed to the underworld, Yomotsukuni, to try to bring her back; he was ultimately unsuccessful, however, and returned alone to the upper world. As Izanagi cleansed himself from the taint of death he washed his left eye, and thus Amaterasu was born. Amaterasu's two siblings came forth in a similar fashion: Tsukiyomi when Izanagi washed his right eye, and Susanoo when he washed his nose. Susanoo, the storm god, was given control of the sea, and Tsukiyomi was the god of the moon.

Susanoo, mischievous and provocative by nature, proved to be a perpetual thorn in his sister Amaterasu's side. On one occasion, Susanoo visited Amaterasu in heaven. Amaterasu was understandably wary, thinking her brother came to challenge her position, and met him with a display of military might. Susanoo, however, insisted he came in peace, suggesting instead that they procreate together in order to cement good feeling on each side. Agreeing to the plan, Amaterasu broke Susanoo's sword into three pieces and swallowed them, before breathing out a mist from which three females were born. Susanoo, for his part, chewed the jewels that belonged to his sister, and breathed out five male children, which Amaterasu claimed as her own.

Although this was meant to increase goodwill towards each other, Susanoo soon revealed his true colours. He carried out a series of increasingly intolerable acts against his sister: breaking down the divisions in Amaterasu's rice fields, defecating on her chair, and finally, the last straw, removing the roof of her weaving room and tossing a flayed horse inside, which led to the death of one of her attendants. This was too much for the goddess. Angry Amaterasu shut herself in a cave and refused to come out, plunging the world into terrible darkness. There she stayed, steadfastly ignoring the entreaties of the other gods. Everyone despaired, and began to think of ways to entice the goddess out into the world again.

The first attempt was to place several cocks outside the cave in the hope that when they crowed the goddess would think it was dawn and time for her to rise. When this failed, the gods tried again; this time they placed a large sakaki tree hung with bright jewels, white clothes and a mirror close to the entrance of the cave, hoping to lure her out with the magnificence of her own reflection. The goddess Ame-no-Uzume, in a trance, danced riotously and started to disrobe, making the other gods laugh and creating a great ruckus. The noise at last piqued Amaterasu's interest and she opened the cave: as the other gods had hoped, she caught sight of herself in the mirror and was transfixed. Another god seized his chance and pulled Amaterasu out into the open, returning light to the world once more. To prevent her from returning to the cave, the gods threw down a sacred rope made of rice straw – *shimenawa* – in front of the entrance.

Amaterasu is also closely linked with the introduction of rice to Japan. It is said that she sent Tsukiyomi, originally meant to rule the heavens with her, down to earth to watch Ukemochi, a food goddess, to see what she was doing. Unfortunately, when the goddess offered him rice, fish and game that she had vomited from her own mouth, Tsukiyomi grew offended and slew Ukemochi. Furious, Amaterasu refused to see her brother again, and the sun and the moon were never seen at the same time from that day. There was some benefit to come from Ukemochi's death, however: when the body of the slain goddess was inspected, it was discovered that various things had sprung forth from it, including silkworms from her eyebrows, the horse and cow from her head, rice from her stomach, and beans and wheat from her genitals. These were brought back to heaven to Amaterasu, who took the rice and created the first holy rice fields in Heaven.

The emperors of Japan to this day claim descent from Amaterasu. The first Emperor of Japan, Jimmu, was said to have descended from Ninigi, Amaterasu's grandson. This celestial connection is reflected in the name of the emperors, Amatsuhitsugi, meaning 'heavenly sun heir'. The Imperial regalia – the Yata no Kagami, the mirror that was used to lure Amaterasu from the cave; the Yasakani no Magatama, her jewels; and Kusanagi no Tsurugi, Susanoo's sword – were also said to have been gifted from Amaterasu to Ninigi, and then passed to the first emperor. The nobility also claim descent from the goddess, via the deities that she and her brother Susanoo produced together.

As further evidence of her status, Amaterasu is worshipped at the most important Shinto shrine in Japan, the Ise Grand Shrine. Millions of visitors and pilgrims visit the shrine each year.

Saule

According to Latvian and Lithuanian tradition, Saule was the sun goddess and also the goddess of life and fertility. She married Menes, god of the moon, but unfortunately he didn't remain faithful to her for long and, according to Lithuanian tradition, had an affair with Aušrinė, the goddess of the dawn. According to one version of the story, Perkūnas, the thunder god, avenged the slighted goddess, tearing the unfaithful moon god to pieces in punishment.

In Lithuania, Saule is mentioned in *The Chronicle* by John Malalas, one of the earliest written sources for Lithuanian mythology. Saule also appears frequently in the *dainas*, Latvian folk songs numbering around 300,000 in total, and which provide much of what is known about folk beliefs in Latvia: at least 1,500 mention her directly. An even greater number of the *dainas* refer to the sun itself, both highlighting the importance of the celestial body and the goddess associated with it, in a mythological and cultural context. It is from these songs that the majority of the information about Saule comes, although there is some debate regarding the balance between what is true inherited folk belief and later invention.

Saule is frequently associated with the colour red: overnight, she is said to don a garment of this colour, and thus rises red in the morning. She was also said to be wreathed in a garland of red flowers during the feast of Ligo, the major festival celebrating the summer solstice and honouring the goddess on 23 June. In many depictions, Saule wears national dress, in silver or gold silk, with a crown on her head, which she hangs on a tree in the evening. Saule is generally portrayed as a benevolent mother goddess, known for showing compassion and pity towards humankind.

In her solar role, Saule makes her daily journey through the forests on a chariot, drawn by inexhaustible horses of varying number: two or three yellow horses, two, five or six brown horses, two grey or even a single small horse are mentioned, depending on the source. As evening comes, and the day draws to a close, Saule pauses to let her horses wash in the sea, and she sits atop a hill with their golden reins held in her hands as they do so. As night falls, she changes her mode of transportation and travels across waters such as lakes, rivers and the sea, riding a golden boat.

Saule was known to cry frequently, these episodes attributed to a number of reasons, such as the departure of her daughter for her marriage, leaves blowing from a birch tree, a golden apple falling to the ground or her boat sinking in the sea. The Žaltys snake was known to be associated with Saule; it was bad luck to kill one, and good luck to have one in your house.

According to one legend, the smith named Teliavelis created the sun in his forge, before throwing it up into the sky.

Utu-Shamash

This Sumerian solar deity was known by the Mesopotamians as Utu, and later by the Akkadian name Shamash or Šamaš, and was one of the most important gods in the Mesopotamian pantheon. Mention of Utu can be found as early as around 3,500 BCE in the first Sumerian writings in existence, and he is referenced in a variety of sources, from royal hymns to documentation of business transactions. So important was he that in the law codes of the Babylonian ruler Hammurabi it is stated that the god was responsible for giving the laws to humankind.

In Sumerian tradition, Utu was the son of the moon god, Nanna, while Akkadian belief names his father as Anu or Enlil.

Utu had a twin sister, Inanna, the goddess of war and love. Some sources also attribute further siblings to the god: a brother, Ishkur the god of storms; and Ereshkigal, the Queen of the Dead, is also sometimes said to be a sibling of Utu. His wife is Serida, or Aya in Akkadian, the dawn goddess. Several children were attributed to the god, including Kittum, the personification of truth, and Sisig, the god of dreams.

Utu is most commonly depicted as an old, bearded, long-armed man, with rays of light shining from his shoulders. He was also sometimes shown as a disc with wings, or the sun itself. The solar disc is portrayed as a circle, with four points in each of the four directions and four waved lines protruding diagonally between each of these points, representing the might and power of the sun. On some cylinder seals, Utu is seen holding a large pruning saw, an arc-shaped blade with large, jagged teeth; another of his emblems.

In earlier references, the god was said to make his journey across the heavens on foot. As time went on, however, this changed to the belief that he rode through the skies in a chariot of fire each day. As each morning came around anew, the huge gates of heaven, resting on a mountain, opened in the east, flung wide by two gods. Shamash took his place in his chariot and rode it across the sky as the day progressed, moving steadily towards the west, marking the path of the sun. Arriving there at the end of the day, the gates in the west were duly opened for him, and he went inside to rest.

Utu's chariot was pulled by four fiery beasts – generally held to be horses or mules, though one argument has been made for them being lions. These beasts were named Uhegalanna, 'the abundant light of heaven'; Uhushgalanna, 'the terrifying great light of heaven'; Usurmurgalanna, 'the dreadful great light of heaven'; and Unirgalanna, 'the noble light of heaven'. The god driving his chariot was named Bunene, and in some accounts he is also Utu's son.

Utu-Shamash was known as the god of justice, and in that role was said to be a just and wise judge. It was a natural role for him to take; just like the strong heat of the sun penetrating everywhere and everything, so the sun god knew and saw everything that went on upon the earth, thus putting him in the unique position to judge humankind and gods alike.

Utu also featured strongly in many sacrificial divination rituals, and the god was frequently asked to help provide an answer to a variety of questions. Around 350 queries survive from the Neo-Assyrian period (9th–7th century) when kings Esarhaddon and Ashurbanipal consulted him frequently, with concerns about illnesses, rebellions and the loyalty of those beneath them. Utu's aid was also called for to help protect against curses and evil wishes.

In one Sumerian poem, Utu is portrayed in a light somewhat different from usual; he attempts – and ultimately fails – to seduce his twin sister Inanna by getting her drunk.

Huītzilōpōchtli

Huītzilōpōchtli was the sun god of the Mexica people, better known by their later name of the Aztecs. He was also the god of war and human sacrifice, and, through his choice of weapon, Xiuhcoatl, the fire serpent, was associated with fire. Huītzilōpōchtli was very much an Aztec-specific god; mention of him is not found outside of the valley of Mexico, and depictions of the god are noticeably absent from the art and artefacts of the rest of ancient Mesoamerica.

There is some debate regarding the exact meaning of his name, but it is generally translated as 'left-handed hummingbird' or sometimes 'Hummingbird of the south', from *huitzilin* – 'hummingbird', and *opochtli*, 'left-hand side'. Some suggest that a more accurate translation is 'the left or south side of the hummingbird'. The god was also known as Xiuhpilli – 'Turquoise Prince'.

In appearance, Huītzilōpōchtli was generally depicted with a hummingbird headdress of blue-green, a golden tiara and white heron feathers. He had blue and white striped paint on his face and a black mask around his eyes, dotted with stars. He was also often depicted holding his fire serpent.

Perhaps the best-known tale about Huītzilōpōchtli is the story of his birth. There are various differences across versions, but essentially the details are thus. One day his mother, Cōātlīcue – meaning 'she of the serpent skirt', due to the skirt she wore made of woven snakes – was sweeping at Coatepec, Snake Mountain. To her surprise, a ball of hummingbird feathers descended towards her. Cōātlīcue caught them in her hand and, entranced by their beauty, placed them in her waistband for safekeeping. When she went to remove them later, however, the feathers had vanished. She had been impregnated by the feathers, and was now with child. When her existing children – the Centzon Huitznahua, the 400 stars of the south, and daughter Coyolxāuhqui – discovered their mother's condition, they were outraged, angered greatly that she had dishonoured herself and them, especially when she refused to name the father of her child. Their mother had brought such shame upon them, said Coyolxāuhqui, that the only thing they could do to rectify the situation was to kill her. Learning of their plan, Cōātlīcue was understandably terrified, but help was at hand. Her unborn child, Huītzilōpōchtli, communicated with her from the womb, assuring her that he was ready to fight to protect her and himself against his treacherous half-siblings.

Thus Cōātlīcue waited atop the mountain for her children to attack. She did not have to wait long, and they came charging up towards her. At the very moment they reached the top, Cōātlīcue gave birth to Huītzilōpōchtli – in some versions her head was struck from her body and the god sprang forth. The god, however, was no mere babe; he came forth fully formed and armed ready to fight for his mother, just as he had promised. Wielding his great weapon, the fire serpent, Huītzilōpōchtli killed his sister and cut off her head, her slain body falling down the mountain to the bottom. He then chased off his brothers, killing huge numbers of them as they tried to escape.

According to Aztec tradition, Huītzilōpōchtli was also responsible for what would become known as the Aztec people establishing their home. He instructed the people of Aztlan to set off on a pilgrimage that would turn out to last for generations, taking them through many hardships, battles and divisions along the way. Their end point was clear, however: they were to establish a new capital in a very specific place. They would know it by seeing an eagle sitting on a cactus eating a snake. Their wanderings finally came to an end in 1345, when Tenochtitlan – 'the place where the gods were created' – was founded.

Controversially, the Aztecs believed that regular human sacrifices had to be made to Huītzilōpōchtli in order to keep the eternal night at bay. According to Aztec belief this was necessary as the god was constantly chasing the stars and moon; if he did not have the strength to fight his siblings, they would be triumphant, and the world would be destroyed.

In 1978, the ruins of the Aztec capital, Tenochtitlan, were discovered beneath Mexico City. The Great Temple, Templo Mayor, was the greatest find, dedicated to Huītzilōpōchtli and Tlaloc, the rain god. Among the finds there was a huge, sculpted stone disc 3.25m (over 10ft) across, showing the events of the sun god's birth and the battle that followed, including a depiction of the dismembered body of his sister at bottom of the staircase that leads up to the Huītzilōpōchtli shrine.

Sól

Sól was the Germanic goddess of the sun, featuring heavily in Norse mythology relating to Ragnarok, the end of the world. Sól was fated to be chased through the sky by the wolf Sköll and, according to myth, a solar eclipse is caused when the wolf draws close enough to snap at her. Sól's brother Máni, the moon, is likewise chased by Hati, the wolves snapping at their horse-drawn chariots until they are finally caught, ushering in the end of the world. All is not lost, however, as it is foretold that before the end comes, Sól will give birth to a daughter – even more brilliant in beauty and brightness than herself – who will shine on in her mother's stead in the new world.

Sól and Máni were originally children of Mundilfari, named after the sun and moon due to their exquisite beauty. But alas, the gods were deeply offended by such a display of arrogance and intervened, decreeing that Sól and her brother should be placed in the heavens themselves. They were charged with driving the two horses that drew the sun's chariot – Arvakr and Alsvior, crossing the heavens each day to mark the passing of the days and years for humankind.

Sól was referred to by several names, including day-star disc, fair-wheel, elf-disc and everglow, and is referenced in both the *Prose Edda* and *Poetic Edda*. Although Sól is referred to as a goddess in several instances, and the sun was generally venerated, it is not believed that there was a Germanic sun cult as witnessed in other areas.

A FATEFUL FLIGHT:
Daedalus and Icarus

According to Greek mythology, Daedalus – his name aptly meaning 'skilfully wrought' – was an architect, sculptor and inventor. Banished from Athens for the murder of his nephew and apprentice, Daedalus found himself in Crete with his son, Icarus. There he was caught up in the great drama attached to King Minos and his family. For Minos had angered the sea god, Poseidon: the god had given the king a white bull to sacrifice, but Minos had kept it for himself. As punishment, the angered god got his own back by making the king's wife attracted to the bull; calling on Daedalus's skill, the queen entreated him to make a wooden cow in which she could conceal herself and thus mate with the white bull. Her plan was successful, and the queen found herself pregnant: in time, she bore the monstrous Minotaur, half-human, but with the terrible head of a bull. Daedalus's talents were again called upon, this time by the king, who ordered the building of the legendary Labyrinth in which to keep the monster far away from sight.

All was well until the hero Theseus arrived – he was intended as a sacrifice to the terrible beast, but things did not go according to plan, as Minos's daughter, Ariadne, fell in love with him. She in turn called upon Daedalus, begging him to reveal the secrets of the Labyrinth so that Theseus could escape with his life. Daedalus helped her and the plan was successful: Theseus escaped, taking Ariadne with him. King Minos was so angered by this that he shut Daedalus and Icarus up in the Labyrinth. The queen released them, but they were stranded, unable to leave Crete by sea or by land as both were under the control of Minos.

Greatly troubled by their exiled condition, Daedalus hit upon a plan. For there was one sphere that the wily Minos did not command: the air. And so Daedalus set to work. He gathered feathers and arranged them in rows: small and short first, increasing gradually in length and size in the manner of a set of reed pipes or, indeed, wings. Thread and wax were used to hold these wondrous creations together: the whole curved into shape in imitation of the wings of the birds whose freedom he envied so greatly.

As Daedalus worked, his son Icarus watched on with fascination, often toying with his father's materials and hindering his progress. At last, though, the wings were complete, and the time of their escape into the sky and freedom drew near. The fearful father gave his son many instructions, the most important being to maintain a course not too high and not too low, for fear that the waves or the sun would bring him to an untimely end. He, Daedalus, would lead the way; all Icarus need do was follow his father and they would be safe and free. Unable to prepare his son any further, there was no more time for delay. Daedalus attached the wings to his son and then himself, before launching himself into the sky.

Those who they passed looked up in wonder, marvelling at what they saw and thinking the pair to be gods as they flew past. Father and son made good progress, and it seemed as if they would make their escape as planned. However, it was not to be. For Icarus, with all the fearlessness and arrogance of youth, found the power of flight too exhilarating: forgetting to be careful, he flew from his father's steady path, straying higher and higher. Alas, he could not continue so: the wax, so carefully applied, melted in the heat of the sun, and the feathers lost their formation, falling away. With nothing now to keep him airborne, the ill-fated young man fell, crying out for his father, into the unforgiving waters below.

Unaware of his son's terrible fate, Daedalus called and called for him, until he spotted the heartbreaking sight of the feathers in the water. How Daedalus wept for his son! Blaming himself most harshly, he retrieved and buried Icarus's body in a place nearby, and the land was afterwards known as Icaria, in remembrance of the one who rested there and all that had been lost.

SUN-GOT-BIT-BY-BEAR:
Eclipses of the Sun

The sun, ever present, has been one of the daily constants for humankind for the entirety of our history. Only, sometimes, this brightly burning star does the unthinkable: it seems to wane, diminishing before our very eyes and even vanishing altogether, plunging the world into darkness with no promise that it will return again. For thousands of years people all over the world have held their breath upon a solar eclipse, creating countless tales and explanations for this fearful phenomenon. Even today, when science provides an answer for the causes of a solar eclipse – when the moon is directly between the earth and the sun and the moon casts a shadow over the earth – we still pause, waiting for the moment that the sun shines bright upon us once more.

In written sources, some of the oldest mentions of a solar eclipse come from Ancient China over 4,000 years ago, where it was believed that an eclipse was caused by a dragon eating the sun: one such early description states that 'the sun has been eaten'. In a common approach to eclipses, people would bang drums loudly and make lots of noise in an attempt to scare the dragon away and bring back the sun.

The idea of the sun being eaten is a very common theme in eclipse folklore across the globe. In Armenia it was also believed that an eclipse was caused by a dragon chasing and eating the sun. A Berber story from northern Africa tells of a huge, winged, evil jinni that lurks in an underground lair. From there it soars skywards, swallowing the sun whole. In a definite case of being careful what you eat, it cannot stomach this hot meal and vomits forth its prize, leaving the sun free to shine again.

In a Chahta tale from North America, a black squirrel is said to be to blame, causing an eclipse of the sun as it nibbles and gnaws at it. The word used for eclipse by the Pomo, the Indigenous people of Northern California, translates as 'Sun-got-bit-by-bear'. In this tale, a bear and the sun have a falling out; the bear bumps into the sun, and when the sun tells the bear to stand aside, the bear refuses, telling the sun in turn that it should be the one to move. As stubborn as each other, neither will shift, and the two fall to fighting. In the ensuing ruckus the bear grabs the sun and, chewing on it, causes an eclipse.

According to Hindu mythology, eclipses are caused by the demon Rahu. Rahu stole an immortality elixir, *amrita*, so he could live forever. He was caught in the act of drinking it, and had only partially swallowed it before Vishnu beheaded him with his flying disc. Rahu's body perished, but his severed head was immortal, never to die or find rest. To this day he floats around the cosmos, causing an eclipse when he consumes the sun. Pots and pans are banged to make him cough up the sun and go away again.

In a Buryat version from Siberia, Rahu, known as Alkha, spent his time chasing after the sun and moon, periodically swallowing them and causing an eclipse. Irritated by this behaviour, the gods finally chopped him in two. Although his lower body dropped down to earth, his head lives on, still munching on the sun and moon, causing their eclipses, although they don't last for long as Alkha has no body to hold them in. Similarly in Polynesia and Indonesia, Kala Rau eats the sun: thankfully he burns his tongue and spits it back out again, the world saved from darkness until next time.

In Korean mythology, both solar and lunar eclipses are caused by *bulgae* or fierce fire dogs. A pack of these creatures was ordered by the king of the heavenly kingdom of Gamangnara – Dark World – to steal the sun so that it could not affect the darkness surrounding his own kingdom. They were not successful in capturing it, but the king did not give up and sent a new dog each time: when the dogs managed to bite the sun, an eclipse was the result.

In South America, the Chiqutoan Manasi people of eastern Bolivia believed celestial serpents attacking the sun caused an eclipse. If they were successful, ultimate darkness would follow: then humankind would be turned into hair-covered animals and eventually be wiped out.

Solar eclipses weren't always caused by the sun being eaten or bitten. According to some Indigenous groups of the Pampas in central Argentina, an eclipse of the sun was caused by a great bird spreading its massive wings over it. For the Fon people of Benin, western Africa, the male sun and female moon love each other deeply, but due to their busy lives, they very rarely get to meet. When they do, they make the most of their time together, but turn off the light so they can be together in privacy. Some believe that an eclipse occurs when the sun itself cannot bear to witness the terrible tragedies of history, and temporarily turns its face away: it is said that the sun was eclipsed during the Crucifixion and when Adam and Eve were expelled from the Garden of Eden. A belief from Armenia held that a sorcerer could enchant the sun – and moon – to stop their light, halting them in their tracks or even bringing them down from the sky altogether.

Understandably, eclipses were generally looked upon as a bad omen, often seen as a sign of great disaster to come. In Ancient Mesopotamia, there was a practice of having substitute kings prepared for when an eclipse was forecast to take place. The 'king' would be dressed in the real king's clothing and treated like the king, even being paired with a young woman as his 'queen'. The real king would retreat into hiding until the eclipse had passed: in a gruesome twist, the stand-in couple were killed before the real king returned to take over his duties once more. On 1 August 1133, Henry I left England on a ship bound for Normandy. As he travelled, a solar eclipse took place on 2 August, and this was seen as a bad omen, predicting that Henry would never return to England alive. He died in France in 1135, heralding a period of chaos and unrest for England.

Due to a variety of negative connotations, many people therefore chose to hide away when an eclipse was taking place. One Hindu belief was that water was the safest place to be during an eclipse, and the very safest water of all was the Ganges River due to its sacred state. In south-western Alaska, there was a belief that during an eclipse, an unclean essence fell to earth. This was said to cause great harm if it landed on utensils or plates and dishes that people might use and eat from, and sickness would result. Therefore at the start of an eclipse, to avoid disaster, dishes, pots and other receptacles were turned upside down so they could not be infected.

HINA:
The Woman in the Moon

According to Polynesian belief, the goddess Hina lives in the moon. In some versions of her tale, Hina and the maidens who worked with her made the finest kappa cloth known to humankind. Day in, day out, the busy Hina was never still; as well as the cloth, she braided mats from the leaves from the hala tree, giving them to members of the household to sleep on, and she also used nuts from the kukui trees to make torches, which in turn were used to illuminate the homes of the highest-ranking of families.

Hina worked so long and so hard, that finally she had enough of labouring among the mortals of the earth. Her own family brought her little comfort: her husband was lazy and did nothing for himself, her sons were troublesome and disorderly, and she found she had little to stay for. So Hina decided to escape. Looking upwards, she spied the tempting path of the rainbow and hatched a plan. She would use it to take her to the sun, where she could rest and escape from her troubles.

Early the next morning, Hina began to climb the rainbow, armed with her calabash packed with her most treasured belongings. But the higher she went, the hotter she became, the strong, powerful rays of the sun beating down upon her so relentlessly that after a time she found she could barely crawl her way along. Still Hina did not give up, but every fraction higher she went it got hotter and hotter. It was no use; she was nearly on fire, and in so much pain that she finally abandoned her attempt, sliding back down the rainbow to the earth once more.

Away from the scorching heat, Hina recovered her strength. When the moon rose and night fell, she decided to try again. This time, though, she would climb up to the moon instead to find the rest she craved. Alas for Hina, she was spotted as she started her new journey, and her husband called to her, telling her not to leave the earth.

Hina would not be dissuaded, telling him that she would go to the moon, who would be her new husband. So saying, she carried on, climbing higher with each moment. Not to be outsmarted, her husband followed, running towards her. She was almost too high, but he jumped and managed to catch her foot. The desperate Hina shook him off, but not without paying a painful price. As her husband fell downwards he broke her leg, the bottom part of it coming away in his hands.

Crying out the strongest incantations she could muster, Hina passed through the stars. The powers of the night hastened to her aid as she was lifted through the darkness until she at last found herself at the door of the moon.

Throughout everything, Hina had kept tight hold of her calabash, and with it she finally limped into the moon. There Hina found her forever home ... and peace at last. When the moon is full, it is said that if you look up you can see Hina there, calabash still by her side. The board where she beat her cloth can also be seen down on earth, turned into a stone at the foot of the fish head-shaped headland known as Kauiki.

MAN, RABBIT, OR JACK AND JILL?
The Many Faces of the Moon

A peculiar trait of humankind is the habit of seeing identifiable images in otherwise random patterns or shapes. This pareidolia as it is known is very common in relation to the moon, and for thousands of years people have been envisaging all manner of figures and characters when they gaze upwards at the earth's only natural satellite. What exactly is seen on the face of the moon – in reality the dark seas and lighter highlands of the lunar landscape – varies from culture to culture, and ideas range from a man, to a hare, to King Mohammed V of Morocco. A splendid array of tales and explanations have sprung forth in support of these ideas: just who do *you* think lives on the moon?

The Man in the Moon

One of the most common interpretations of the face of the moon in Europe is that it looks like a man. Old and wizened, the Man in the Moon is generally seen as bent over, often carrying a load of sticks upon his back. The idea of there being a Man in the Moon is an ancient one, dating back thousands of years, with many differing suggestions regarding the man's identity and just how he came to be on the moon in the first place.

A popular theme is that the man serves as a warning to others, a cautionary tale not to follow his bad example. In a tale from Germany, the man was cutting sticks for fuel in the forest one Sunday and, after he had finished, slung them over his shoulder on his staff. On the way home, he met a man dressed in Sunday best heading in the direction of church. 'Do you not know that you should be in church as it is Sunday?' the man

demanded of him. Unimpressed, the old man just laughed, saying that Sunday was just the same as any other day to him. Well, said the younger man, in that case he could carry his bundle forever! With that, he was banished to the moon, a reminder and warning to all who might be tempted to break the Sabbath. Some link the tale to the story in the Bible in the book of Numbers that relates how a man was caught gathering sticks on the Sabbath and was sentenced by Moses to be stoned, although there is no mention there of the moon.

In some versions, the man is guilty of stealing from a neighbour and is likewise punished. In North Frisia, Germany, a man was guilty of stealing cabbages on Christmas Eve from his neighbours. He was caught in the act and as punishment the people used magic to send him up to the moon. In another version it was willow boughs that he stole, but the result was the same. According to a Dutch tale, the man was caught stealing vegetables.

Another idea with German origins says that there are both a man and a woman in the moon. The man was guilty of laying thorns and brambles across the path to stop people getting to church on a Sunday. The woman was not much better, as she broke the Sabbath by making butter on that day. Both were banished upwards to the moon, the man still seen holding his thorny bundle and the woman with her butter tub.

In Malaysia, the man is busy braiding bark to make a fishing line. If he completes the line, he will use it to catch up everything that is upon the earth, a disaster that must be avoided at all costs. Fortunately, there is a rat that gnaws at the line so that it cannot be finished, and a cat that chases the rat in turn, making sure between them that balance is maintained and disaster averted.

Although seeing a Man in the Moon is very common in the northern hemisphere, he doesn't make an appearance in stories from the southern hemisphere. This is because the moon is seen differently depending on which hemisphere you are in, and thus the markings and lightness and shade upon the moon's surface are perceived in a different way.

The Fox

In Peru it is said that the animal on the face of the moon is actually a fox. Many, many years ago, at a time when it was common for animals to talk, Fox had a dream: more than anything, he longed to visit the moon. He watched it and gazed at it, and day by day his desire to go there grew and grew. Finally he confided his wish to his friend, Mole, and explained his plan to get there.

Mole, more interested in eating worms than in thoughts of what went on in the sky, was not very keen on the idea, but Fox convinced him with the promise of fresh moon worms, and so the pair went about carrying out Fox's plan. According to Fox, all they needed to do was fashion a rope out of grass, hook it over the moon when it was in its crescent form, and then use it to climb upwards. It sounded so simple, and the pair worked hard to braid grass into a rope long enough, they thought, to reach the moon. With the rope finally completed, then came the wait: they waited patiently as the moon passed through its phases, until at last they were rewarded with the sight of the crescent moon in the sky, the hooked end beckoning them enticingly. How close they were, thought Fox, to getting there!

But, alas, it was not as easy as he had first thought. Try as they might, they could not throw that rope high enough to hook over the end of the moon. Time and time again the rope went so high, but then crashed back down to earth before them. The disappointment! Mole would have welcomed giving up at this point, but Fox would not be dissuaded even then. At a loss, they went to ask Bear to help them. Bear could climb higher than any animal, but even when at the top of the highest tree, he couldn't quite reach to hook the rope over the moon as they wanted. The same went for Llama – although he could climb to the top of the highest mountain, it just wasn't quite high enough. Finally they asked Condor and, lo and behold, the plan finally worked and the magnificent bird managed to hook the rope securely over the end of the moon.

Making sure to secure the other end to a tree, Fox and Mole then started to climb. Fox went ahead, but Mole was more hesitant, lamenting how dizzy he felt if he looked down. Fox admonished his friend and told

him not to look down but to keep going, and up, up, up they went, ever closer to reaching their goal.

Now there are different versions of what happened next. Some say that Mole, in his nervousness, slipped and was caught by Condor, who then flew him back down to earth. There the other animals teased him, and Mole hid in the ground where he lives to this day. In another version, as they were climbing, Parrot came to jeer at Mole, saying that he would never make it all the way to the moon. Mole retorted that Parrot was just jealous that he was not going to the moon with them. This angered Parrot and he pecked at the rope until it broke, sending Mole falling back towards the ground. Luckily Condor caught him and brought him back to earth safely.

As for Fox, in all accounts, he continued on upwards, safely reaching the moon, where he can still be seen to this day.

The Water Carriers

Some see two children in the shapes on the moon's face. In the 13th century Icelandic *Younger Edda* written by Snorri Sturluson, there is reference to two such children. Named Hjúki (meaning 'the one returning to health' in Old Norse) and Bil (meaning either 'moment' or 'instant'), the pair were on their way from the well Byrgir, carrying a bucket between them on the pole known as Simul on their shoulders. Máni the moon god, spying them, took them up from the earth to be with him, and that is where they are now, following him through the heavens. Based on this, it is said by some that the figures seen on the moon are none other than these two children.

Very little else is known of the elusive Hjúki and Bil, as they are not mentioned outside of the *Younger Edda*, though Bil is mentioned later on in the same text as a minor deity, along with the sun goddess Sól. It has been suggested that the pair might represent the phases of the moon, but the more accepted theory is that the two children are an explanation for the craters and shapes on the moon's surface as seen from the earth.

There is some speculation that Snorri took the idea of the children from a now unknown folk tale, or that he invented them altogether. Due to the similarity in names, the water-carrying aspect of the story, and the hill, there is a theory that the two children are actually referenced in the popular English nursery rhyme, Jack and Jill.

There is another Siberian story that tells of a young girl who is kidnapped by the moon when carrying a pitcher. She clings on to a willow bush in an attempt not to be taken, but to no avail; she can still be seen in the moon, clinging to the shrub.

The Toad

Out of all the animals seen in the moon, a toad or frog is one of the most common. The idea is particularly prevalent in China: this motif is recorded in the *I Ching*, or 'Book of Changes', from over 2,400 years ago.

There are many variations and differences in details to the tale, but the essential story involves a woman named Chang'e or Chang Er and her husband Archer Yi. Yi had obtained the herb or elixir of immortality from the Queen Mother of the West, but Chang'e took the herb for herself and consumed it, before floating off to the moon. In some versions Chang'e turned into a toad, and there she remains in that form.

In some tellings, Chang'e is beautiful yet vain and haughty, in stark contrast with her pious husband. Her punishment for stealing the elixir from him is twofold – not only is she banished, she also loses her greatly treasured beauty when she is transformed into a toad. There are other versions where the roles are reversed; it is the husband who is vain and arrogant, turning over time from a hero of the people into one of the worst tyrants imaginable. Desperate for the elixir so that he can be immortal, he will stop at nothing: knowing how dangerous it would be for a man such as her husband to have eternal life, Chang'e takes the elixir so that he cannot, and floats off to the moon, thwarting him as he tries to shoot arrows at her to bring her down.

The woman's original name was actually Heng'e, but this was changed to Chang'e after using the name Heng – meaning 'eternal' – became prohibited when a Han emperor used it in his title. Some believe that Chang'e is a moon goddess, but there is also an argument that she is the moon spirit itself: a toad in earlier versions of the story. It could be that the toad was the earliest creature or person to live in the moon in China.

According to some, Chang'e is not entirely alone in her lunar exile. There is the Jade Rabbit there to keep her company, pounding the very elixir she took in its pestle and mortar. There is also a woodcutter, doomed to forever hack at a cinnamon tree that heals each cut every time he makes one.

A toad is also associated with the moon in a tale attributed to the Sqelix or Salish from the Pacific coast of North America. Once there was a wolf in love with a toad, so obsessed with the toad that he followed her everywhere he could. The toad wasn't interested in the slightest, and hid from the wolf, leaving the bereft creature to pine alone. Wolf finally asked Moon to shine so he could find Toad, and Moon did so: the joyous wolf chased after the toad throughout the night once more. Poor Toad! She ran and ran and ran and was nearly caught, but with one last burst of energy she leapt as high into the sky as she could. She reached the moon, and is there even today.

Another tale from the Sqelix people tells of how the moon invited all the people to a great feast. Toad, offended when she was told there was nowhere for her to sit, went home and made it rain heavily. Eventually there was nowhere dry for people to shelter, until they saw a light and went to Toad's house. Finding it dry, they crammed inside, and Toad leapt onto Moon's face. Try as they might, people could not pull her away, and the marks from Toad are said to still be on the moon's face today for all to see.

The Hare

Another common idea is that a rabbit or hare lives on the moon, a motif found in several cultures. The Sea of Tranquillity is seen as the rabbit's head, while the seas of Fertility and Nectar are the ears.

In a story in the Buddhist *Sasa-jātaka*, the hare had three friends: the otter, jackal and monkey. Hare told his companions how it was good to give alms, and how, on the forthcoming fast day, they should give food to any beggar who asked for it. When the next day came, the deity Sakka – ruler of the Trāyastriṃśa heaven, and a protector of Buddhism according to Buddhist belief – came down to earth disguised as an old man, and asked for food to test them all. Otter, Jackal and Monkey all readily gave food that they had to hand, but Hare, having nothing to gather but grass, knew this would not do, and offered himself upon a fire for Sakka to eat. For his faithfulness, Sakka did not allow the hare to perish, but plucked him from the flames and set him in the moon. In some versions, he used the essence extracted from squeezing the mountain to draw the image of the faithful hare on the moon for all to see. There are other very similar stories about a self-sacrificing hare in other cultures, with different animals being listed as his friends.

In a tale from Sri Lanka, Buddha was lost in a wood. Hare offered to help him find his way, but Buddha said he was hungry and poor and could not pay him for his services. Hare immediately offered himself to eat; when Buddha made a fire, Hare threw himself onto it, but Buddha, using his powers, saved the selfless creature and sent him to the moon where he is today. There is a similar tale in Japan, where the rabbit is known as Tsuki no Usagi, and the Man in the Moon comes down to earth disguised as a beggar. The other animals present him with food, but the rabbit, with only grass to offer, sacrifices himself on the fire for the beggar, who then transforms into his original form and takes the rabbit up to live with him in recognition of his selflessness. This is a popular Japanese tale, and often told to children in September, at the time of the Harvest Moon and the Mid-Autumn Festival.

In a different vein, according to a tale from South Africa, the hare is responsible for the fact that humankind is doomed to die. Moon sent Hare down to tell people that just as she, the moon, 'died' when she faded away each month, only to return again, so would humankind. But Hare did not deliver the message correctly; instead, the flighty creature told people only that they would die. When Moon found out what Hare had done she was so angry she attacked him with a hatchet, intending to split him in two. She only succeeded in splitting his lip, however. Hare, angry in turn, lashed out with his claws, scarring Moon's face, which can still be seen in the dark shapes on the moon today.

According to Aztec tradition, the gods gathered to appoint a new sun after the fourth sun came to an end. The choice was between two gods: proud, handsome Tecciztecatl and lowly, ugly Nanahuatzin, and the one to become the sun had to throw themselves into the fire. At the last moment, Tecciztecatl hesitated, leaving Nanahuatzin to make the sacrifice first. Recovering himself, Tecciztecatl then followed, but this then left a situation where there were two suns. The remaining gods threw a rabbit at Tecciztecatl, leaving the mark on his face and making him much dimmer than Nanahuatzin. Tecciztecatl could only be seen at night, and thus became the moon.

THE MORNING STAR AND THE EVENING STAR:
A Romanian Tale

Once upon a time there was an emperor and empress who longed to be blessed with a child. They stopped at nothing to achieve their desire, consulting with witches and wizards and others with such skills, but to no avail. Finally, the desperate couple gave themselves over to fasting, praying and the giving of alms to the poor, in the hope that this might do some good for their plight. One night, the empress dreamed that the Lord himself appeared to her, bringing the news she longed to hear. He promised her that she and the emperor would be blessed with a child unlike any other, but only if they would follow certain instructions. According to the empress's dream, the emperor was to take a hook and line to the brook; when he caught a fish, the empress was to prepare it herself and eat it, and this would ensure she was with child.

Overjoyed, the empress woke her husband and told him what had occurred. The emperor wasted no time and leapt from his bed, and they hurried to the brook and did as instructed. The couple waited with bated breath. A short while later the cork started to bob. The line was pulled in, and to their amazement and great joy, at the end was a huge golden fish.

The empress continued to follow the instructions from her dream, and soon had the fish prepared and cooked. The pair ate it, and the empress immediately knew that she was indeed with child as she had been promised. Unbeknown to the royal couple, however, when clearing the table, a maidservant spied a fish bone left on the empress's plate. Giving in to temptation, she sucked it, curious to know how the dish from her mistress's table tasted.

Time passed, and the empress gave birth to a perfect baby boy. That very same night, the maidservant also had a boy: and guess what? The two children were so completely identical, that no one could tell them apart. The prince was named Busujok, the maid's son Siminok.

These two boys, so alike in looks, and bringing such joy to those around them, were each other's constant companions as they grew up. They learned together and played together and, as the years passed, grew into fine young men, charming, handsome, eloquent and brave. Still no one could tell the difference between them, and one was often mistaken for the other.

This difficulty plagued the empress, as even she very often could not tell her own son from the other youth. One day, when the men decided to go out hunting, the anxious mother called her son to her; stroking his hair, she secretly knotted two locks together, before sending him on his way with his friend.

The two young men played in the fields, watched bees and butterflies dart through the air, gathered flowers and, when finally starting to tire, drank water from thirst-quenching springs. The pair then ventured into the woods, gazing around in astonishment at the vast beauty of the forest around them. As they wandered they discussed what they would hunt, and quickly agreed that they would only hunt wild beasts, leaving the birds and other animals to go free. It had been a long, wonderful, yet intense day, and the prince was suddenly overcome with tiredness, too weary to stand a moment longer. He lay down, placing his head in Siminok's lap, asking him to stroke his hair.

It was in doing so that Siminok came across the knotted locks; exclaiming in surprise, he alerted the prince to the fact that his hair had been tied together. The prince was very confused, and did not like this discovery. He was so confounded that he declared his intention to go out into the wide world, as he could not fathom why his mother had tied his hair so.

Siminok tried to dissuade him, saying that the empress would not have done so for any evil cause and must have some innocent explanation. The prince would not be talked around, however, and he did not back down. Busujok bid his closest friend and brother farewell, giving him a handkerchief. He told him that if he ever saw three drops of blood on the handkerchief, then Siminok would know that he, the prince, was dead.

Embracing, they parted, Siminok returning to the palace to break the news to the empress and emperor. The poor empress was inconsolable, weeping and wringing her hands with great grief. The presence of Siminok, looking so much like her son, was some comfort, but that did not last. Siminok, glancing at the handkerchief one day, noticed three drops of blood upon it. Declaring that this meant his brother was dead he took off in search of the prince.

On and on he travelled, across fields and through forests and beyond. Finally Siminok reached a small hut, where he discovered an old woman. The woman informed him that Busujok was now the son of the local emperor, married to the princess.

Siminok made his way to the emperor's palace with all haste. As he approached, however, the princess saw him, and of course mistook him for her own husband, Busujok. Siminok told her that he was not the prince but in fact his friend, and that, upon hearing that he was dead, had come to find out what had happened. The princess was not convinced; she was certain that Siminok was indeed her husband and was playing a trick on her. Siminok declared that the Lord himself would reveal the truth: the sword that hung on a nail nearby would scratch the one of them who was wrong in their belief.

Of course, the sword cut the princess: she accordingly believed him, and accepted him as a guest. During the course of his inquiries, Siminok discovered that Busujok had gone out hunting, but he had not come home. Siminok wasted no time in taking a horse and some hounds and set off after him, riding on and on across the kingdom. At the forest, he encountered the Wood Witch. She ran away when she saw him, but he gave chase, finally catching up with her at the foot of a tall tree. The witch fled upwards, hoping to be safe in the protective branches.

Siminok was not easily dissuaded, and simply set up camp at the foot of the tree, made a fire and started to eat; his greyhounds settled nearby, accepting the occasional bite of food. Eventually the witch complained of being cold, and when Siminok suggested she join him by the fire, she expressed fear of the dogs. He told her they would do her no harm and she wavered, finally telling him to take a strand of her hair and tie the dogs up with it. Siminok agreed but instead put the hair in the fire. The witch, suspicious, asked if he had burned the hair, but Siminok denied the fact, saying he had done as she requested. The witch believed him and came down from her refuge, moving closer to the fire. When she told him she was hungry, Siminok asked what she would want to eat; in an expected moment of treachery, she told him she would eat him. Siminok was ready for her, however, and let the hounds go to tear her apart.

The witch, knowing she was caught, cried for him to call them off, promising that she would give the prince back if he did so. Siminok quickly called off his hounds, and the witch, true to her word, swallowed three times. To his amazement, up came Busujok, along with his horse and dogs too. Once they were free, Siminok set his hounds on the witch again, and they tore her to pieces.

After her demise, the prince related how he had been asleep, and Siminok in turn told him of what had occurred during his absence. Unfortunately, the suspicious prince believed that the princess had turned her affections to his brother instead, and nothing would dissuade him of this notion. In his madness, the prince declared that each of the brothers should cover their horses' eyes, mount, and let the horse carry each of them where they chose.

Siminok agreed, and the two duly bound their horses' eyes and their own. After a time, Busujok heard a groan; the prince halted his horse and freed his eyes. He looked all around for his brother, but there was no sign of him: alas, he had fallen into the spring and drowned.

Busujok made his way home and interrogated his wife on the story that Siminok had told him. She of course told him the exact same tale and, just to make extra sure, the prince told the sword to scratch whichever of them was wrong. It did so, scratching his own middle finger.

Too late, the prince regretted his jealousy and suspicion. He lamented and pined, overwhelmed by the weight of his grief at the loss of his dear brother. He could not, he decided, live without him any longer: he bound his eyes and those of his horse, before setting out to the forest where Siminok had died. Once there, the horse fell into the very same spring, and Busujok likewise drowned.

At that very moment, the emperor's son Busujok appeared in the sky as the morning star, and Siminok the maid's son appeared as the evening star. And that is how they came to be.

THE SEVEN SISTERS:
Orion and the Pleiades

There are perhaps no two arrangements of stars that have more captured the imagination throughout history than the Pleiades and Orion. Tales and superstitions regarding them both abound, with striking and intriguing similarities between disparate cultures and lands.

The Pleiades asterism consists of around 3,000 hot, blue, relatively young stars, about 115–125 million years old. To the average, well-sighted person, however, today only six are visible to the naked eye. Considered one of the most stunning sights in the night sky, the Pleiades can be found on the shoulder of Taurus the Bull.

The Pleiades was one of the earliest asterisms to be named: mentioned by Ancient Greek writers Homer and Hesiod, they are also one of the few asterisms outside of the Zodiac mentioned in the Old Testament, and the stars are also referenced in the New Testament. The oldest symbolic representation of the Pleiades is believed to be found on the Nebra Sky Disc; this artefact, discovered in Germany and thought to have been made around 1600 BCE, shows six stars arranged around a seventh, which are believed to represent the Pleiades. Archaeological evidence also speaks to the important role the Pleiades played in many cultures, and it is believed that the Temple of the Sun in Mexico, Egypt's Great Pyramid and the Parthenon in Athens, Greece, were among those monuments aligned with the Pleiades or built with them in mind.

With strong links to the phases of the agricultural year, in many cultures the rising and setting of the Pleiades has been used to mark important stages in the calendar. For many of the pastoralist groups in South Africa, the Pleiades are known by various names that translate to the 'Digging' or 'Ploughing' stars. When they first appear in the sky, it is seen as the signal for hoeing to begin, ready for the agricultural year ahead. To some of the Indigenous groups of Borneo, Southeast Asia, the disappearance and return of the Pleiades each year marked the passing of the seasons and determined their agricultural pursuits; likewise in

Peru, the appearance of the Pleiades also governed the crops and harvest. According to belief in both Belarus and Lithuania, it was time to sow corn after the asterism had risen. The Pleiades were also relied upon by many Indigenous groups across America, a connection strengthened by the fact that the stars themselves were thought to look like a heap of seeds: they were actually called 'the seeds' by the A:shiwi of New Mexico. Some Japanese nomadic cultures used the celestial movements of various stars and bodies to judge when to move and where to find food; the Pleiades – or Subaru – was an especially important asterism in this regard.

Unsurprisingly then, the Pleiades were also linked with the ability to foretell the weather, especially where rainy seasons were concerned. According to a Swahili proverb from South Africa, 'If the Digging stars set in sunny weather, they rise in rain, if they set in rain, they rise in sunny weather.' The Khoikhoi of South Africa used the Pleiades to forecast the start of the rainy season, while the Tapirapé people of Brazil believe that when the Pleiades disappeared it is a sign that the rainy season is coming to an end. The Pleiades were generally used for marking the passage of time: for the South African AmaXhosa, they marked each fresh year of adulthood for men of the tribe. For several Indigenous Australian groups, the heliacal rising of the Pleiades marks the beginning of winter.

The Pleiades have also long had navigational links, used in particular by sailors to find their way across the wide dark seas. To reflect this, in Ancient Greece they were known as the sailing stars, and in Germany today they are still known as *Schiffahrts Gestirn* – Sailors' Stars – along with their official name of Plejaden. In some Polynesian cultures, this asterism also played an important navigational role, as people used the stars to guide their journeys during the night.

But who exactly were the Pleiades and how did the stars get their name? According to Greek mythology, the Pleiades were the beautiful daughters of Atlas and the nymph Pleione. Orion the Hunter fell deeply in love with the girls and wouldn't take no for an answer, pursuing them relentlessly wherever they went. With no help forthcoming from their father, who was condemned to hold up the earth until the end of time, the maidens despaired. Zeus, however, took pity on them and heard their pleas; he turned the girls into doves, and they flew up into the sky where they became the stars of the Pleiades. Even now Orion hasn't ceased his pursuit; he can be seen today, still chasing them across the night sky. In another, more sinister, version of the origin tale, the sisters committed suicide out of sadness for their father, and were then placed in the sky.

This idea that the stars represent seven or six people, usually sisters or young women, is one of the most popular and common explanations across the globe for the Pleiades. According to a tale of the O-non-dowa-gah or Seneca people of North America, the Pleiades were seven young sisters, transformed into stars because they stayed too long when visiting a magical fountain. A Prussian tale has the Pleiades as the wife and daughters of a tyrannical husband who turns into a cuckoo. In Belarus, the stars are known as Siem Malciev, 'seven men'.

One of the most intriguing aspects of the Pleiades is the wealth of tales suggesting there were once seven stars clearly visible to the naked eye and that one of these stars at some point in history ceased to shine brightly enough to be seen, leaving the six that we see today. Some scholars believe that the strong similarities between such tales from Europe and Australia suggest that they originated from before the time when the ancestors of both cultures migrated out of Africa, which would date tales of the missing star to before 100,000 BCE.

This detail features in stories across such disparate nations and cultures that it is very probable one of the stars used to shine more brightly at some point than it did later, and missing Pleiades stories are found in African, Asian, European, Native American and Indigenous Australian cultures.

According to Greek mythology, it was the sister Merope who left the group: she felt such disgrace after marrying a mortal that she withdrew from her sisters. Another tale holds that it was Electra who vanished, hiding her face in grief when the city of Troy fell. In the belief of Indigenous groups in Australia there are many variations on what happened to the missing Pleiad, usually involving one, or sometimes even two, sisters either being abducted, dying or going into hiding.

In a tale from the Mono of Central California, six women discovered onions while out picking herbs one day. They tasted them and enjoyed

them so much that they ate as many of the onions as they could find, only returning home when it grew dark. Their husbands – returning from a day hunting cougar – were not impressed with the smell, and made the women sleep outside. Despite this, the next day when the men went out hunting, the women went out again to eat more onions as they had enjoyed them so much. The men returned home angry and tired; they had not managed to catch any cougar, they said, as they smelled like the onions and scared away the prey.

A week passed in such a fashion, with the wives eating onions and the men catching nothing. The men were increasingly cross because of this, and the women were fed up and angry too because they could not sleep well outside in the cold. On the seventh day, the women took ropes with them when they went out. Resting at the top of a large rock nearby, they decided to leave their husbands. One of the women whispered a secret word, and then threw her rope straight up into the sky. Like magic, it hooked over a cloud, with the two ends hanging down towards the women. The others tied their own ropes to it, and as they sang a special song, their ropes began to swing, taking them up into the sky. The men returned in time to see them and were instantly sorry; they too used magic and started to follow their wives up into the sky. The women were not happy with this, and shouted at them to stop – they did so, just a little way behind them. The women were turned into stars – six bright ones and one fainter one, the little girl of one of the wives. The men are also still there to this day, represented in the constellation of Taurus.

Another popular motif is that the Pleiades represent a mother hen and her chicks. This idea can be found across a large portion of central, western and southern Europe, West Africa, the Sudan, north-east India and south-east Africa. According to some Indigenous groups of Borneo, the stars are six chicks, followed by their invisible mother. Once upon a time there were seven chicks, but one went down to the earth and was given food. This greatly angered the mother hen, and she threatened to destroy both her chicks and the people on earth. In Hungary, the stars are also said to be a hen and chicks, and likewise to the Imohag, a Berber group of the Sahara, they are also chickens. In a similar vein, the names for the Pleiades among several groups located in northern Russia all mean 'nest of eggs' or 'of a wild duck' or 'flock of ducks'. In Thailand, the stars are called Dao Luk Kai, the 'Chicken Family Stars'.

In a tale from Croatia, there was a church that was threatened with destruction by its enemies. In the dead of night, the intruders were creeping up on their target when the hen, Kvočka, flew down from her tree outside the church, screaming and flying about to alert the people of the impending attack. The church was saved, and its would-be destroyers fled, but could not be found. Again, Kvočka saved the day: the people heard her clucking and followed the sound to the place where the enemies were concealing themselves, and they were apprehended. At that moment, someone happened to look up at the sky, and noticed that a group of stars there looked like Kvočka, and so they have been named ever since.

Another popular idea is that the constellation represents a sieve in the night sky, with the stars being the holes in the sieve. This explanation for the Pleiades can be found in Western Ukraine, south-east Poland, the Balkans, Russia and Western Europe. In the Slutsk and Homiel regions of Belarus, the sieve was where souls were sifted, the good going to heaven, the bad to hell.

In some tales, the sieve is linked to Mary, mother of Jesus. In Poland, it is said that the three Magi left the sieve that they used to sift their horses' oats in Bethlehem, and Mary used it, then hung it in the sky. In Lithuania, Mary used the sieve to sift flour, but one day it went missing, stolen by the Devil. St Mark was charged with returning it, and he and the Devil got into a fight. The sieve was retrieved, but damaged beyond use, and Mary hung it in the sky. In the folklore of Lithuania and Latvia, the sieve was likewise also sometimes stolen from a sky god.

Other explanations for the Pleiades are varied and equally intriguing. A Polynesian tale tells how there was a star that shone so brightly in the sky that the god Tāne grew greatly jealous. He threw Aldebaran, another star, at it, and the star broke into six pieces, each in turn becoming its own star. In the Near East and North Africa, the Pleiades are known by the Persian-Arabic word *soyraya*, meaning 'chandelier' or 'cluster of lamps', while to the Söl'kup, native to Siberia, they were hare's droppings. In Russia, Ukraine, Bulgaria, Hungary and the Volga Region, the asterism is seen as a beehive.

What then of Orion, the constellation so closely linked to the Pleiades in many myths and legends? Orion is likewise mentioned in the Old Testament, and the Ancient Greek writings of Homer and Hesiod. Who was Orion, and why is his constellation so important? According to most sources, he was Boeotian by birth, a giant and a hunter. Tales of his birth vary: according to some sources he was the son of Poseidon the sea god, and Euryale, and had the ability to walk on the waves of the sea. In another tale, when three gods visited King Hyrieus of Thrace, they were impressed by the king's hospitality and granted him a wish. He wished for children, so the three gods urinated on the hide of an ox that the king had sacrificed, the skin was buried, and from it was born Urion – later known as Orion. Although far from one of the largest constellations – Orion is only 26th in line – it is the constellation recognized most by people, his club, lion skin, belt or girdle, and sword easily located in the night sky. Unlike some constellations, Orion is visible across the globe.

Orion's pursuit of the Pleiades has a long history; Hesiod, circa 700 BCE, refers to his chase of the ill-fated sisters across the sky. There is some dispute over who exactly Orion is chasing after, however; Hyginus said that it was actually Pleione, the mother of the Pleiades sisters, that he was chasing.

In some traditional Indigenous Australian tales, most cultures have associated Orion with a man, or a group of young men, and there are many stories centring around Orion trying to catch the Pleiades. In Arnhem Land, northern Australia, there were stories that portrayed the Pleiades as the partners of the men who make up Orion. In New South Wales and Victoria, the girls of the Pleiades make music, and in some stories the boys of Orion dance at night to it.

In one Greek tale, the great hunter set his sights on marriage to Merope, daughter of King Oenopion of Chios. Orion carried out many tasks to help the king, including ridding the area of beasts, but the king did not really want his daughter married to one such as Orion, and continually put off the day that the pair would marry. One night, drunk and out of control, Orion forced himself upon Merope; when the king discovered this, he asked his father, the god Dionysius, for help. The god obliged, enlisting the help of the satyrs to put Orion into unconsciousness, and with him in this state, the king blinded the hunter who had done his daughter such wrong. Orion sought help from the god Hephaestus for his condition, and was told that he needed to travel to the place where the sun rises, and to let the sun bathe his afflicted eyes. With the god's assistant as his guide, Orion went where he was bid and regained his sight: seeking revenge, he went after the king, but he was hidden underground and Orion could not reach him.

After a colourful and varied life, there are several different versions of how Orion met his end. According to one tale, he died at the hands of Artemis, goddess of the hunt, in punishment for raping one of her handmaidens. In another, Orion and Artemis were lovers, and the hunter sought to marry her. Apollo, Artemis's brother, was not happy with this, and came up with a scheme. He bet the proud goddess that she would not be able to hit the target he indicated far off in the sea. She took aim and fired, hitting the target true, only to learn that it had been Orion's head, bobbing in the water as he swam. In another, it was Orion's own boasting that brought about his death; he had bragged that he would hunt all the beasts on earth, and this was displeasing to Gaia, Mother Earth, and so she sent a scorpion to slay him and remove the threat. Whatever the cause of his death, Orion was placed in the stars where we still see him today.

Interestingly, the constellation of Orion has links with dismemberment in various myths across the globe. At Orion's right shoulder is the bright star with a reddish glow, Alpha Orionis or Betelgeuse, the second brightest within the constellation. In Arabic, its name is said to mean 'shoulder' or 'armpit of the giant' or 'central one'. To the Taulipang of northern Brazil, the constellation was a man called Zilikawai, and his wife hacked off his leg – the shoulder is seen as a leg as the constellation appears sideways. There is a similar tale told by the Warao of the Orinoco Delta, who also say it is a leg, this time from a man named Nohi-Abassi. To the North American Lakota, Betelgeuse is also a limb, an arm of a chief, ripped off as a punishment.

According to one theory, Orion actually used to represent the Greek hero, Heracles. According to the Sumerians, Orion was Gilgamesh, fighting a giant bull – Taurus. Gilgamesh was the Sumerian version of Heracles. According to Egyptians, Orion's belt marked the resting place of the soul of the god Osiris. In a story from the Indigenous Australian group the *Yolŋu,* the three stars that make up Orion's 'belt' represent three brothers in their canoe. They were blown up into the sky by the Sun-Woman as a punishment when they ate a kingfisher, a creature sacred to their people, which violated the law (known as *Madayin).*

HOW THE MILKY WAY CAME TO BE

There are many tales from folklore and legend that attempt to explain the existence of the Milky Way, that winding, twisting galaxy in which our solar system is found. According to this story from South Africa, it is not made from stars at all, but from embers and ashes.

Many, many years ago, when it was night time, there was no light whatsoever in the sky, and the world was plunged into darkness at the end of each day. In time, however, resourceful humankind learned how to make fire, and they used it to bring light and warmth to themselves during the long dark-filled hours.

One night, a young girl sat before her wood fire, playing with the ashes as she warmed herself there. Taking some of the ashes in her hands, she cast them upwards into the air, watching them dance and swirl prettily, floating away into the air above. As she watched them go, the girl added more wood, stirring the fire to keep it going and making bright sparks dance and waft into the air after the ashes. How beautiful they looked! Hanging in the air, the sparks formed a bright road made from, it seemed, diamonds and silver, sparkling bright for all to see.

Called by some the Milky Way and by others the Stars' Road, it is still there today as splendid as ever, reminding us of the girl who threw those ashes and sparks up into the sky – a pathway of light shining brightly in the darkness.

SOARING SOULS AND SHOOTING STARS: Star Superstitions from Around the World

The enduring habit of humankind to attach meaning to signs and occurrences stretches back into the mists of time. When it comes to superstitious belief surrounding stars, it is tantalizingly apparent that such beliefs and ideas regarding the significance of the stars are shared across the globe.

Shooting Stars

Spotting a meteor, or shooting or falling star as they are commonly known, is a time-honoured pastime. Interpreted in many different ways, it is widely believed that catching sight of a falling star as it streaks across the night sky is an omen of good things to come. As well as a general sign of good luck, spying a shooting star can also have a variety of more specific interpretations.

According to superstition in Kentucky, USA, if a falling star was seen, someone in the family would marry soon. In Montenegro, Serbia and Macedonia, a falling star could indicate the escape of a person from imprisonment or captivity. Upon seeing a star it was important not to draw attention to the fact in order to help the person stay free: instead, it was advised to either remain silent, or say, 'Behind the thorns, behind a bush hide!' According to the Yolŋu people of Arnhem Land, Australia, a meteor was a sign to a family that a relative had arrived home safely.

Being lucky enough to see a falling star could also help with health concerns. According to Marcellus of Bordeaux, writing in 350 CE, they

could cure pimples. To be free of the affliction, one should observe a shooting star and then wipe a cloth over the spots; the pimples would then transfer to the cloth and your face would be clear. There was an important caveat, however: make sure not to touch your face with your hand, otherwise the spots would simply be transferred there instead. In another example of a cure, Pliny, in his *Natural History*, stated that if a corn or callus was cut when a star was falling, it would be quickly cured.

What actually is a shooting star? Although science now tells us that the phenomenon is caused by tiny specks of space dust burning up as they enter the earth's upper atmosphere, there are many other explanations to be found. According to Romanian belief, a falling star was actually an angel flying to help someone in need. People, being sinful, could not see them, and so only saw the star. According the Karajarri people of Western Australia, the night sky was a dome, made of hard rock or shell. Each star in turn was a nautilus shell, housing a living fish; a meteor was a dead fish falling from its shell. The Indigenous Australians near the Pennefather River, Queensland, believed that a falling star was the spirit of a woman watering yams to aid their growth.

Falling stars were not always viewed positively, however. A common belief was that a falling star signified either a death had occurred or was to happen soon. This was particularly the case if a shooting star was seen when at a sickbed or on the way to visit a sick person: one mother from Yorkshire, England, related how she knew her child was going to die because she saw a shooting star the night before they passed. A popular belief in Belarus held that it was a bad idea to look at falling stars on 5 February, as it would mean a death would follow soon after. In Russia it was also taboo to look at shooting stars on 5 March (20 Feb in the old Russian calendar) for similar reasons.

Meteors have also been associated with evil magic and spirits. According to the Tiwi of Australia's Northern Territory, the spirit of a falling star searches for living things to consume. It is told how one old woman placed infants in a bag tied about her neck to hide them from the eyes of these evil spirits. Another practice among some peoples was to kiss a baby on the forehead if they saw a meteor, so the child wouldn't be seen. In the Halliste region of Estonia, it was believed that a shooting star was caused when an old demon threw his hot stones high up into the sky. A particularly strange meteor spirit known for its malevolence, the Jubena, was found in Eastern Cape York Peninsula, Australia. It cooked eggs and burned them on the coals, and these were seen as falling stars. The spirit was known to hunt people down and tickle them to death. According to the Arrente people of Australia, mushrooms were fallen stars imbued with evil magic; because of this, they were considered taboo and not to be eaten.

According to belief in Ukraine, if looking at a falling star, be sure to say 'Amen' three times. This means when it lands it will solidify as rosin and be harmless. Otherwise it will transform into a devil, causing great harm to people in the area. In Bulgaria, the Kervanka, or Lazhi-kervan, is the name given to a bad star of evil spirits and disaster. People followed this star as they set off in the morning and often ended up dead, attacked by evil spirits on the road.

It is also very important to show a shooting star respect. According to Belarusian belief, you shouldn't laugh at a falling star, or it might burn down your house!

Wishing on a Star

Another popular star superstition is the practice of wishing on a star or shooting star in the hope that the wish will come true. A belief found across many places and cultures, it is not always as straightforward as just making a wish, and varying conditions could be attached. The most common and widespread caveat is that the wish must be made before the star is gone from sight in order for it to come true, a belief found in nearly all areas where this superstition is followed.

It is also sometimes said that the precise star you wish on is important. The most popular choice to wish on is the first star seen in the evening. This belief is captured in the now popular rhyme:

Starlight, star bright, first star I see tonight.I wish I may, I wish I might, have the wish I wish tonight.

The position of the star when the wish is made is also said by some to be important – if the star is on the right-hand side, then good luck will follow and the wish will come true, but if it is on the left, then bad luck should be expected.

Some say that you should wish on a certain number of stars in order for your wish to come true; for instance, a belief recorded in mid-20th century Swansea, Wales, held that counting nine stars on nine nights in a row would ensure that you got what you wanted.

What you did after making the wish was also important. Certain prohibitions were named in a collection of superstitions gathered from a sample of US college students; these variously specified that after wishing you should not look at the star again until you see a specified number of others, that you should throw kisses to three other stars before speaking, or that you shouldn't speak until you are asked a question that you can answer 'yes' to.

In Russia, a shooting star was said to be an angel, on its way to collect a departed soul. They did not refuse wishes at that time, so it was a good time to make a wish; as long as you could still see the falling star, the wish was likely to come true. The speed the star flew at also indicated how quickly the wish would be granted: the faster the better!

Stars are also said to be able to predict what the future might hold. Some believe they can predict how many children you will have. Just hold a piece of cloth up and look towards the evening star; the number of little stars you see around it will predict the number of children.

Pointing at Stars

According to widespread belief, pointing at stars is a big no-no. Although the precise reason for this is not clear, there are several suggestions for why pointing at the stars is a really bad idea. A popular theory is that, according to ancient belief, the stars were actually gods up in the skies. To point at one could imply disrespect – and who would want to risk angering a god? This is linked to similar beliefs of how it is taboo to point at other celestial bodies, such as the moon or rainbows.

In Germany, it was a commonly held practice to bite one's finger after pointing at a star, potentially to avoid the star having to bite the persons finger. Biting the finger would, in theory, prevent it from falling off. Superstition in Estonia decrees against pointing at a star as it falls: if you do, you might find your finger starts to decay! It was also considered bad luck to count the stars in the sky, so pointing and counting might be doubly unlucky. In the mid-19th century in Derbyshire, England, children would dare each other to count the stars, with the belief that the counter would be struck down dead upon reaching a hundred.

As with every rule, there are some exceptions. According to lore in Kentucky, USA, if you want to find something you have lost, just count a hundred stars without counting the same one twice. Counting seven stars for seven nights in a row could help with finding love; according to superstition, the first potential partner you shake hands with will be your future spouse. Similarly, sleeping with a mirror under your pillow after counting nine stars for nine nights in a row will make you dream of the person you will marry.

Passing Souls

There is a long-held connection between human souls and the stars. In Classical belief, when the world was created, the creator divided the left-over material into a number of souls equal to that of the stars in the heavens; each soul was assigned to a star. Those who lived a good life would, at its end, return to their star for a blessed existence, but it was a different story for those who did not learn the lessons they were supposed to during life: their soul would return again and again in lesser forms until they passed the test. The Ancient Greeks believed that shooting stars were falling or rising souls, depending on which way the star was going, and this belief held for centuries.

A very common belief even today is that a falling star is a soul either falling to earth or ascending into heaven. In some South Slavic and East Slavic areas, a falling star marked the death of the person it belonged to. In Bulgaria, when someone dies, the star that started to shine at their birth, will fall into their tomb. In 19th-century Yorkshire, it was believed that falling stars were the souls of babies coming down from heaven. Similarly, in Romania, stars were the souls of unbaptized children shining in the sky. To help the soul of the unbaptized child, it was important to cross yourself or give the soul a name to help it on its way. A common belief among many Indigenous groups in Australia was that a falling star was the spirit of someone who had died, falling from the sky. Some groups believed that if the sight of the star was accompanied by a loud crash, then it signified the death of a great medicine man.

The direction the star was travelling was sometimes said to be significant. If a star fell downwards, then it marked a death; if going upwards, then a birth had occurred. If a star fell towards the left, then the departed soul was that of a wicked person, and had gone straight to hell. In Belarusian belief, the sight of a falling star could mean that the deceased had not reached heaven, and their soul had returned to earth in order to put right the wrongs done in their previous life.

The star's direction could also signify *how* a person had died. In Belarus, if the star fell in a slanting direction then the person died a natural death, while if it fell fast and straight, they had been killed.

A slowly falling star indicated that the deceased had been ill for a long time before their passing.

Some believe that the way a star fell was linked to the character of the person who had died. If it fell in a straight line then they had been an honest and good person during life. A jaggedly falling star, however, indicated that the individual had been unkind.

According to the Wardaman people of Australia, after death a person's spirit passed through a hole in the sky. There it would shine as a star, watched over by the Rock Cod star, Munin (Arcturus). When its time came, the spirit fell down to earth as a shooting star. Landing in a stream, the Rock Cod looked after it once more, until the spirit was united with its mother and reincarnated as her baby.

In Lithuania, it was believed that if the star had a tail, then it belonged to a rich person, whereas a simple star signified a person in a less healthy financial position. A large star could belong to a grown-up, while children had smaller stars.

Have you ever heard the phrase that someone must have been born under a lucky star, used about those who seem to have a charmed life with everything going their way, or those who rise to great heights? Equally, there are those who seem to be constantly suffering, experiencing mishap after mishap, with nothing going right. Although obviously not supported by fact, according to some, this might not be a coincidence, and there is a belief that the star someone was born under influences their entire personalities and life ahead. In Romanian belief, the star of an emperor, for instance, was bright and large – a *luceafar* – while a small, faint star signified a poorer, less-important individual. In Bulgaria, a sickly child is said to be of a weak star, or *slabozvezdo*. In contrast, many cultures believe that a leader or great person will have a bright star that shines clearly in the sky.

Dragons in the Sky

Another popular explanation for falling or shooting stars is that they are dragon- or serpent-like spirit creatures, blazing their way through the night sky, often wreaking havoc and destruction when they hit the earth.

In Belarus, if a star is seen falling fitfully rather than in a straight line, this is a strong indication that the star is actually a *zmej*. These creatures are often linked to evil magic; when a fireball is seen, it is said to be the *zmej* or devil carrying gold or silver for a witch or wizard, and that the star will fall over the location of the sorcerer's house. Likewise in Russia, it is said that a *zmej* or fireball is actually a flying witch or sorcerer. The Romanian *zmej* or *balauri* were malevolent creatures, waiting in the dark to leap on those people rash enough to be wandering alone at night, to disfigure or even kill them.

In Serbia, Bulgaria and Macedonia, the *zmej* is often known as *ala* or *hala*, which means 'snake' in Turkish. This creature can come down as a thick fog that stops corn from ripening and brings bad weather in general, such as great winds and storms. They live in caves out of the way of humankind when they can, guarding their treasure jealously. At the end of their lives, they become so large and filled with power that they cannot be contained on earth any longer; they leave altogether, and can be seen as shooting stars in the sky as they fly.

In Russia, the *zmej* or *zmey* as it is also known there, targets women who either pine too heavily or for too long for missing men-folk, or those that are dead. The *zmey* appears in the likeness of the missing man to the woman (though no one but her can see it), and is said to have sexual intercourse with her. Malevolent meteor spirits in the form of dragon–serpents were recognized by several groups in the Northern Territory of Australia. They hunted for the souls of those who were ill or dying.

Such dragon spirits associated with meteors aren't always seen as malevolent beings, however. In Belarus, there is the *khut*, a household spirit that brings good fortune and wealth to a family. Likewise in Lithuania, the *aitvaras*, another meteor dragon, brings good fortune and wealth to the household it patronizes.

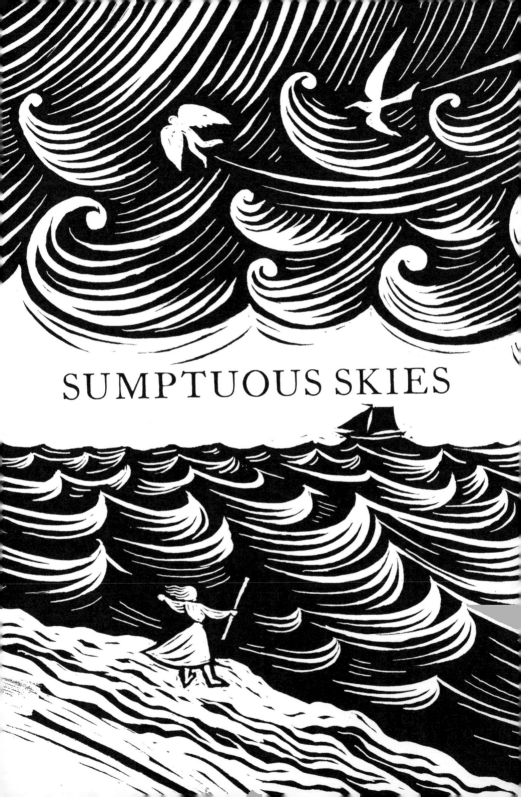

SUMPTUOUS SKIES

STALLIONS OF THE SKIES:
Pegasus and Other Soaring Steeds

Myth and folklore abound with tales of winged horses, sweeping majestically through the skies, often taking their riders on glorious and perilous adventures to far-off lands where anything can – and quite often does – happen.

Without a doubt, one of the most famous and well-known winged horses is Pegasus of Greek mythology. Linked with the adventures of more than one Greek hero, this divine steed was a brilliant white, with large, resplendent wings that unfurled to an enormous width.

There are several different variations of the birth of Pegasus. In one account, the winged horse sprung forth from the spray of blood created when Perseus lopped off the head of the Gorgon Medusa. In some versions, Medusa was actually portrayed as a mare; Pegasus was foaled after her decapitation. In another, Pegasus came to be when Medusa's blood and pain mixed with sea foam, and is said to have been fathered by the sea god, Poseidon, who was also the god of horses.

According to one myth, in Lycia, a terrible, fire-breathing monster known as Chimera was causing great terror and destruction across the land. The king despaired of finding a hero who could slay the creature, when the hero Bellerophon arrived at the palace with letters of introduction from Proetos, the king's son-in-law. Those letters were a double-edged sword, however, as they also asked the king to slay Bellerophon, due to the fact Proetos felt his wife was giving the hero too much attention. The wily king quickly saw a solution: send Bellerophon to face the unstoppable monster.

As the king had hoped, Bellerophon accepted the impossible task. He took the advice of a soothsayer, who counselled him to find and master Pegasus, a great winged horse, and that he should start by spending a night in the Temple of Athena. Bellerophon did as he was instructed and, while he slept, the goddess came to him with a golden bridle. It was not just a dream, however: the bridle was in his hand when he awoke.

From there, Bellerophon went on to find Pegasus. He finally located the horse drinking from a stream; upon seeing the bridle, Pegasus allowed Bellerophon to mount him, before flying off into the air. They found the Chimera and Bellerophon defeated the terrible creature, bringing an end to its reign of terror. After that, Bellerophon went on to successfully complete many more trials with his faithful steed, and finally the king gave his daughter as his wife.

Pride comes before a fall, however, and fall Bellerophon did; when he attempted to fly high enough to enter heaven, where only the gods could dwell, Zeus punished his presumption by sending a gadfly to sting Pegasus. The startled stallion threw his rider, and Bellerophon fell to earth, where he lived out the rest of his days, lame and blind. After the fall of Bellerophon, Pegasus was taken up to Olympus where he lived in Zeus's stables, carrying thunderbolts for the god. He served Zeus so faithfully, that after a time he was rewarded by being turned into a constellation and placed among the stars. Pegasus can be seen today from the northern hemisphere from late summer throughout autumn, and in the southern hemisphere in late winter and into spring.

It was said that Pegasus had a power that meant wherever he stamped his hooves, a fresh water spring would flow from that spot. The most famous occasion of this was the creation of the Hippocrene – meaning 'horse spring' – fountain. On Mount Helicon, during a contest with the daughters of Pierus, the Muses played such beautiful music and sang so enchantingly that the earth and heavens themselves stilled: the mountain rose upwards, ascending towards where the gods lived. As with Bellepheron, such presumption could not be left unchecked: Poseidon, angered that the mountain moved without his say-so, sent Pegasus to the summit, where the great horse stamped his hooves to stop the mountain in its tracks. Water gushed forth from the spot, becoming the sacred fountain of Hippocrene.

Another snow-white winged horse is the Hindu Uchchaihshravas. This sacred steed was sometimes said to be the *vahana* – vehicle – of the king of the gods, Indra, and was, like Pegasus, pure white.

Indra is not the only god that Uchchaihshravas is associated with. In the *Bhagavad Gita*, he is identified with Krishna, when this god likens himself to Uchchaihshravas among horses, i.e., that Uchchaihshravas is king of the horses. In the *Vishnu Purana*, Uchchaihshravas is also named as king of the horses. Uchchaihshravas was also said to have been taken by Bali, king of the demons, who used the horse for many nefarious purposes.

How did Uchchaihshravas come into existence? According to the *Mahabharata*, Uchchaihshravas was created during the Samudra Manthana – the churning of the milk ocean – which also led to the appearance of several other great treasures, including the elixir of life, known as the *amrita*.

Uchchaihshravas was the focus of a bet between Vinata and Kadru, the wives of Kashyapa, over the colour of the horse's tail. The stakes were high: whoever lost the bet was to become the servant of the winner. Vinata bet that the tail was white, while Kadru chose black. Leaving nothing to chance, Kadru cheated; she instructed her serpent sons to cover Uchchaihshravas's tail, making it appear black as she had predicted, thus securing her victory.

According to the traditional tales of several Turkic-speaking nations, the Tulpar is another winged horse, known for its great speed. It is thought that this fantastical beast came about through the amalgamation of horses and birds of prey, used together for hunting in Central Asia. They were merged into one in the popular imagination, creating the mythical beast known as the Tulpar.

The most well-known tale involving the Tulpar concerns the creation of the *morin khuur*, the Mongolian horse-headed fiddle. A sheep herder named Namjil is given a winged horse, magical and special, that went by the name of Jonon Har – Black Jonon. Busy with his master's sheep by day, come night time it was a very different story, as Namjil would mount his magical steed and fly to a far-off land to meet with the love of his life. Namjil's happiness, however, was destined to be jeopardized as one woman, overcome with jealousy, plotted his downfall, and employed someone to cut off Jonon Har's wings. Finding his beloved steed dead, the distraught herder created the fiddle from the horse's bones and skin, and used it to play songs about his lost friend for all to hear.

The Tulpar also features in the national emblem of Kazakhstan. Officially adopted in 1992, the emblem is circular in shape, with a *shanyrak* – an arched, cross-shaped top of a yurt – on a blue background. Sun rays or supports radiate from this, and on either side of the yurt is a Tulpar. According to the official website of the President of the Republic of Kazakhstan, the Tulpars represent bravery and the wings the dream of a nation that is prosperous and strong. The wings are also marked like sheaves of corn, representing the 'labour of the people of Kazakhstan and material welfare of the country'. Although the Tulpar could fly, the wings of a Tulpar were actually sometimes linked to the speed of the horse, not flight itself.

Another winged horse is the Qianlima, found in the Chinese classics, known throughout several countries of East Asia. Variously also known as Chollima and Cheollima, its name translates to 'thousand-li horse', referring to the fact it is said to be able to travel this distance – approximately 400km (250mi) – in the space of one day. Also from Chinese folklore is Tianma, or 'heavenly horse'. This horse was sometimes depicted with dragon scales, and some sources say that it was able to sweat blood.

BIRDS OF MYTH AND LEGEND

Birds, those natural denizens of the sky, are frequently featured throughout folklore, and they have come to stand as both symbols and portents in familiar and not so familiar tales. From the self-regenerating phoenix to Odin's ravens, here are some of the most wonderful and revered birds from myth and legend.

Caladrius

The Caladrius is a bird found in Roman legend, purported to have both prophetic and healing powers. This wondrous bird would be brought to the sickroom: if the bird turned its head away from the sufferer, then this was bad news and meant they would surely die; but if the Caladrius looked into the person's face then all would be well, they would recover and live. The Caladrius was said to actively aid in the recovery of the sick; it would absorb their sickness and then fly upwards to the sun, where the illness would be burned up and removed from both the sick person and the bird itself before it returned to earth.

Dung from the Caladrius was also believed to have restorative properties and to cure people of blindness. There was one catch, however: the dung had to be rubbed into the eyes of the afflicted person. This was sometimes commuted to having dung rubbed on the thigh bone, which may have been in order to make the practice less distasteful, or due to a confusion or mistranslation between *fimus* ('dung') and *femur* ('thigh bone'). Pliny the Elder named the bird *icterus* due to its yellowish colour, and said it was skilled at curing jaundice.

In medieval bestiaries, the bird was frequently used as an allegory for Christ, both in turning his face away from sinners who refused to repent and also due to the pure whiteness of the bird as represented in the volumes. This link is further cemented in the idea of the bird taking on people's sickness, representing Christ's saving of humankind.

The appearance of the Caladrius varies between sources. In medieval bestiaries the bird was often represented as either dove- or seagull-like in appearance, and was pure white. Mentioned in histories of Alexander the Great from the same period, the bird was shown with tan or yellow feathers and, in general in non-religious texts, the Caladrius was shown in varying colours. Other depictions of the Caladrius include a sculpture from the 12th century in St Mary's Church, Alne, near York, and a 13th century stained-glass window in the cathedral of Saint-Jean-Baptiste, Lyon, France.

The origins of the Caladrius are unknown and disputed; some believe it may have been based on a real bird, and potential contenders include the heron, dove, skylark or wagtail. Aristotle and other early Greek writers described a bird known as the charadrius; this creature was a water bird, or a bird that lived in a cave, and it is possible the Caladrius was developed from this bird.

Interest in the Caladrius seems to have died out by the 15th century, but curiosity about this mythical bird has seen a resurgence in recent years, and it is used in several health-related logos and symbols, such as that of the Isle of Wight Health Associates Cricket Club and the coat of arms for the Medical University of Southern Africa.

Huginn and Munnin

The name of Odin, king of the Norse gods, is a familiar one to many from myth and legend and, more recently, the highly popular Marvel movie franchise. How many know the details, however, of his two faithful feathered companions?

In Norse mythology, Huginn (meaning 'thought' in Old Norse) and Muninn (meaning 'memory' or 'mind') were two ravens, one perching on each of Odin's shoulders. The god would send them off each day with the dawn, and they would spend their hours flying across Midgard – earth – before returning to him in the evening. During their flight covering the whole span of the earth, these ravens would hear of everything that was happening, and report back to their master who had, according to some sources, given them the power of speech. In this way, Odin was greatly knowledgeable of all that went on across the earth, and learned a great deal from the two ravens.

Another link between ravens and Odin is the Raven Banner – a flag that was flown by some Viking chieftains and rulers in Scandinavia between the 9th and 11th centuries. With a rough triangular shape, the outside edge was rounded with tassels on it. Some believe that the raven depicted symbolizes Odin, with the purpose of terrifying the enemy.

Ravens are common throughout Norse mythology and belief, and have a strong connection to war and death, frequenting battlefields and being attracted to carrion there. Odin is likewise linked to death and battle. He receives half of those who have died in battle in Valhalla, while the other half go to Freyja in Fólkvangr.

Ziz

The Ziz is a mythical bird from Jewish tradition. This giant creature was a sight to behold – when it spread its wings, it was said that it blocked out the very light from the sun, causing a solar eclipse. Standing on the floor of the deepest ocean, the water barely reached its ankles, with its head reaching up to touch the sky.

In appearance, the Ziz has been likened to the legendary griffin. It has the head and wings of a bird, with the back legs of a lion. The Ziz is often linked with the other great beasts, Leviathan who rules the sea and Behemoth who rules the land, with Ziz named as the ruler of the sky, the third creature in a mythological triumvirate.

According to a tale in the Babylonian Talmud, a group of travellers in a boat caught sight of the Ziz standing in the water close by. They assumed the water was shallow as it was only reaching as far as the bird's ankles. Tragedy was averted when a voice from above called to them, warning them that the water was not as it appeared; a carpenter's axe had been dropped into that very spot seven years ago, and the axe had not yet reached the bottom!

Another tale pays further testament to the great size of this bird. Once an egg belonging to the Ziz fell from its nest, smashing as it hit the ground. The contents of the egg were so great that it destroyed 300 cedar trees and flooded 16 cities.

Fenghuang

The Fenghuang is a mythological bird found in Chinese, Japanese and Vietnamese cultures. First depicted in art around 8,000 years ago, the Fenghuang has a long history, as splendid and varied as the bird itself.

The Fenghuang is said to be six chi – 2.7m (9ft) – tall. In appearance, descriptions of the bird vary: originally, the Fenghuang was said to be a composite of several creatures, with the head of a cock, a swallow's beak, the neck of a snake, a tortoise's back and the tail of a fish. In more recent times, a common description includes the head of a golden pheasant, a parrot's beak, crane's legs, the body of a mandarin duck and wings of a swallow. Colour-wise, there are also variations: the bird is variously described as black, white, red, yellow and green.

The different parts of a Fenghuang are each said to stand for a different aspect of space: the feet represent the earth, the head the sky, the back the moon, wings the wind, tail the planets and eyes the sun. It is generally accepted that the Fenghuang has actually shifted gender over time, moving from yang (male) to yin (female). In modern times, the female Fenghuang is a familiar sight, paired with the male Chinese dragon.

Misleadingly referred to at times as the Chinese Phoenix, the Fenghuang is one of China's most famous mythical birds. The links with the phoenix are misleading, as the two birds are actually entirely different and have different origins. The connection between the two birds is believed to have arisen due to 19th-century textual translations from Chinese to English, and highlights the difficulties and impact of cultural assumptions and misinterpretation: the Fenghuang is culturally specific to Chinese culture and cannot be cleanly translated into a Western cultural experience, so the word 'phoenix' was used frequently to be more easily understood by Western readers. This conflation or interchangeability of the two birds is still seen today: in the 2020 Disney film *Mulan*, a phoenix represents the Fenghuang.

The Fenghuang was said to govern one of the four quadrants of the heavens, one of four sacred creatures to do so; Fenghuang ruled the southern quadrant. It made its home in the K'unlan Mountains, living there within wu tung trees. The song of the Fenghuang was believed to be such a magical sound that its song was the inspiration for the Chinese harmonic scale itself.

A peaceful creature, the Fenghuang was known for eating bamboo seeds. Associated with summer, the sun and fire, from the Zhou dynasty onwards it was also linked with harmony, peace and political prosperity. Seeing a Fenghuang is said to be a sign of good luck, a good omen for times ahead. The bird was also believed to only appear during times of prosperity and during peaceful, well-governed reigns. No one knows for certain where the Fenghuang myth originated, but it has been suggested that it might actually be based on a real creature, such as an ostrich-like prehistoric bird.

One popular legend relating to the Fenghuang is that it appeared before the death of the Yellow Emperor, Huangdi, in the 27th century BCE. The bird is also said to have appeared at the grave of Emperor Hongwu, founder of the Ming Dynasty.

Today, the Fenghuang is a familiar decorative choice for religious ceremonies and weddings, and is also popular in jewellery design.

Firebird

The firebird is perhaps the most iconic and well-known bird from Slavic folklore and fairy tales. In appearance, the bird was described as having bright, crystal-like eyes, and it glowed as if on fire; in some cases, it was actually said to burn. The firebird's plumage is resplendent in shades of reds, yellows and oranges, a dazzling display that captivates all who see or hear of it. The feathers of a firebird are said to remain glowing even when they have come loose.

There are many versions of the firebird story due to the fact that such tales were originally conveyed in oral form. There are common themes throughout the tales of this elusive bird; it is often the treasured prize in a quest by a hero, who sets off to find the bird either after finding one of its tail feathers or being tasked with finding it by an authority figure, such as a father or the king or the tsar himself. The first written recorded version of the firebird tale was from the mid-19th century, *The Firebird, the Horse of Power and the Princess Vasilisa*. Tales of the firebird were obviously in existence much earlier, however.

The themes of hunting a difficult treasure, or being on an arduous quest or journey, are also common themes associated with the bird. The firebird was known for stealing apples from the garden of the tsar; in some versions of the tale, events revolve around attempts to stop the bird, with the tsar charging his sons with solving the problem. In another tale, a terrible magician is holding 13 beautiful princesses captive in his castle; the young Ivan discovers this when he captures the firebird and sets it free, and is given a feather in reward for granting its freedom. Ivan falls in love with the fairest of the princesses, and ultimately defeats and kills the magician with the aid of the protection of the magical feather.

The firebird is a mixed blessing; it is seen as a positive force, a treasure, a gift, but this can also turn and leave the quester wishing they had never come across the bird or its feathers. For it can also stand as a symbol of misfortune, peril and ultimate doom.

In more recent times, the firebird has erroneously come to be conflated in some cases with the legendary phoenix, but the two birds are very distinct creatures. Although they share some similarities, the big difference is the phoenix's self-combustion and resurrection every 500 years.

THE FIREBIRD

Long ago in Russia there was a girl called Marushka. This young orphan was a good-natured girl, gentle, modest and quiet, and none could fault her. She was also wonderfully skilled with a needle, and no one could do such fine embroidery as she. Marushka made many beautiful items for people, from shirts to sashes and much in between, using silks and beautiful beads made of glass. Whatever she was paid for her work she was content, and never complained, even when it was worth much more than she was offered.

Many merchants from both near and far-off lands heard of Marushka's talent, and many came to witness it for themselves. Amazed, they gazed on in awe, never having seen work so beautiful in their lives. Captivated, each visitor asked Marushka to leave her life to live with them, and each offered her things they believed she could never refuse. But the girl surprised them all, telling each simply that she was content where she was. She would not leave her village, she told them, and riches held no interest for her. She would continue to sell her work to those who wished to own it, but she would remain where she was.

The rejected merchants were greatly disappointed, but there was nothing they could do, and each went on their way, telling those they met as they went on their travels about the girl with the unforgettable embroidery. In this way, word of Marushka eventually reached a wicked, wicked sorcerer, none other than the terrible Kaschei the Immortal himself. This terrible man immediately flew into a great rage, angry beyond measure that there dared to exist such beauty in the world that he had not personally witnessed.

Kaschei transformed his appearance into a young, handsome man, and flew his way across all manner of terrain to the cottage where the unsuspecting girl lived. He asked then to see her needlework, and Marushka duly laid out everything she had: handkerchiefs, towels, shirts and veils – each item more beautiful and impressive than the last. She told the sorcerer that he could take whatever he wished, and if he had no money with him then, it was no issue: he could pay her later when he was able to. If there was nothing that appealed to him, Marushka continued, he had only to tell her, and she would make something that fit with his requirements.

Rather than being impressed by her kindness and the quality of her work, Kaschei grew still angrier. For all the fine things he owned, how was it that this simple girl from the countryside could make things so much finer than anything he possessed? He was the greatest of sorcerers and had whatever he wanted, but he just could not compete with Marushka's splendid work.

Determined to have what he wanted at all costs, the sorcerer applied all his wit and cunning to the situation. He told Marushka that if she came with him, he would make her a queen, filling her head with all manner of wonderful and precious things that she would have if only she would leave her home and go with him. Gold plates for her meals, a bejewelled palace, and an orchard with golden apples and beautiful birds singing the sweetest songs known to humankind were among the things he offered her, certain that Marushka would not be able to say no.

The sorcerer was wrong, and Marushka rejected him, not tempted for one moment by all that he dangled before her. She had no need of such riches or the things he offered: for right where she was she had the woods and fields where she had lived since she was born, and there was nothing sweeter to Marushka. Not only that, but she would never willingly abandon the graves of her parents, or leave the people who found such joy in her work. No, Marushka told him firmly, she would not embroider for one man alone, whatever riches he offered her.

The furious Kaschei could not believe anyone could defy him so. In a rage he shouted that Marushka would be a maiden no longer, but instead would be a bird for evermore. No sooner had the words left his lips than a firebird appeared where moments before Marushka had been standing. In turn, the sorcerer transformed himself into a giant black falcon. In this form, he soared high into the sky before swooping down to capture the firebird, strong, cruel talons gripping her tight.

But Marushka would not be beaten, and would not leave her homeland without leaving some long-enduring memory of herself there among the people and places that she so loved. As she rose she shed her brilliant feathers, and they fell, one by one, down to the ground below. Landing in the forests and the meadows, there they lay, a rainbow reminder for all to see of Marushka and her beautiful embroidery.

COME RAIN OR SHINE:
Weather Lore and Superstitions

The state of the weather has always been a vitally necessary preoccupation of humankind, the effects of fair weather or foul affecting our daily lives and, quite literally in some cases, determining our very survival. Unsurprisingly, therefore, there is an equally long history of belief that certain signs in the natural world can predict what weather will follow, with a vast number of superstitions, sayings and adages growing from these signs and predictions. Passed down through the spoken and printed word, some hold scientific backing, others decidedly less so, but regardless, many remain deeply entrenched in our collective psyche today. Some beliefs and sayings prove to be almost universal, while others are relevant only to the particular weather and climate conditions of specific countries. The wide glut of weather-related superstitions and sayings in existence are far too numerous to cover in their entirety, but here is a tour through some of the most popular – and some less well-known – weather sayings and superstitions from around the world.

For obvious reasons, the appearance of the sky features heavily in weather lore. One very familiar idea is that if the sky and clouds are tinged red at specific times of the day this is a sign of either rain or fair weather to come, as in the ever popular: *Red sky at night, shepherd's delight, red sky in the morning, shepherd's warning.*

The belief that red sky has great significance has a long provenance; in the Bible in Matthew, 16:3, Jesus says: 'When it is evening, ye say, fair weather: for heaven is red. And in the morning foul weather today: for the heaven is red and lowering.' Theophrastus recorded beliefs about the importance of red skies in the 3rd century BCE, stating that a red sky before dawn would mean rain either on that day, or within three days. A red sky at sunset would also potentially mean rain within three days, though this was less concrete.

'Evening red and morning grey are sure signs of a fine day. Evening grey and morning red, put on your hat or you'll wet your head,' is another instance of red skies being cited. According to another saying, 'Red morning skies fill the well, red evening skies dry it,' meaning red sky in the morning heralded rain. According to some, a red morning sky on New Year's Day was said to mean thunderstorms and general bad happenings would occur.

What causes these red skies in the first place? Scientifically, red skies at sunset are caused by blue light being scattered when dust and small particles are caught in the atmosphere by high pressure, and often does indicate fair weather the following day, as it is a sign of high pressure moving in from the west. According to Germanic mythology, a red sky in the evening was caused by a giant doing battle with the spirits of light. Another explanation was that the Virgin Mary was making cakes for Christmas.

The shape or form of the clouds is also considered important when it comes to predicting the weather. One widely held belief is that clouds looking like the scales of a mackerel predict certain weather, for instance in the saying: 'Mackerel sky, mackerel sky, never long wet, never long dry'. Another similar idea was that 'Mackerel sky and mares' tails, make lofty ships carry low sails,' warning that a storm and high winds were on the way and that the sails should therefore be lowered.

Don't let us forget the significance of the sun, moon and other celestial bodies when it comes to being harbingers of weather to come. Black spots on either the sun or moon were said to be a sign of rain, but if the spots were red, then wind was due instead. A halo around the moon or sun is also a sign that wind is due. If there is a break in either halo, take note of its position: the wind will come from that direction.

Another common method of predicting the weather is the less scientific yet equally popular belief that weather at certain times of the year can predict weather at a different time of year, with one being dependent upon the other. Such seemingly spurious ideas actually shed an important light on the impact weather can have on humankind as a whole: a vast number of such correlating predictions involve predicting whether the coming winter will be harsh or mild, reflecting the grim fact that at many times this could very often be the difference between survival or otherwise.

One belief with a long heritage is that of the predictive abilities of the weather in early February. It is said that the weather at this time can predict how much longer the winter will continue. In many countries, including England, Germany, France and Scotland, it is believed that the weather on Candlemas Day, 2 February, will predict how long winter will continue. One popular saying is: 'Candlemas Day be fair and bright, winter will take a second flight', meaning that if the weather is fine on Candlemas, then winter will come back for a final harsh spell before finally giving way to spring.

In both England and Germany there has been a belief since at least the 16th century that the day upon which Christmas Day falls will determine how the winter weather pans out. For example, if Christmas Day falls on a Thursday, the winter will be a windy one, whereas Christmas Day on a Friday means a winter of hard frosts and snow. In Sweden, weather on 30 November, St Andrew's Day, is also an important predictor, as in '*Anders slaskar, julen braskar*', i.e., 'slushy Anders, frozen Christmas'. Another belief is, 'If ice in November can bear a duck, the rest of the winter'll be slush and muck'.

According to the Hispanic *cabañuelas*, the first 12, 18 or 24 days of January or August will predict what the weather will be like for the rest of the year.

It is not only in the skies that we look for these patterns of cause and effect: we have extended our horizons to the behaviour of birds, animals and even insects, finding correlations between their actions and the weather. Animals are said to be particularly sensitive to changes in the air or temperature, and are believed to be able to feel approaching weather before we do. Whatever the truth of this, they are frequently credited with the power to unwittingly forecast the weather, a belief reflected in the wide abundance of sayings linking the two.

If an ass has its ears forwards and downwards, then rain should be expected, and the same if the animal is rubbing against the walls or braying more often than usual, as reflected in the saying from Tyrol, modern-day Austria, that '*Wenn oft die Esel schreien kommt schlechtes*

Wetter'. In Bergamo, Italy, it was said that when asses pricked their ears or sneezed, a change in the weather was due, and rain was on the way.

Cattle are also believed to know when rain is coming: a popular belief is that when they are lying down – sometimes specifically in the morning – rain will follow soon. In a proverb from Ariège, France, if cattle huddled together, then rain was due. This could also be true if cattle sniffed the air, lay on their right side, or licked their front feet. A Venetian proverb states that: '*Co la vaca tien su'l muso, Bruto tempo salta suso*'. Meaning that if a cow sniffs the air with its nostrils turned upwards, then bad weather is to be expected. The same is true if they lie on their right side or lick their forefeet.

According to Bretagne lore, '*Chien qui se roule annonce du vent: s'il mange de l'herbe, il pleuvra*' – if a dog is rolling on the ground, then a strong wind is said to follow; but if it eats grass, rain will come. A saying from Germany holds that if dogs bark at the moon, then it's time to wrap up warm, as a severe cold snap will soon be on the way.

Hedgehogs might seem a surprising candidate for weather prediction, but according to various beliefs they are said to have foreknowledge of when windy weather is due. The animal is said to make two holes underground, one towards the north, and the other towards the south. If the hedgehog blocks one of the holes, then that is the direction the wind will be coming from. Be especially wary if the hedgehog blocks both holes – violent wind is not far away. It is also said that whichever way the hedgehog builds its nest, the wind will blow from the opposite direction.

Snails are believed to forecast rain: if there are lots out in the evening, then it will be a rainy night. There is some basis in fact: snails do come out when it rains, as do slugs. An intriguing snippet from Georgia in the *American Meteorological Journal* refers to a certain type of snail that changed colour when rain was due, but no further information was available on this intriguing occurrence.

Frogs were commonly believed in German-speaking areas of the world to be able to predict the weather. If green frogs chirruped in a tree, or if toads were taking a bath or making a lot of noise, then rain should be expected. If a tree frog is croaking on its own in the early dawn, then a storm is coming.

Out at sea, dolphins diving and then reappearing several times when near land are said to predict rain or a storm, as does the appearance of a large number of jellyfish.

How do birds fare against their fellow creatures in the prediction department? A common belief found in South Africa, Ukraine and other areas regarding swallows is that when they fly low then rain is due. Another belief is that when cranes take flight and don't return, then good weather is ahead. If cranes appear early in the autumn, however, then winter will be harsh, while cranes soaring quietly is another reason to expect good weather – but if they are loud, then a storm is due. Corvids are also said to be handy barometers: crows, diving or hovering over water, or a raven making a whirring sound and shaking its wings, or flying high and screaming, means rain. Likewise, if a lone raven makes three croaks, then repeats this over and over, rain is due. If a crow caws three times at the break of dawn, it is a good sign: fair weather is coming. Generally, when non-water birds bathe, then rain or a storm should be expected. In Australia, when kookaburras call in winter, it is said that rain will fall, as is the case when black cockatoos fly and call.

A common belief from the coastal areas of many countries is that gulls will head for land when bad weather is due. This is reflected in such sayings as: 'Seagull, seagull, sit on the sand, it's never good weather when you're on the land.' In some areas of the United States, this is believed to the extent that some people will leave a beach when they see gulls leaving in large numbers.

The cuckoo – also called the rain cow in the USA – is one of the best-known harbingers of rain in the animal kingdom, a belief found in many countries across the world. This is a long-held idea: according to Hesiod, when one was heard, three days of rain were to be expected. In South Africa, the Burchell's coucal, a type of cuckoo also known as the 'rain bird', is also said to be heard when a storm is forming.

In a popular belief from the Cape Peninsula, South Africa, bad weather is expected in the afternoon if the bokmakierie calls before dawn and carries on for several hours. An AmaXhosa belief states that the bird's sound changes to a trill when rain is due. There is also rain due if the southern boubou calls while sitting under a bush.

And what of insects? If ants have an anthill in a hollow and are seen to carry their eggs to higher ground, it is said that there is rain to come. If the ants carry their eggs downwards, however, then fair weather is to be expected. In a belief from Australia, if ants travel in a straight line, then expect rain, but expect fine weather if they move in a more scattered form. Bees are said to 'never swarm before a storm', so if you see bees swarming then it is probably safe to venture out without your umbrella!

Humans themselves are also said to have some ability when it comes to predicting what weather lies ahead. This is often said to show itself in physical indications in the body: swelling feet, for instance, is said to mean that a southerly wind is due, potentially in some cases even a hurricane. Aching joints in general is often believed to mean bad weather is on the way.

Finally, signs can also be found in other, everyday items. Smoke falling from a chimney is said to mean a storm, as does a water-filled pot causing sparks when it is set on the fire. If a fire has embers looking like hailstones, then hail is to be expected. Fire or a lamp that cannot be lit despite repeated attempts is a sign of a storm, whereas a lot of ash means snow. A lamp burning quietly during a storm is a sign of good weather to come. Cobwebs dancing means wind is coming. In Iceland, if you leave a rake in the yard with the prongs up, beware: you might cause it to rain!

SOMEWHERE OVER THE RAINBOW: Rainbows in Myth and Legend

There is little that can compare with the brilliance of a rainbow arching across a sunlit sky. This multicoloured optical phenomenom, caused by light striking water droplets in the air, often lingers for only a few moments, but this brevity only adds to its mystery, fuelling the myriad tales and beliefs in existence about this awe-inducing phenomenon.

One of the most familiar ideas from Abrahamic traditions is that the rainbow represents a covenant or promise: in Genesis in the Bible, the rainbow symbolizes God's promise never to destroy all life on earth with floodwater again. Aside from the story of the Nativity, the story of Noah and the ark is perhaps one of the most popular Bible stories taught to children from a young age, the image of the rainbow one of the earliest introductions to the Bible.

Another motif linking rainbows with the heavens is that they are a connection between the worlds of the gods and humankind. According to Norse mythology, a burning rainbow bridge spans the space between Asgard, where the gods reside, and Midgard, the realm of humankind. The resplendent bridge known as Bifröst or Bilfrost is so huge in size that it can be seen not only from Midgard, but from all of the nine realms.

Bifröst is guarded by the god Heimdallr or Heimdall who lives at Himinbjorg, at the Asgard end of the rainbow bridge: the perfect sentry, Heimdall needs very little sleep, is said to be able to see a distance of 100 leagues, and can hear the sound of grass growing. He is also said to possess a horn called Gjallarhorn – the yelling horn – so powerful, it can be heard in every realm. Heimdall guards Asgard against the Jötnar from the realm of Jötunheimr, an ultimately futile effort as their coming is foretold along with Ragnarok, the end of the world. The destruction of Bifröst is also foretold: Heimdall's horn will warn that Ragnarok, the terrible war to end the world, is starting, and on that day, the rainbow bridge will be no more.

In pre-Hindu Indonesian belief, the rainbow was also a connection between the gods and humankind, enabling contact between the mortal world and the gods. From the Torajan people of Indonesia, there is an image of a priestess in a trance next to a sick person, using a rainbow as a boat or a bridge to ascend to heaven to obtain spiritual strength on their behalf. Priests from the Ngaju people of Borneo drew a map of the Other World, showing a rainbow as a link between earth and heaven.

Many cultures have deities or spirits that are described as the personification or representation of the rainbow. The Greek goddess Iris is one such figure, acting as a link between the realms of god and man. Iris is portrayed in a variety of ways, the most common being as an actual rainbow, or as a young woman with splendid golden wings. Iris used rainbows to transport her as she carried messages between the gods and the mortal world, and was also known as a messenger goddess. In addition, Iris was charged with transporting water in a ewer from the River Styx, to be used when a god or goddess needed to make an oath. Woe betide the deity who dared lie; the water would leave them unconscious for the period of a year.

Another personification of the rainbow is the Mesopotamian Manzat, one of the main goddesses in Elamite culture in southwest Iran. Her name means 'rainbow' in Akkadian, and it has been suggested that she might have been a protective goddess towards women. In Hawaiian tradition there is Anuenue, another rainbow messenger goddess. She delivers messages from her brothers, the gods Kanaloa and Tane, and is able to move in the twinkling of an eye. Sometimes she is depicted as being wrapped in the colours of the rainbow, and sometimes she is the rainbow itself.

Rainbow serpent deities are common among the cultures of many Indigenous Australian groups; their names are many and differ from group to group, but they are frequently considered to be creator deities and are also often said to control the rain. There are also rainbow spirits found within several West African religions, such as the Ayida-Weddo from Haitian Vodou in Benin and Oxumere, from the Ifa religion of the Yoruba people.

As with several other bodies in the sky, it is a popular belief that you should not point at a rainbow: one researcher discovered this belief was common to 124 cultures across the globe. The consequences of breaking this taboo vary: depending on where you are, the offending finger could be bent like a rainbow, be overcome with maggots, or even fall off altogether! To the Karen people of Burma and Thailand, if a rainbow was accidentally pointed at, then a person would press their finger into their navel in order to avoid it falling off. Less specific consequences include the belief that general bad luck would befall the pointer, or someone related or significant to them. Pointing at a rainbow could also risk bringing rain back again after it had stopped.

According to a belief recorded in Shetland, Scotland, in the early 20th century, a rainbow arching over a house meant there would soon be a death either within the house or of a relation of the family who lived there. There is also the belief that 'a rainbow in the morning will give a sailor warning, a rainbow at night is the sailor's delight'.

What lies at the end of the rainbow and how to get there are questions that have taxed many. The Leprechaun – a mischievous supernatural being from Irish folklore – is said to live there with his fabled pot of gold. Although many have searched, they are doomed to failure: it is impossible to find the end of the rainbow, as it is actually a circle!

Rainbow-bridge imagery is often used today when a beloved pet or animal has passed. They are said to have crossed over the rainbow bridge to the afterlife, where they meet with other pets who have gone before, and where they will be waiting to meet their owners when their time likewise comes.

Today the rainbow is also a symbol of hope, inclusion and diversity, in particular for members and allies of the LGBTQ+ community. It was also a popular symbol of hope and unity during the recent Covid-19 pandemic.

THE LUCKY RAINBOW AND THE INDALO MYTH

This intriguing image of a man holding a rainbow was discovered in 1868 in the cave of Los Letreros, Almeria, Spain. Discovered by Antonio Gongónia y Martinez, the symbol became known as the Indalo Man, and is believed to date back to prehistory.

One interpretation of the Indalo image is that it shows a prehistoric god. According to this theory, the rainbow represents a covenant of protection between the god and mankind. Others believe that the Indalo is actually a depiction of a hunter holding a bow above his head.

The Indalo is linked to the revival of the Almerian town of Mojácar in the mid-20th century, following intellectual, artistic and financial improvements in the area. The artistic movement there took the Indalo as their symbol, and it was thus linked to rejuvenation and hope.

Today, the Indalo is the recognised symbol of Almeria and Mojacar in particular. Fully embraced by inhabitants, it is a familiar sight on the front of houses, believed to offer protection from bad weather and the Evil Eye, as well as being a general protective symbol. The Indalo is also popular among tourists, depicted on numerous souvenirs.

SHIMMERING LIGHTS AND WALRUS HEADS:
The Folklore and Legends of the Auroras

Over 19,000km (12,000mi) apart at opposite poles of the earth, fantastic displays of flashing bright lights in myriad colours and patterns swirl and dance across the sky, leaving those who witness them awestruck at their grandness and beauty. These mystical lights are known as the auroras: those at the North Pole are called the aurora borealis, or the northern lights, while aurora australis is the name by which the southern lights at the South Pole are known. They are caused when solar winds and the earth's magnetic field collide; the particles this creates in turn collide with gas atoms and the energy created is released as light. For a great deal of history, however, this was unknown, and the lights, both feared and revered, have been interpreted in many different ways by many different peoples.

The northern lights, aurora borealis, were named after the Roman goddess of the dawn and god of the north wind respectively. The aurora borealis is visible mainly from Finland, Norway, northern areas of Sweden, Iceland, southern Greenland, Alaska and Canada.

A common belief about the northern lights was that they were the souls of the dead. According to belief in some Inuit groups, when someone died their soul went to either the upper world or the under world. In a reversal of more typical associations, the under world was the better

option; warm, comfortable, with food in abundance, there were none of the shortages and bitter cold those in the upper world had to suffer. Those who were lucky enough to go to the under world were known as the *arssartut* or 'ball players', as there these souls played a game of ball with the head of a walrus. The aim of the game was to kick the skull and make sure it fell with the tusks downwards, sticking in the ground; it was this impact that caused the lights in the sky. The sound the lights made was also explained by this game: the noises were made by the footsteps of the players on the frosty ground. If you wanted to have a close encounter with the lights you need only whistle: they would then come closer to investigate. Another explanation for the noises of the lights from the Inuit peoples near Hudson Bay was that they were the spirits of the dead as they tried to speak with those left on earth: if you wanted to send a message to the dead, it was said you should whisper it in return.

A spectacular display of the aurora can also be seen from the Hebrides in Scotland. There the lights were known as the Nimble Men or the Merry Dancers. Giant but graceful, these groups sometimes danced together, and at other times warred against each other, creating the lights as they moved. The heroes of the Nimble Men were split into two clans; one wore garments of white, while the other was clad in a shade of pale yellow. The females of both groups wore various colours, brightly arrayed in greens, reds, silvery white and resplendent purples.

The Inuit of the east coast of Greenland believed that the lights were the dancing souls of children born dead, premature or murdered. In some beliefs, these spirits were playing ball with their afterbirth, thus causing the lights.

Another common belief was that the lights were fires lit by groups of people. To the Anishinabe of the north-eastern United States and south-eastern Canada, in particular the Anishinaabeg, the lights were a sign

from the creator of the world, Nanabozho. When he left them to head northwards to live, he reassured his people that they would always be of great importance to him: he would light fires from time to time as proof of this, and they would see the reflection of those fires in the sky.

The Kwih-dich-chuh-ahtx or the Makah Nation of Cape Flattery, Washington, believed that the lights were the fires of a small tribe that lived on the ice; the lights came from the fires they boiled whale blubber upon. The people were said to be half the height of a canoe paddle, but despite their diminutive size they were known for their great strength – it was said they could catch whales with ease with their bare hands.

Some believe that these lights are caused by foxes dashing through the snow, sparks flying from their tails as they pass. Reflecting this belief, in Finland the lights are known as *revontulet*, or 'fox fire', and the 2019 short film *Fox Fires* is a beautifully animated retelling of the Finnish story of the origin of the mysterious lights.

Although the lights are mostly visible from coastal areas, at times the northern lights can be viewed from further inland. In areas where the lights were seen less frequently, they tended to be perceived with more negative connotations, often seen as terrible omens, foretelling death, destruction and disaster. In northern England, they were often seen as fiery spears, particularly in Northumberland. There they were also referred to as Derwentwater's lights – it was said that the lights had been bright and vibrant in the sky after the young, popular Earl of Derwentwater was executed for treason in February 1716.

Even those who were more used to the lights did not always see them positively. To the Inuit of Point Barrow, Alaska, the lights were greatly feared, and people would carry a knife for protection against them.

There are fewer tales of the southern lights, by dint of there being fewer people to observe them in those areas, but there are some intriguing similarities between the origin stories of the southern and northern lights. Some northern Australian groups believed the lights to be fires from the feasts of the Oola Pikka – ghostly spirits that spoke to male elders through the aurora. In New Zealand, it was said that Māori travellers voyaged far south in their canoes but were trapped; generations therefore remained there, and the lights were from the bonfires they lit. The lights were known as Tahu-nui-a-Rangi – 'Great Glowing of the Sky'.

FLYING CRYPTIDS

Throughout history there have been tales of strange creatures seen flying through the skies, beings that terrify us and yet at the same time intrigue us, with each fresh sighting further fuelling the desire to know more and, perhaps, even see them for ourselves. These 'cryptids' – animals or creatures whose existence is unsubstantiated or disputed – have a huge following today, peppered throughout popular culture and in some cases even being huge tourist pulls. Here are two of the most famous and well-known cryptids from the United States of America.

The Jersey Devil

The creature known as the Jersey Devil is said to frequent the New Jersey Pine Barrens in the USA. Reports of strange noises, wailings and sightings coming from the forests have been reported for decades, with those who believe they have witnessed the creature describing a two-legged beast, often kangaroo-like in appearance, sometimes with a face like a horse and a head like a collie dog. It is generally said to have two short front legs that it holds up when walking – and, of course, wings. It has also variously been described as either like a bat or a pony.

Although many are familiar with the name, it might surprise people to know that the Jersey Devil is actually one of the USA's oldest cryptids, its origins dating back to over 250 years ago. The 'devil' was not known as the Jersey Devil then however, but the Leeds Devil, named, according to some, after an association with Daniel Leeds, a 17th century Quaker-cum-Almanac writer who got on the wrong side of the Quaker authorities and left the church under a cloud due to his mystical writings. Referred to as 'evil' on more than one occasion by contemporaries, and with the connection further fuelled by the inclusion of a winged monster on the Leeds family crest, by the close of the 18th century the Leeds Devil was firmly established in Pine Barrens folklore.

The most common explanation for the 'devil' is that it was the child of 'Mother Leeds'. With 12 children already, and expecting her 13th, some say she cursed the child, either while still pregnant or during labour, declaring 'let it be the devil'. After birth, the child was said to have turned into a terrible winged creature and flown off up the chimney, and thus the Leeds Devil was born.

In some versions, the creature stayed with the family for some years before flying off. In others, Mother Leeds looked after the creature until she died, at which point the devil flew off into the forest, where it has lived ever since. Often, Mother Leeds is said to have been a witch, the father of the child being Satan himself.

Some believe that the story stems from Daniel Leeds' son Japheth and his wife Deborah: the couple had 12 children, and some say that this was the origin of the story. According to some versions, the beast killed the whole family before it flew off.

Supposed sightings and encounters continued throughout the years. One of the stranger reports was in the 1870s, when a fisherman said that he saw the creature in the company of a mermaid. In 1893, in another encounter, a railroad engineer claimed that his train was attacked by none other than the Leeds Devil, the creature having a face like a monkey.

Some famous names also claimed to have seen the devil, one being the brother of none other than Napoleon Bonaparte. Joseph Bonaparte, former King of Spain, moved to America in exile after his forced abdication in 1813. He built a mansion at Bordentown, New Jersey, and according to the tale, when he was hunting alone in the woods near his home one day he spotted some strange tracks in the snow. Noting that one footprint was slightly larger than the other, he followed them until they came to an abrupt stop: hearing hissing, Bonaparte turned to find a large creature with a horse-like head, wings, and legs like a bird. After a tense moment where they stared at each other, the creature hissed again, before flying off.

It was not until the early 20th century that the creature's name changed from the Leeds Devil to the Jersey Devil, marking the modern era of the legend. In perhaps the most well-known sighting of the devil, in 1909, E.P. Weeden, a local councilman in Trenton, New Jersey, woke one January morning to flapping wings outside his bedroom window.

When he went to investigate, cloven footprints were in the snow outside. This sparked off a spate of sightings of strange footprints and hundreds of people came forward to say they had seen the creature that made them. The Jersey Devil sightings spread to even further afield, to Delaware and Pennsylvania, until the mania finally died down.

The Jersey Devil, however, was not forgotten. In 1937, in Downingtown, Chester County, there was great excitement when Cydney Ladley, his wife, and a neighbour of the couple dashed into town one night, declaring they had seen the Jersey Devil on a back road near where they lived. According to Ladley, the creature – the size of a kangaroo, hopping, with long hair and terrible eyes – had jumped across the road in front of his car. In response, around two dozen men and a pack of dogs set off armed with guns and clubs to try and find the creature; their hunt was ultimately unsuccessful. In 1939, the Jersey Devil was given the honour of being declared the official state demon for New Jersey, further cementing the creature's fame.

There are still sightings of the devil today, with people insisting they have seen the creature. In 2015, for example, Dave Black of Little Egg Harbor captured what he claimed was photographic evidence of the devil: he witnessed it running through trees, before spreading large, leathery-looking wings and flying away over a golf course. The photo is considered unconvincing by experts. There is still a reward waiting for anyone who can capture the devil; in 1960, Camden merchants offered $10,000 to anyone who could bring in the creature. Unsurprisingly, it has yet to be claimed.

Mothman

Although having a more recent pedigree than the Jersey Devil, Mothman has gained a firm place as one of the most popular and well-known flying cryptids in the USA.

The first sightings of the creature that came to be known as Mothman came in November 1966, when on 12 November a humanoid flying creature was reported by a group of men near Clendenin, West Virginia. Three days later, two couples were driving together through the back roads near the old TNT plant at Point Pleasant. They got more than they bargained for when they caught sight of a huge humanoid creature with large, bat-like wings. It appeared to have its wing caught in a wire, and was pulling at one wing with large hands, trying to get it free. After watching for a while, the couples drove off, but it appeared again in front of their truck, forcing them to stop; they drove on, but the creature spread its wings and flew after them – according to the witnesses, it was flying at over 160km/h (100mph).

Word of the encounter spread, sparking a spate of sightings over the next few days: interest was slow to abate, and there were said to have been over a thousand reported sightings in the next year. Mothman was also blamed for all sorts of strange occurrences in Point Pleasant; one man said that the buzzing of his television and the disappearance of his dog were caused by the creature, and strange lights in the sky, power shortages and strange sensations were also attributed to it. Many people said they experienced a strange feeling of dread after witnessing Mothman, leading to belief that the creature was a bad omen.

Early reports of Mothman described a winged, humanoid creature with red eyes. Between 1.8 and 2m (6–7ft) tall, with large wings like a bat, it was also said to have long legs, which stretched out behind when it was flying. Other sightings described a creature that was similar to an owl in size. Intriguingly, some witnesses reported that, after seeing the creature, they were visited by strange 'men in black' at their homes. With a dull, robotic tone, these strangers probed witnesses for details, before warning them not to reveal their sighting to anyone else. Phone calls from the same robotic voice were also reported.

The last of this particular spate of sightings of Mothman came in December 1967, after the collapse of the Silver Bridge, a tragedy that led to the deaths of 46 people. Due to this supposed correlation, the two became linked in the minds of many, leading to the theory that Mothman had appeared to either predict or even cause the disaster. Not everyone believes that Mothman's presence was a negative one, however: there are those who say that he actually came to warn people of the tragedy.

Fresh interest in Mothman was sparked in 1975 with the release of John Keel's book, *The Mothman Prophecies.* Interest surged again in 2002 with the film of the same name starring Richard Gere, and sightings continue of this elusive being. In 2017, there were over 20 reports of a similar creature being sighted between April and July in Chicago.

The origins of the name are unclear, but are generally attributed to a reporter who was inspired by the Killer Moth character from the popular *Batman* comics at the time.

Explanations for Mothman encounters vary. With the initial sightings, the Sheriff of Mason County put forward the theory that people were actually seeing a 'shitepoke', a name given to a type of heron that was much larger than average. Another explanation is that people were actually seeing a sandhill crane which had been blown off course on migration – this giant bird, with a wingspan of around 2m (7ft), would have been an unfamiliar sight, causing confusion and fear in those who unwittingly witnessed it. The crane stands almost as tall as a man and is the second largest crane in America. This theory is backed up by the fact that in 1966 two witnesses said that the creature they had seen was definitely a giant bird.

It is undeniable that Mothman is firmly entrenched in the psyche and folklore of Point Pleasant. This is reflected in the 3.7m (12ft) metallic Mothman statute commemorating the legend in Gunn Park, Point Pleasant. Then there is the annual Mothman Festival, which takes place on the third weekend in September and attracts thousands of visitors each year.

People don't have to wait until September, however, to get a Mothman fix. The Mothman Museum in Point Pleasant is an invaluable source of information for anyone interested in learning about Mothman, containing a wide range of documents, images and artefacts relating to the enduring legend.

CONCLUSION

When the ideas for this book series were still forming, fresh and full of possibilities, we were inspired to create something that uncovered a profound truth about humanity – as that is what folklore is inherently about. Now, in bringing together this collection of tales, traditions and beliefs we hope to have emphasised the unity we all share.

Our myths, legends and folk tales hold age-old wisdom. This learning has been gathered over centuries and encoded into symbols, archetypes and stories that make those truths of life easier to understand. It is easier to remember and pass on this information with a tale, to anyone who might wish to listen. Our customs, beliefs and traditions show our reverence of nature and its spirits, and we use these rites and rituals to breathe meaning into the world in which we live. We use them to mark important events in life, to show how times like the birth of a child, or the joining of two people in marriage, are different and special events. In this book, we have seen many stories and many rituals. We have seen how these customs vary greatly from place to place across the world. Yet, we have also seen how they all come inherently from the same place within ourselves as humans.

In our journey through these pages, we have traversed many landscapes. We have traced the pathway into the folklore of our vast oceans, our deepest woodlands and into the timeless skies whose stars map our most ancient myths in the heavens. Through the stories and traditions of the rivers and seas of the world, we have heard tales of sacred rivers and the threat of pollution that they face. We have seen that the fate of legendary river dolphins across the world – from India to Brazil – lies within our hands. We have looked upon the face of the spirits of our waters, and while they might look different – from Mami Wata to Poseidon, from the fossegrim to the naiads – their role in our lives is the same. They aid us when we are lost. They offer us healing. We plead and bargain with them for their gifts and blessings.

The waters of the earth course through our very veins; necessary, vital, the essence of life. When we, as humans, are brave – or foolhardy – enough to gaze upon their mysteries, we see our very image reflected back up at us: tempestuous, changeable, dangerous and painfully beautiful, a shared consciousness and acknowledgement of the turbulent forces within us.

Then on land come the trees, standing tall and majestic, enshrined in their cloaks of leaves. Our forests spread wide, reaching up to touch the heavens while at the same time burrowing deep into the earth beneath us. The world trees of global spiritualities tie the land to the sky, the heavens to the underworld, and we – as humans – are said to be free to move between these realms. We see this link between the two again and again, both in the trees themselves and through the creatures that live underneath their branches. In folklore, trees can transcend both time and space. They are the vessel of the very gods and goddesses that come down to earth, and a way for us to ourselves transcend the boundaries that bind us. These tales teach that, through the trees, we can discover our own animalistic natures once more, embrace the wild world around us in all its glorious forms, and ascend to the heavens themselves.

Above the seas and woodlands, the firmament of the skies towers over the land, the vault of the heavens emblazoned with shining stars, the clouds in constant flux. Looking upwards, we are reminded how humanity is bound together – gazing at the same moon, wishing on the same stars that influence our lives from the heavens.

Since humankind first walked this earth, the skies have been used to ground us in our own sense of place and time. The stars help us navigate the seas. The shadows cast by the sun allow us to measure the sands of time as they ebb away before us, it's rising each morning providing a constant as it illuminates our waking hours. More than that, the sun provides the heat and sustenance for our crops to thrive, nourishing our own bodies and maintaining life on earth. At the end of each day, the moon rises to take her turn, and as darkness falls, providing a time of reflection as we lie down to rest, safe in the knowledge that the skies are intrinsically linked with the ebb and flow of our lives, day to day, season to season.

We project our stories on to the skies, looking up and seeing the face of the gods watching over our small human lives from the heavens, as the Man in the Moon too watches on. Across the ages, humankind has strived to reach the heights: to soar into the air with the birds and rise higher than our destined lot. In this way, the skies remind us of our place in the world and show us opportunities to attain greatness – to achieve more than we think we ever could.

Throughout our journey into these timeless tales of our landscapes, and the traditions that span the earth, we have seen how folklore – our stories, customs and beliefs – can help us look at our world with fresh eyes. We see things in ways we have never seen them before, the world reframed by our myths and legends: we can see it anew as it is brought to life, watching the magic with which it has been imbued for millennia with the wonder and awe it deserves.

So now we have reached the end of our journey together; following the breadcrumb trail to safely return to our daily lives. But this is far from a farewell; before we go our separate ways, pause a moment to savour what we have found together. Take with you a little of the wildness we found in the forests. Keep watching the skies with wonder as you wish on the first star you see each night. As you close your eyes, hear the roaring of the oceans, and remember: when our own ebbing and flowing life journeys are finally over, we will rejoin with the earth once more – in the same way that all rivers one day meet the sea, pouring their magic and mystery back into the vast blue beyond.

ACKNOWLEDGEMENTS

As with all books, this one would not have been possible without the help of so many special people.

We'd like to thank everyone in the #FolkloreThursday community for their continued support and enthusiasm since we started in 2015.

We'd like to thank especially the #FolkloreThursday Twitter hashtag day hashtag hosts, the editing and web team, to the Patreon supporters, and to all of those who have contributed articles to FolkloreThursday.com over the years. Thank you also to our wonderful families, who have seen us through the process from initial dream to making #FolkloreThursday a reality.

We'd like to give a special thanks to Shanon Sinn, author of *The Haunting of Vancouver Island*, and Rosaria Tundo for their help with fact checking and proofreading. Also to staff at the Church of the Latter Day Saints Church History Library for providing access to documents that have aided in our research. Finally, a thank you to the whole Batsford team, and everyone over at Sprung Sultan for their support over many years.

Index

First published in the United Kingdom
in 2024 by
Batsford
43 Great Ormond Street
London
WC1N 3HZ

An imprint of B. T. Batsford Holdings Limited
Copyright © B. T. Batsford Ltd, 2024
Text copyright © Dee Dee Chainey and Willow Winsham, 2024

Illustrations by Joe McLaren

ISBN 9781849949217

A CIP catalogue record for this book is available from the British Library.

10 9 8 7 6 5 4 3 2 1

Reproduction by Mission Productions, Hong Kong
Printed and bound by Dream Colour, China
Edited by Rebecca Armstrong

This book can be ordered direct from the publisher at
www.batsfordbooks.com, or try your local bookshop

This collection first appeared in three separate volumes: *Treasury of Folklore: Seas and Rivers* (2021), *Treasury of Folklore: Woodlands and Forests* (2021) and *Treasury of Folklore: Stars and Skies* (2023).